Mango
Samba

DAWNE A. ALLETTE

Photography by Mark Reutter.

Printed in the United States of America.

Book Vine Press
2516 Highland Dr.
Palatine, IL 60067

DEDICATION

This is what I've done
With the gift You graciously flung
Diamonds in the sun
From Heaven

S*amba* is an infectious dance and style of music that dates back to the 16th Century. It was brought to Brazil and the tropics by enslaved people. The word Samba is derived from the West African word, Semba, which means "touch of the bellies" or a physical invitation between a man and a woman.

CHAPTER ONE

Windward

The island appeared out of nowhere. It was as if it had just sprung up from beneath the ocean, shook itself off and settled in the morning sun—a mass of sharply angled hills like broken crystal, set against a backdrop of lush emerald forests. The itinerary said it was Windward, the last of the islands that the *SS Tropical Sea* would visit before returning to Miami. But Kate was so lost in her misery that she was startled by the island's sudden appearance.

Leaning on the railing of the upper deck, she pulled her sunglasses from the top of her head to shield her eyes from the piercing sun as the island materialized before her. Buildings of all shapes, styles and sizes clung to the hills like barnacles, and splashes of scarlet from the blooming flamboyant trees seemed to suggest that a million bonfires were ablaze. Fishing boats nestled against the sea wall came into view, completing the fantasy that this place could possibly be a port of calm.

Kate Carrington had not traveled alone. She was accompanied by Madge Sorenson, her next door neighbor from a manicured Maryland suburb. Kate had booked the 10-day cruise to the Caribbean for herself and her husband Colin in a last-minute attempt to save their unraveling marriage. Colin assured her that he needed the time away to untangle himself from the web of bile and deceit in which he had become immersed. True to form, however, he begged off at the last minute. Kate was left with the sinking feeling that he had never intended to accompany her in the first place and that he was not about to stop his surreptitious dealings in Baltimore. Desperate to escape, she had turned to Madge, the only person available on such short notice.

Kate and Madge's friendship was not a particularly close one. Kate could not share secrets of her troubled marriage with her, knowing full well that Madge, a two-time divorcee who dabbled successfully in real estate, would snatch Colin for herself without a moment's hesitation. Madge was attracted not only by Colin's wealth and charm, but also by his refined sexuality. The kind that accompanies power and position. In her cool and confident way, she seemed to salivate whenever Colin walked into a room.

Kate O'Neil had married Colin Carrington right after they graduated from the University of Baltimore. After ten years together, things had gone from uninteresting to questionable. As she watched the last island on the cruise close in on the ship, she thought back to what had changed everything. The proverbial straw that broke the camel's back.

She had walked into her husband's home office to return some documents he had absently left on the kitchen counter when his phone rang. She paused for a moment to call out to him, but realized that he was still in the shower.

Kate had never answered her husband's private line before, but her hand, without her conscious consent, reached for the receiver.

Before she could even say "hello," a gravelly voice said, "Don't talk, Colin. Just listen."

Kate wanted to say, "Sorry, this isn't Colin," but she didn't.

"We've hit the jackpot," the strange voice rumbled. "Them two kidneys you removed yesterday are fetchin' a fortune. Keep 'em coming, old man. Keep 'em coming. We just got a very eager buyer in London, and our people are ready for action. Things are moving along like a well-oiled engine."

Kate inhaled audibly into the receiver.

"Is that all you have to say?" the voice demanded. "You can talk now. Whaddya think?"

Kate was silent. She couldn't find the words to reply.

"Colin?" the voice asked with mounting frustration. "Colin?"

Horrified, Kate slammed the receiver back in its cradle and walked out of the room.

Later that day, she confronted Colin and demanded an explanation. He was aware that there was no way that Kate would go along with his involvement in something she considered heinous. He also knew that he had no intention of discontinuing. The solution to the problem troubled and excited him. Removing kidneys from dead bodies was not only personally satisfying it was a very lucrative business that brought in lots of cash to the Carrington household. It was also relatively easy since corruption was so rampant in the city. Hell, if he wanted the kidneys before the person was dead, a man in his position could easily get away with it in a city sometimes nicknamed Bodymore.

"This cannot go on, Colin," Kate warned him. "I won't let it."

Now looking down at the ocean below her, she thought about how easy it would be to just slip away. She could easily slide over the railing and sink into the ocean before the other passengers even noticed. One thing she knew for sure was that she could not live with a man who sold pieces of human beings for profit. Just the thought of it made her sick. It was demonic. Their marriage was bad enough as it was, but this latest revelation was beyond the pale. The life that she had gotten used to was over. There was nothing worth salvaging. She felt depressed and alone. She searched in her head for something to live for but came up with nothing.

Kate stared at the ocean again, expecting it to be as dark and turgid as her thoughts. To her surprise, it was an extraordinary blue. Even with her sunglasses on, it sparkled as if God had thrown handfuls of diamonds down from heaven just for the hell of it. It was not the kind of water in which to die.

People were soon rushing past her, heading for the ramp. She allowed herself to get carried along with the throng. Over her shoulder, she watched Madge as she trotted down the gangplank with a young Hispanic man. He looked like the bus boy that she had picked up like a hot real estate listing the night before.

Then she saw him. The man in whose cabin she had spent the night trying to forget that her marriage was over. He had been chatting her up since they boarded the ship in Miami. Kate had never sought affection outside of her marriage, but desperate as she was to feel sexy and desirable again, she relished his attention. Since Madge had deserted her right after boarding the ship, in her own quest for husband number three, Kate felt the need for some kind of company. The pain in her heart combined with one glass of Chardonnay too many in her head had pushed her into Ross Winter's arms. A few hours with a young, attractive man was supposed to bring her vindication and relief. Instead, it just served her a platter of shame and disgust.

She winced as she recalled their frantic attempt at lovemaking. Moving with legs leaden with regret, she shot a mournful glance at Ross as he disappeared into a bus with the words, *Come Let We Go*, painted in large curly letters on its side. He had obviously bought the all-day package tour of the island to avoid her.

She walked off the ship and slowly along the harbor that had presented itself earlier as a hallucination. The boats and small skiffs creaked and groaned on their anchors. Buildings of weathered brick and rough concrete fronted the narrow street that was crowded with people, vendors selling souvenirs and tourists. She found a seat near a life-size bronze statue of what appeared to be a saint and made the sign of the cross in case it was. Kate looked at the statue's outstretched arms, burnt dark amber from the sun, and wondered if they were welcoming her.

She sat down and let the soft breeze caress her skin. Her thoughts came to rest on her husband again. She had fallen in love with Colin the moment she first saw him. He was the life of the party, and Kate wanted to dance. A football jock, Colin usually went for the blond, cheerleader type, but when he saw Kate's eyes, he was smitten. They were the most striking of her fine features—a piercing, penetrating green that could rival any emerald worth its salt.

She had dark brown hair cropped short, long slender legs, milky-white skin and deceptively soft features. She was often referred to as a Scarlett O'Hara look-alike. But she dressed a whole lot simpler than Scarlett and was a bit of an introvert. Her life, when she chose to call it that, was uneventful. She had no siblings and grew up in The Valley, a patchwork of old and dying factories near downtown Baltimore. Desperate to escape the tomb that was her parent's home, Kate jumped straight into the arms of the golden boy from suburbia. Soon after graduation, they were married and living in a gated community in the suburbs. Their combined salaries afforded Kate all of the luxuries she thought she wanted and needed. Expensive clothing, weekly manicures and pedicures and trips to the theatre. She lived in a gilded cage as the years dragged on.

Reluctant to release his vanishing youth, Colin had become engrossed in an affair with a younger woman he had met at an office party in Baltimore City. The affair had rendered him physically absent two or three times a week and emotionally absent the rest of the time. He thrived, however, in his position as chief medical examiner for the Baltimore City Police Department. Kate had closed her eyes to the truth about her marriage and looked the other way, burying herself in her work as a pediatric nurse at Johns Hopkins Hospital—especially after her best friend, Hanna Gamble, confirmed her husband's infedelity.

A pair of seagulls perched on the shoulders of the bronze statue disturbed her ruminations. They watched her intently with their heads cocked sideways, no doubt wondering if she had any spare crumbs in her purse. Suddenly she realized that she was as hungry as they appeared to be.

"Miss, lemme take you on a tour aroun de town." The voice came from a man who appeared in front of her wearing a remarkably tall knitted hat of yellow, black and green wool. The hat appeared to be reaching for the sky while knowing it was futile. Kate realized that the rising tower housed the man's hair because a stray rope of matted hair had escaped its woolen ward and hung freely just above his knees.

"Dey call me Roy," he announced politely, amidst a spray of spittle.

"Thank you, Roy," Kate answered just as politely, ducking slightly so that she would not be doused. "Dey call me Kate." Despite her melancholy, a smile tugged at the corners of her mouth.

Casting an apologetic look at the seagulls, she walked behind Roy's ropy hair, all the while trying to decipher his singsong words as he pointed out various points of interest.

He suddenly turned back to look at her. "You want food?"

At last there was a word she understood. Her stomach churned in anticipation, causing her to emit a surprisingly loud burp.

"Woi," said Roy, jumping back with more exaggeration than was necessary.

"Excuse me," she said, placing her fingers over her mouth.

"No worries," said Roy, amused that such a stately looking white woman could make the same sound as any fisherman on the wharf. "Dis is carnival day in Windward," he told her. "People, people everywhere, yes."

Dodging and weaving their way between masqueraders dancing in the street dressed like toucans, butterflies in various forms of metamorphosis and drunken sailors, he led her into a clapboard shack that had miraculousy managed to squeeze itself between a store selling tee shirts all saying "New York Yankees" and a shop hawking an array of women's underwear, fishing equipment and car tires. The sign above the shack read: "We Sell Spirituous Liquors." Painted around the sign was a flock of birds in flight, as if to suggest that the spirits sold within had the capacity to make you soar. She felt immediate relief from the blistering sun.

Hazy streaks of light poured in through the unevenly spaced wooden panels. The floor was made of padded-down earth, and when she reached down to remove her sandals, she found that the ground felt like cool, smooth tile.

When her eyes grew accustomed to the darkness, Kate took in the interior of the place. There were five wooden tables each surrounded by cheap plastic chairs. A dozen drinkers and equal amount of diners filled up the space. In the far corner of the room was a battered counter behind which an exotic-looking proprietress wore a multicolored headwrap like if it was a crown.

Despite its dubious decor, the restaurant was filled with merriment. The people spoke as if they were singing and they grinned at Kate because they thought she understood their song.

She and Roy squeezed their way to a table where two men were arm wrestling. The one who was losing immediately pulled his hand away from his opponent's and happily offered them the table. The other one nodded at Kate quickly, grabbed his opponent by the scruff of his neck and ushered him outside.

"Fight, fight," someone shouted, and everyone emptied out onto the sidewalk, some to watch and others to place bets on the winner. Kate and Roy suddenly had the place to themselves.

Roy took it upon himself to take charge. He called out to the proprietress who was shaking her head with amusement as she watched the fight outside the door. "Bring two goat roti and two sweet drink. Red Spot—not Fanta. You hear?"

Kate wondered how he would eat with so many of his teeth missing.

When the food and drinks were brought to the table, he turned to Kate and said, "Pay de lady, eh."

"No worries," said Kate, proud of her new lingo. She hungrily took a mouthful of the hot curried concoction. It tasted absolutely divine.

Roy leaned back in his chair and chewed noisily.

After their meal, they continued further into the town, which rose vertically in a crosshatch of narrow streets. She was not quite sure when she lost him. She just turned around and he was nowhere to be found. This left her prey for the Jab Jabs and the Short Knees left over from the early morning's J'Ouvert celebration. The Jab Jabs, or devils, were painted in oily black from head to toe. Kate stood still as they came towards her with their jagged gait, wearing their fiercest faces.

She thought of trips to New Orleans at Mardi Gras where the masqueraders sometimes left her uneasy. This was like nothing she had ever seen or imagined before. It was Mardi Gras multiplied 100 times and then some. The Jabs Jabs held long chains in their hands and had large horns on their heads, courtesy of some bulls that had long since been killed. Their extended tongues hung out of their mouths, long and red, and their eyeballs were glazed from drinking too much rum in the sun.

They wore skimpy shorts that refused to fully cover their private parts. Gyrating, they made menacing gestures at Kate as if they wanted to make her one of them. At first she tried to run away, but was shocked to find that she was not afraid of them. She found an odd comfort in their company. The Jab Jabs seemed equally surprised that the white woman they had surrounded was not fazed by the terrible figures they tried to cut.

"You is one brave lady, oui," said the Jab Jab with the battered enamel chamber pot perched precariously on his head.

She wanted to tell him how much those words meant to her. Instead, she simply said, "You are nothing compared to what I left behind."

As was their custom, they smeared her arms with black tar and glared at her one last time before stamping away. Their slurred, ragged song filled the air.

Kate much preferred the Short Knees who followed in their wake. The men danced around in a wide circle and flung white face powder on anyone who was not light of foot.

When they stamped their feet, tiny bells around their ankles rang out. They sang a sweet, catchy tune as they pranced around her. They had wire-netted masks over their faces and they wore satiny over-sized clown suits unto which were glued lots of little, round glass mirrors, sequins and large colored buttons. The Short Knees were as cheery as the Jab Jabs were scary. She tapped her feet to the beat that strummed like a guitar in her belly. She would have followed them anywhere if they had asked her.

Later that night, when midnight approached, the same masqueraders would dance their final measure before Lent demanded that they stop for 40 days. Through the dark streets, the King Jab Jab would leap high into the air like a Watusi warrior in a fantastical farewell to the carnival. The boys and dem would chorus back in voices as shrill as the night frog's and give tongue to a testimony of rhythm and ancestry reaching all the way back to Africa.

CHAPTER TWO

Windward

K ate continued on her walk, away from the celebration. The chanting and the drums grew fainter—wafting to her ears only in gusts. She felt like she had found an enchanting place. She climbed a hill that was so ridiculously steep, she had to laugh out loud. "This is straight out of *National Geographic*," she told herself. No sooner had she gotten to the crest of the hill than she saw that she would have to descend a path that was just as absurdly vertical. In the distance the ocean gleamed before her. A million more diamonds had obviously been dropped down from heaven since she left the ship. She waited for a minute or two to catch her breath after that incredulous climb, then took off her sandals and padded down the hill comfortably. At the bottom of the hill, a marketplace presented itself. Beautiful women of color strolled around sometimes arm in arm buying fruits that were just as exotic as they were.

"Spices, dahlin?" someone sang out. She turned around to face the songstress—a busty woman wearing a large straw hat made of dried banana leaves. Stuck in the front of the hat was a thin stick on which a long-legged chickadee made out of straw swayed back and forth. The woman was seated on an old plastic crate. Before her was a large wooden tray filled with all kinds of spices. In the middle of the tray there were stacks of gnarled ginger, hills of broken cinnamon sticks and mounds of nutmegs still housed in their mace. Neat clusters of cloves, mauby bark and bouquets of dried sorrel decorated the four corners of her display.

As soon as Kate inhaled one scent, her nose was assaulted by another. Every vendor had a supply of mangoes that threatened to overpower everything with their sweet scent. She thought of all the shopping she had done at the Giant Supermarket back in Baltimore. The produce aisle was a vision of opulence. She could find a dozen different fruits washed, waxed and sprayed intermittently by automatic nozzles to keep them looking fresh. She had seen mangoes before, but never remembered them ever having a smell.

"Wha kind you looking for?" asked the songstress.

"Kind?" asked Kate perplexed. "There are kinds?"

Her question caused the market women to howl with laughter. They slapped each other on the back, then proceeded to bend over holding onto their stomachs. When they finally straightened up from their merriment, the busty one said, "You have Julie. You have Ceylon. You have Rose and Calabash. You have Mango-vert and Mango-peche. But Julie is de best. Dey sweet, sweet, sweet," she said. The straw chickadee bobbed up and down on her hat as if in hearty agreement.

"I'll take two Julies then," said Kate, smiling as she handed her money over.

"Nice," said the woman. "I have a sistah dey in Brooklyn, New Yak. If you don't mind, tell her I say hi when you go back to America. She living right there in Flatbush."

Kate nodded and touched the woman's hand. There was no sense in telling her that Brooklyn was about a four-hour drive from Baltimore. On an island measuring about eighteen miles from shore to shore, how would they understand what a span of 200 miles meant?

"Me, too," said her companion, eager to join in the conversation. "Tell my uncle I good. He living in California. Not too far from Brooklyn. You can't miss him if you try. He look just like me." This remark caused them to throw themselves on each other and laugh heartily again.

Kate felt a longing to linger in the women's world. She took a seat on a spare crate and listened to their ditty. Every few minutes she buried her nose in the paper bag to get a whiff of the Julies with her eyes closed. The women occasionally glanced over at her, giggled and continued talking to each other. Once in a while, Kate heard a musical note that resonated. She lost track of time.

The distant horn of the cruise ship brought her back to reality.

"Mam, you go miss de boat if you don't come wid me now," Roy spoke from somewhere behind her head. She did not know how much time had passed.

"Oh my goodness," Kate gasped. "I almost forgot. Let's hurry."

Roy directed her back up the hill and then down again. When she finally got to the water's edge, she realized that the ship was anchored on the opposite side of the harbor.

She stood there panting, flustered, and dirty from the Jab Jabs and the long walk. She wondered if she should swim across the water to the ship. She quickly dismissed the idea.

Even for her, a winner of college swimming trophies, the ship was too far away.

"Excuse me, but can I be of help to you?" came the most melodious sound she had yet heard.

"What?" she asked, turning toward a small skiff bobbing along the seawall.

"You will miss that ship unless you let me take you to it."

The owner of the voice was shirtless. He was standing in his boat looking like a young Sidney Poitier. He had muscles that could be counted down his bare torso. His grin revealed white teeth with a splice of gold that caught the late afternoon sun and glinted for a second before he spoke again.

"Why don't you let me help you get back to America?" he asked, his legs spread and swaying from side to side to keep the boat balanced. He wore faded denim shorts that seemed too small for so strapping a man. His hair was a waterfall of dreadlocks that framed a handsome, smooth face. His eyes were deep and brown, his lips generous.

"You are an American, not so?" he asked with a grin.

His voice brought her back to her senses. "Uh, yes," she stammered. "I am."

He beckoned to her with his arms and she leaned into them. She felt him grip her strongly under her armpits as he lifted her up and then lowered her into his boat. Their bodies touched as she slid down the length of him to the hull of the boat. She knew that she should thank him, but the words got stuck under her tongue. The man smelled, she realized, like nothing she had ever smelled before. She felt intoxicated.

Kate sat facing him, one hand tightly gripping the side of the boat and the other clutching her purse and bag of mangoes. He sat opposite her and began rowing towards the cruise ship. She kept her eyes on his swaying dreadlocks as he pulled on the oars. She dared not glance down further, guessing that his cut-off shorts only partly covered things up.

She looked at him again and their eyes locked together. He was looking at her in a way that no one else had ever looked at her before. A comforting wave washed over her.

The fisherman's eyes went to work. They did a quick inventory of Kate's body that caused her to shiver in the hot Caribbean sun. His eyes rested first on her breasts, then travelled slowly down to her long legs, which were splayed out to keep her balance in the boat. As she watched him watch her, she wondered if she was wearing anything. The fisherman didn't seem to think she was.

The man smiled broadly as he pulled on the oars. Here was a woman with the greenest eyes he had ever thought possible. The words of Bim Bim, the village Obeah woman, flashed through his mind. She had told his grandmother that he would meet his soul mate at the water's edge and she would be a foreigner with green eyes. No one in the village had ever seen or even believed that anyone could actually have eyes that were green. That was just not possible. Absurd, the fisherman believed. Until now. Yes, she was dirty, disheveled and smelled like a ramgoat, but silhouetted against the setting sun, she was the most beautiful sight he had ever seen.

He rowed in silence as he drank in her presence.

When the fishing boat reached the cruise ship, he pulled up to the floating ramp so that she could get out. He stood up to give her a hand, but Kate did not move. Their eyes locked again. He waited with his arms extended. Still she did not move. Not a muscle.

"No worries," the fisherman said to break the silence. He sat down and picked up the oars. Turning the boat around with great ease, he headed back towards Windward's shore.

CHAPTER THREE

Windward

The fishing boat, named *Come With Me*, glided up to the seawall. The man got out and leaned over the boat with a length of rope and pulled it in closer. He tied the rope to a piece of jutting concrete that housed a large iron hook and secured the skiff. Kate sat stiffly in the boat as it rocked back and forth. The waves made a slapping sound as they fussed at the seawall. There were a few discarded bottles floating in the water that would eventually break into little pieces and become glistening glimmers of coloured glass.

The man stretched out his hand to her. She tried to grasp it, but the churning water conspired against her and she fell back and landed flat on her bottom, still clutching her purse and the bag of mangoes. She looked up and saw that the man was laughing. She had to laugh at herself.

He stooped down and held out his hand to her again. She put her upper body in his grasp and allowed him to pull her on to the seawall. He held her, not wanting to let go. She tried to move away from him, but she could not. He tried to step back from her, but failed. Something held them in a vice like a determined vine that wraps itself around a tree trunk, twisting upwards and imprisoning the tree. They stood like captives in the path of a raging wild fire. Motionless. When the fire finally abated they reluctantly moved apart, both looking down at imaginary pebbles on the ground.

"Where do I go now?" she wondered as they watched the ship slip through the mouth of the harbor.

"Well, Miss Green Eyes," he smiled, "seems like your ship has sailed."

"Seems like it did." She chuckled nervously and then waited for him to continue speaking.

He was silent.

She searched his handsome face but all she could read was his apparent amusement.

"Come, let's walk, yes," he finally said. Taking her hand in his, he steered her across the busy street.

She swayed on her feet. Not here, she told herself, I will not fall down here.

Seeing her discomfort, the man led her to an old wooden bench and sat her down. "Wait here," he instructed. "I going and find you some coconut water to drink. It will fix you up. Don't move."

Kate watched him walk away with a stride that made her suddenly blush. She looked at the people dancing by to the rhythm of calypso music that was riding on a soft breeze. She did not want to go back to America.

"I should fly back home tomorrow. What choice do I have?" she asked herself. "I couldn't possibly stay here," her logical mind continued. "I don't belong. What would I do? How would I live?"

Kate let out a loud sigh. For now, she told herself, just enjoy the moment. Looking up at the sky, which was a tender blue, she felt a strange anticipation. She closed her eyes tightly, unaware of the smile on her face.

"Like you feeling better or what?"

She was startled by the fisherman's voice so close to her ear.

"Yes, I am, actually," she answered.

He handed her a green coconut. "It ain't have no straws to drink it wid, so just drink out of dat hole right dere," he instructed, pointing to the top of the coconut.

Kate lifted the fibrous shell to her lips. The sweet liquid was cool and comforting. What didn't land in her mouth bathed her neck and chest.

The man found that very entertaining and watched her intently.

Licking her lips, she handed him the empty shell.

They stood together at the side of the road not caring about anything but the burning desire that had come up between them again. Thinking like the person she was said to resemble, Kate told herself, "Tomorrow is another day, after all."

"Come," he said. "I will take you to my house. You can rest there until…"

All she could manage was a slight nod.

They walked back into the town to look for transportation. When they got to the market where rows of buses were vying for attention, he took her hand in his and with a firm grasp, propelled her through the throng towards a brightly painted truck masquerading as a bus. He placed both of his hands on her bottom, pushed her up into the imposter and then helped her onto a hard wooden seat.

The used-to-be-a-truck was named *Come Who Going*. It filled up quickly with passengers. The fearless conductor, a mere boy determined to be a dare devil, hung out dangerously from the side and yelled, "Marabel. Come who want to go."

They sat on what appeared to be the last available seats on the bus. Kate could not understand why the conductor was still hanging out of the bus calling out to passers by. She wondered where another person would sit. Seconds later she found out when three women climbed aboard. The smallest one told her good evening and promptly sat in her lap. The second one, larger than the first, sat on top of the boy conductor. The third looked around sweetly, then tried to squeeze her big bottom between Kate and the fisherman. This resulted in most of her rear appendage resting comfortably in his lap. He rolled his eyes in frustration and tried without success to remove himself from under it. Resigned to his fate, he settled in for the ride. The boy conductor, obviously used to being mistaken for an available seat, managed to wiggle his way out from under his new mate.

The bus rumbled along, sometimes too close to cliffs as they made their way up the coast. Kate watched in amazement as they drove past children splashing about in the ocean and fishermen hauling in their catch. The sand was extraordinarily white and seemed to run for miles. The coconut trees swayed in the breeze as the bus sped by. Along the road, all kinds of exquisitely colorful flowers competed for attention. Splashes of bright reds and yellows played among different shades of green. A veritable smorgasbord of color appeared everywhere. The bus negotiated the narrowing path with goats and donkeys as the road swung from the sea and climbed uphill towards the rain forest. Kate stared in amazement at women sitting in their yards shelling peas and tossing rice in the air from gourds in preparation for the evening meal. Every so often, a monkey appeared in an overhanging tree to watch the bus grind by as it wound its way uphill towards Marabel.

"Bus stop," the fisherman called out. Kate did not see any signs suggesting there were any bus stops anywhere. But, like the woman in her lap, passengers just said, "bus stop," and the driver would screech to an abrupt halt, throwing everyone headlong on top of everyone else. Bus stops seemed to be anywhere you wanted them to be.

Kate and the fisherman gratefully hopped off the truck-bus and he took her hand again. He led her to a narrow dirt road and they walked in silence. They passed a few cows that were swiping flies with their tails. One of them mooed, which made Kate giggle and caused the fisherman to squeeze her hand tighter. Big bushy trees lined the road, their fruit-laden branches rustling in the steady breeze from the Atlantic Ocean. A riot of heliconia, lobster tails and birds of paradise showed off some feet away and some unfamiliar birds flew overhead—a whir of gaudiness.

She looked at one of the trees quizzically.

"Oranges," the fisherman said, reading her thoughts.

"Oh," she replied with a short laugh. "I've never seen green oranges. I just never thought of them as ever being green."

A brave little marsupial that the natives called manicou, ran across her path. The fisherman's wooden hut sat in the middle of the green confusion looking like something out of a fairy tale where only spirits lived. She stepped on to the verandah and followed the fisherman through a painted red and yellow door. The door was kept shut by a small bit of wood nailed to the frame, making Kate suddenly think of Baltimore with its security doors and burglar alarms. Her face broke into a comical grin.

There were two large rooms inside. One served as a kitchen, dining room, living room and office, judging from the table covered with papers and a typewriter. The other was his bedroom. Within its whitewashed walls was an iron bed with a clean cotton sheet embroidered with a picture of the Eiffel Tower. There was a wooden dresser in the corner of the room with a missing space where a drawer once held some of his clothing.

Perhaps his underwear used to be in that drawer. Or maybe he doesn't wear any, Kate shamelessly thought as she licked off the sweat that had made little shiny beads on her upper lip. On the other side of the bedroom was a small wooden table. In the middle of it was a flowered enamel pitcher filled with water. Next to it was a basin and a neatly folded white face towel. This room obviously had a woman's touch, she thought, adding some tremelous beats to her heart's already crazy rhythm. A small window was propped open with a long stick. A red-and-white checkered cotton curtain danced back and forth to the beat that the breeze brought in. The floor was bare and clean.

"You hungry?" he asked.

"Famished," she answered, shocked that a word had emerged from her lips.

He led her into the kitchen towards a table with two chairs, which were obviously built by someone who built tables and chairs as an after-thought or on a dare. There was a frosted glass pitcher with beads of water on the outside to suggest that the water inside might still be a little chilled from melted ice cubes. The pitcher was covered with a white paper napkin. Next to the pitcher was a glass turned upside down against the marauding flies. A single plate covered by another plate was carefully placed on a tablemat made of straw and plastic strips.

"My grandmother does cook for me," he said proudly. "Sit. I know it have enough for two."

She sat down as he lifted up the covering plate. The smell of the food cooked in coconut oil and spices filled

27

the room. She inhaled deeply. The food was still warm, so his grandmother must have just left the house. She happily discarded the idea of the woman she had imagined when she was in his bedroom.

"Good, eh?" he asked her as she savored the spoonful that he put into her mouth. He reached over and blocked some gravy that was trailing down to her chin with his finger. He then put his finger into his mouth and licked it clean. She blushed beet red as the pit of her stomach churned, causing her to squeeze her legs together. They shared the food, he feeding her every other spoonful until they were done.

"I don't know what…" she began, but he had put his fingers to her lips to keep her quiet.

"I don't know what either," he whispered in his rhythmic singsong. "Lemme show you where the shower is. You are the dirtiest woman I have ever seen," he laughed.

She allowed herself to be led through the back door to some steps made of concrete blocks.

Kate was startled when she realized she would have to shower outdoors from a pipe and hose. There was no surrounding wall, just a galvanized barricade on one side facing the house.

He handed her a piece of yellow soap that smelled of coconut. "I will wait inside. I will not watch you. I can't, however, vouch for the chickens," he said in his delicious voice.

There were no houses in the immediate area, and so only the animals watched her as she undressed with newly found abandon. She threw her clothes on a tree branch, got under the water and grimaced in its cold embrace. Naked under the last rays of the tropical sun with clean spring water pouring down on her, she thought about her Victorian-tiled bathroom and Chippendale bathtub in Maryland. She was forgetting who she was, where she came from and why she was where she happened to be, when a little green lizard took the opportunity to jump on her foot. She screamed, dropped the soap and bolted toward the house.

Hearing the commotion, the man ran out and caught her in his arms.

She was slippery and soapy, scared but elated.

"Let's get you back under the water," he said. She clung to him as he held her steady under the spigot. She watched as her hands reached out and began to take his denim shorts off. Tossing them aside, their mouths hungrily found refuge in each other's. The cold water did nothing to douse the flame that engulfed them. He ran his hands over her body, relishing every curve, as he washed the soap away. His fingers sought places she had almost forgotten existed and her body trembled with joy. She soaped him down, letting her hands slide down each stomach muscle and finally come to rest on the place that rendered him helpless. He kissed her cheek, then her eyelids and pulled her urgently from the water. He laid her down on the grass under the breadfruit tree as a goat and some chickens watched.

From the hut came the strains of Bob Marley's, *Satisfy My Soul.* She got lost in his sultry voice and the constant dependable beat. They moved as one, in and out, back and forth, above and beneath each other. They clung and bit and pulled and strained as the fire burned with a flame that scoured every inch of their bodies and made them utter sharp animal cries.

The chickens ran for cover, but the goat held his ground.

When they finally pulled themselves up from the grass, the man tenderly carried her indoors and laid her on the iron bed. Kate slept the sleep of the dead, only awakening as if in a dream to the chickens squawking and a rooster crowing. She had never heard these sounds outside of nature shows on Maryland Public Television.

The morning green was dusted with a cool mist and the sun was popping over a mighty palm tree. Kate pulled herself to a sitting position. The man, fully dressed, was staring at her.

"Mornin," he said softly. "My name is Tsekani but dey call me Breed. Wha dey call you, Green Eyes?" he sang softly.

"What interesting names you have," she said, lowering her eyes so she would not seem to be staring back at him. "I've never heard those before."

"Well," the man explained. "Tsekani is an African name. It means something that is close to you. My mother is of African descent and my father is an East Indian. In dis country almost everybody get a nickname. Mine was Half-Breed on account of my mixture. Dey soon got tired of dat, so they shorten it to just Breed."

"They call me Kate," she smiled. "My name is Kate Carrington, once O'Neil. No interesting story attached to it. But I like your name. It suits you."

"An Irish colleen," he said, gazing into her eyes. "OK, Miss Green Eyes from the Emerald Isle. You can sleep some more. I going to town to do some business. On my way back, I will pick you up something to wear. We can't have you walking round naked. Tink of wha people would say," he chuckled at his own humor.

"Thank you. I rather like being clothed myself," she answered between giggles.

She heard the rickety door squeak shut and Breed's footsteps fade into the morning cacophony.

"Have I utterly gone mad?" she asked herself out loud. "Have I lost my mind? Have I died and gone to heaven?"

She sat up on the hard mattress stuffed with coconut fibre and pulled her legs toward her body. Instinctively she placed her hands over her stomach. Her heart pounded in her chest. As her hands caressed her still warm stomach, she felt that she was no longer alone.

When Breed got to Boysie's rum shop, the political meeting was already in session in the back room. He had an extra pep in his step that his comrades noticed. They were meeting to talk about the problems the farmers faced selling their crops. They were being eased out of the world market by bigger countries that could export much larger numbers of bananas and other tropical fruits to Europe and the United States. The meeting was to discuss ways in which the government could better integrate Windward's crops into the world market, but when they saw their comrade walk in so jauntily, they set aside their weighty discussion to address his unusual enthusiasm.

"You do wha?" asked Marshall dumbfounded. "You have a wha in yu wha?"

"Cool yourself man," muttered Breed as he tried to explain how it was that he had a white woman staying with him.—The oppressor's woman…The Eve who had come back for her mango. The ultimate trap for a revolutionary black man.—All those words came from the mouths of his comrades.

"Man, I don't know what happen. I just know dat dis one different. It have something about her," he explained to the doubtful bunch.

"All I want to know is," demanded Boysie, "how you go liberate de people wid the enemy in yu bed?"

"You can count on me. I am committed to the struggle. Dis woman won't stop me," Breed said with a flash of anger.

"And what you planning to tell Debbie, eh?" Boysie asked. "Dat woman been waiting for you to married she all dis time."

Marshall, his closest friend, snorted the air as if smelling imminent danger.

"I don't want to be on dis island when Debbie meet up with you white woman."

"I can deal with Debbie," Breed snapped back without much conviction.

CHAPTER FOUR

Baltimore

Like millions of men around the world, Colin Carrington dreamed of killing his wife. In his sleep images flashed before his eyes about how and when he would do it. The why was no longer important because he knew she was privy to his secret shenanigans. If only she had not picked up the phone that day, he wouldn't have to eliminate her now. So vivid were his night dreams that Colin sometimes had them in the middle of the afternoon. Once when he was closing up a dead body after removing its kidneys, he thought he heard the corpse curse him. "That's what I get for dissecting the dead in the city of Poe," he chuckled to himself. Leaning closer to his victim, he whispered, "It was a dark and soundless day in the morgue of Dr. Carrington."

Colin was fully aware of the illegality of his activities. Selling body parts could land him in jail indefinitely, not to mention end his good name and celebrated career. He knew it would be only a matter of time before Kate turned him in, especially since their marriage had disintegrated. But he also knew that he could get away with murder because of his position and his acquaintances. "I hope you drop dead," were his last words to Kate before she got in the taxi to begin the cruise. Yes, Kate would have to die so that he could prosper.

This morning he was a bundle of nerves. Pacing back and forth in his living room, he looked at his watch for the hundredth time. The *SS Tropical Sea* should have docked in Miami by now and still he had not heard from Ross.

Ross Winter. A man he had met by chance in a bar. A man with a smooth façade and a deadly purpose. For a handful of bills, he could make a person disappear.

While trying to keep his imagination in check, Colin couldn't help wondering. What if Kate had put up a struggle? After all, she grew up in a neighborhood where fights broke out every Friday night. Kate O'Neil might look delicate, but she wasn't afraid of throwing a punch. His heart raced and he could hear its tell-tale beat as he thought, "No. Impossible."

Colin mopped the beads of sweat on his forehead with a paper towel and poured another shot of Johnnie Walker from the sideboard. He was filling his glass for yet another drink when the phone finally rang.

"Hello," he said into the receiver.

There was a brief silence.

"Is anyone there?" he asked anxiously.

"It's done," said the caller, giving his prearranged answer.

Colin exhaled loudly.

"Same place. Be there tomorrow night at eight," Ross Winter said before the phone went dead.

Colin raised the glass to his lips and downed the whiskey in one gulp. He had already concocted the story he would tell their mutual friends and Kate's cohorts at Johns Hopkins Hospital. He'd say that she had just upped and left him. Met a man on the cruise ship and never came back to Baltimore. He would say that he was so devastated that he could not talk about it. She left without an address or an explanation. No foul play thank goodness. Just a case of a wife gone mad.

Her family did not matter. No one would press him for an explanation of Kate's whereabouts. Kate always said that if someone looked up the word 'dysfunctional' in the dictionary, the person would see a picture of her family staring glumly back at them.

Madge. He'd forgotten about Madge. What would he tell Kate's friend who went on the cruise with her? Or more disconcertingly, what might Madge tell him? Colin took another shot of whiskey and thought, "I'll deal with Madge later."

Madge had feigned indifference when Ross Winter had knocked on her cabin door shortly after the *SS Tropical Sea* left Windward for its return to Miami. She reluctantly opened the door and invited him in.

"I've come to collect Kate's luggage," he said with a crooked grin that Madge interpreted as post-coital. In Madge's life everything was either pre- or post-coital.

"Help yourself," she told him, standing still so that he would have to brush against her to gain access into the small cabin.

"So, eerrr," she purred.

"Ross," he answered, holding out a large hamlike hand. Madge licked her lips.

"Kate is in my cabin," he volunteered. "She will be staying with me for the trip back. And then, forever, I hope."

"Well, well," Madge said in shock. She had no idea that Kate, whom she thought she knew, had it in her to run off "forever" with a man she had just met. But then again, look at the man. Madge would have run off with him herself had he asked her.

Ross collected Kate's bags hurriedly. Running his fingers through his thick red hair, he again offered Madge a wry smile.

"I hope you two are happy," Madge offered. "Tell Kate she knows where to find me, should she care to," Madge hissed, shutting the door behind him.

Why didn't she say something, Madge idly wondered. She could understand why Kate would leave Colin. Hell, she should have done that a long time ago for the way he treated her. But at least she could have dropped by to say "caio."

Madge did not like being ignored. That seemed awfully close to being stood up. She was starting to feel sorry for herself when she remembered Jose, the laundry boy, was waiting for her downstairs on a pile of dirty clothes. She grabbed a bottle of wine from the nightstand, slipped out of her underwear and left the thought of Kate behind.

When the ship got back to Miami, she thought she saw Kate walk down the ramp. She recognized the broad straw hat. The one with the blue polka-dotted headband Kate had bought at Hutzler's two weeks before they left Baltimore. Kate had insisted it was chic. Madge hated it but went along good-naturedly. She watched the hat disappear into a taxicab without the wearer ever turning around once.

"That's it," Madge said out loud. "I don't like getting the shaft, sister. You're dead to me, Kate Carrington!"

CHAPTER FIVE

Windward

Breed left the rum shop and walked down the foothills toward the village of Marabel. Following him were the shouts and laughter of his comrades, especially the loud-mouthed Peter.

"You better watch your back, Breed. You know Debbie already kill a man in Wacuzi. Watch you not next." The men slapped each other on the back, then settled down to their business.

Breed was familiar with the gossip that his so-called woman had killed a man because he had cheated on her. She was never jailed because no evidence or body could be found. Everyone believed that she worked black magic courtesy of Bim Bim, the Obeah woman, to leave no trace. Breed chose to ignore the rumor. Debbie had the face of a rosy ripe Ceylon mango and a bottom that would make a preacher drop his bible. He thought about her as he went into the shop to buy clothing for the naked white woman he had left in his bed.

The shop was busy as usual because it sold everything from hot food, chamber pots, machetes, ground provisions, building supplies and clothing. Buckets and roofing galvanize were stocked at the front entrance. A few chickens walked about freely, happy that they had escaped yesterday's stew.

Nothing stays secret in the village, so when Breed went up the counter with two panties, a bra, two cotton shifts, a toothbrush and a pack of French letters, everybody knew about it.

Including Popo Le Grande, Breed's formidable grandmother. Popo lived about 10 minutes from her grandson's house. She made that walk every day to clean, wash the wares, cook and make sure her grandson had clean clothes to wear. Although she had taught him since he was a boy to do all of these things for himself, it still gave her pleasure to do them for him. Because he knew it made his grandmother happy to help him out, he accommodated her. Today, Popo decided to go a little earlier to the house because she had some unexpected business in town. Striding through the front door she was greeted by an almost naked white woman.

"Morning, Miss," Popo said, courteously and with raised eyebrows.

"Good morning," Kate stammered, clutching tightly to the sleeves of a cotton shirt she had retrieved from the closet. "I am so sorry, but I am waiting for Bruce to come back."

"Breed," corrected his grandmother, not missing a beat. "His name Breed."

"Oh God," Kate thought. She had just spent the night with a man and she could not remember his name.

She was about to cry when she noticed that Popo had a broom in her hand and had begun sweeping the already clean floor. She had an amused look on her face.

"I'm sorry," Kate stammered again.

"No need to be sorry, Miss. Breed is my grandson, but I make a point to not meddle in his business."

Now Popo understood the message she had gotten just minutes earlier from an out-of-breath gossip. Still she did not expect to see what she saw.

"Dey call me Popo," she nodded amiably.

Kate was unable to look Breed's grandmother in the face. What does she think of me, she wondered. Despite all of the conflicting feelings she experienced since arriving on the island, what she didn't feel was shame, or guilt. Instead, she felt a strange and invigorating joy. Exhaling fully for the first time in years, Kate held out her free hand to Popo while clutching the shirt around her body with the other.

"Abigail. Abigail Fisherman," she blurted out with a smile. "And I have come here to—to stay," she added with a confidence that astonished her.

Kate had always liked the name Abigail. Fisherman came in a flash of inspiration as she saw Breed approaching the house. Breed was a fisherman and so she would be.

Breed walked into the kitchen where his grandmother and Abigail stood facing each other. He handed her the bag of clothes and turned to embrace his grandmother.

"We go talk later, Breed," Popo said. "I see you are well."

She walked towards the door and turned back to look at Abigail.

"So long, Abigail Fisherman," said Popo, making a gesture with her fingers to encourage Kate to cover herself. "It was good to, ahh, see you. I guessing I will see more of you since is stay you come to stay." She directed the last part of her remarks at her grandson, and with a regal turn of her wrist she bade them goodbye.

"Abigail?" Breed asked after his grandmother was out of earshot. "What has become of Kate Carrington, once O'Neil, my dirty colleen? I liked her."

"Kate Carrington walked out on me" was her answer.

"Bye bye den, Kate, and hello Abi," said Breed as he wrapped her in his arms. He asked no more questions. He didn't need any explanations. Nothing mattered to him but the desire he felt for the recently christened Abigail Fisherman. The two of them stood locked in a kiss. The shirt fell to the floor. Their lovemaking was sweet and fast. The hard wooden floor did not spare their backs and elbows, but they did not care.

When they spoke again, Breed looked at Abi and mumbled, "Let's get you clean and put some clothes on you." In fact he had no particular desire to get up from where they lay entangled.

"I'm clean now," Abigail said, her eyes twinkling mischievously. "But just to make sure, let's go out and bathe again. I like the cold water."

Breed chased her outside, scattering the chickens in the yard as they raced towards the open galvanized shed. There he rubbed her down with the coarse, yellow soap and she returned the favor. She felt full of life when they turned the tap off.

Abigail put on her new dress over her new panties and bra. The bra was a perfect fit for her.

"And how did you know what size to get me?" she asked Breed shyly, as he snapped the fasteners at the back for her. She was trying to adjust to this new person that had emerged from somewhere deep inside of her. She closed her eyes to embrace her newness. She wanted to scream with joy, but instead her face crinkled up. The pressure of the last 24 hours found an outlet through her eyes. Tears poured in streams down her cheeks.

Breed dried her tears with his lips. He had waited for her all of his life. He had not been able to make a commitment to any woman because he felt that the special one had not yet come along. He had tried to fall in love, to experience the feeling of belonging to someone, but there was something different here. Although women came in droves because Breed LeGrande was a handsome man and rumor had it that he was sweeter than a Julie mango, he always felt that something was missing. Until now. The woman with emerald green orbs had changed everything in what seemed like the blink of an eye.

"What are you daydreaming about?" Abi breathed in his ear. "I still want to know how come you knew what size bra to buy." She tickled his nose with hers.

"I made a cup out of my hands," Breed grinned. "I took the bras out of the bucket one by one until I found one that fit into my hands. I knew that was the size to get. My hands will never be the same again."

"Here," he said cupping her breasts firmly in his hands, "dis will always be where my hands belong."

They stood together for a long time and then reluctantly separated themselves from each other.

"I have to go to Seaview," he told her. "I must take care of some business. Will you be alright alone?"

"I'll stay here," Abigail assured him, her eyes never leaving his own. "I'll introduce myself to my new surroundings."

"OK, but listen Miss Abigail Fisherman," Breed warned. "De people round here are peepers, so keep the door closed. I assure you dey will be hovering around outside trying to see wha going on in a place that does not concern dem. Dey like looking into other people's affairs. Someone ought to make a calypso about all dat peeping dat taking place."

"Why would someone make a song about that?" asked Abigail curiously.

"Our songs are like social commentaries," Breed replied in his melodious voice. "We learn what is going on through our calypsonians, who put everything that's happening to words and music that make you want to move your hips."

He grabbed Abigail and danced her around the room, singing in her ear and flinging his hips this way and that. She let him guide her and buried her face in his neck. They twirled and dipped. Breed placed each of his palms on either side of her hips and wound them around and around so that they ground into his groin.

"What dance is this?" she moaned, trying to keep up with his fast steps.

"This is the Samba," he told her. "A gift from Africa via Brazil. A dance of liberation."

"Then please liberate me," Abi pleaded, trembling with desire.

He moved her around so that her back was against him and pressed himself against her. She closed her eyes and was lost in the electric surges that came over her body.

He swung her towards him and kissed her, his dreadlocks covering her face. His arms held her with a skill and understanding that was both reassuring and frightening. Then he guided her limp body to the bed with her eyes still closed. When Abi woke up he was gone.

CHAPTER SIX

Baltimore

Colin arrived at the bar early to give himself enough time to think about what he had done. What he had paid Ross Winter, a complete stranger, to do.

He thought back to how easy it had been to find a hired gun. He had been drinking at a tavern in Fells Point when Ross Winter wandered in. As was usual in the bars in Baltimore, the two men became engrossed in a conversation about crime in the city. Soon they were laughing together and getting drunker and drunker. He must have said something to trigger Ross's remark.

"I'll do her for you," his newfound friend blurted out.

"Do?" Colin exclaimed in a guttural whisper. "I don't want her screwed. I want her d-e-a-d," he said, spelling out the last word. His brow was wet with anticipation. He was excited about the prospect of getting rid of Kate but there was also an excitement he did not want to identify. One that made him squirm uncomfortably on the bar stool as he looked at Ross' taut body. One that caused him to dig in and rearrange his briefs.

"Yeah, I hear you," Ross nodded casually. "I'll do it. Let's talk money. Then tell me when and what she looks like."

Colin pulled a photograph of Kate from his wallet and showed it to Ross.

"That's a nice piece. Why you want her dead?"

"I'm not about to discuss my personal affairs with you. You want the job or not?" Colin asked, irritated.

"O.K., my man. Cool your jets. I just like to know that the person I am about to whack deserves it. That's all."

"I can tell you this," Colin said in measured tones. "She knows something she has no business knowing. Something that can cause me to lose everything I have worked for."

"Say no more," Ross said, satisfied with the explanation.

The men met two more times to finalize the details at an all-night diner on Aliceanna Street where shadowy figures darted in and out of warehouses and docks with regularity. By his own testimony, Ross was a seasoned pro who was no stranger to murder-for-hire. He had a questionable portfolio of more than half a dozen women who had lost their lives by his hand. The agreement was for him to drive himself to Miami to avoid the paper trail of an airplane or train ticket, book a cruise on the *SS Tropical Sea*, introduce himself to Kate and find a way to kill her and to dispose of her body, preferably in the ocean. He was also to make sure that her friend Madge remained clueless in the Caribbean.

Ross was very impressed with Colin's plans. "Great decision, Doc," he said. "Guys in my line of work know that cruise ships don't only pollute the ocean and the sky, they provide great cover for crime. Once you're 20 miles off the shore, you're in international waters. Then it's the law of the pirates, man. Like we say in the business,

> If you can't find your gun
> And you don't have a potion
> Just take her on a cruise
> And toss her in the ocean."

As Colin waited on the bar stool, the thought flashed across his mind that Ross would walk in with two cops, their guns drawn, and a pair of handcuffs. Alarmed, he got to his feet unsteadily—Johnny Walker was doing a jig in his head. He stumbled out into the open air to make a dash for his car.

"Going somewhere?" A strong arm restrained him. "Can't wait a minute for a guy to get through this city traffic?"

Colin stared for a long time at Ross's very tight jeans and pink flowered shirt before they walked back together into the bar.

"Are you alone?" he asked, looking around to make sure no one was watching them.

"I always travel alone, Doc. Always."

The men sat at the bar in the same seats they had occupied when they last met and got down to business.

"It was not difficult," Ross reported, rubbing his chin reflectively "She didn't struggle. I strangled her after she was dead drunk. Then I waited till all was quiet, took her out of the room up to the deck. I waited till I saw sharks in the shadows, then I tossed her in."

"How can I be sure you're telling me the truth?" asked Colin.

Ross reached into his shirt pocket, took out Kate's wedding band and handed it to Colin. She had guiltily taken it off her finger and forgotten to retrieve it when they had sex in his cabin.

Colin exhaled.

"I have her luggage in my car," he continued warily. "I brought it back with me on the train. What should I do with it?" he asked Colin with a smirk.

Colin tried to feign interest. He pulled out a thick white envelope filled with hundred dollar bills from his briefcase and gave it to Ross.

"I don't care what you do with her damn things. Throw them in the harbor. Give them to the homeless. Or wear them," he added cynically as he observed Ross's obvious flair for things feminine.

Ross did not respond. He had already removed some of Kate's frilly bits for himself, including the hat with the blue polka dotted headband, which he had worn when he got off the ship in Miami.

"Goodbye," Colin gurgled thickly and walked out of the bar. He was not happy with the effect that this man had on him. It was not new and it was unwelcome.

Ross patted the envelope with a satisfied smile and called out for another drink.

"Make it a double shot, my good man," he said to the indifferent bartender.

Colin got into his car and drove towards Lombard Street for the long drive back to the suburbs. He felt relieved but still tense. He turned on the radio full blast and sang along with Diana Ross. By the time he merged into the Russell Street traffic, his shoulders relaxed a little. He reached into his pocket and, waiting for the midway point of the bridge over the railroad tracks, he rolled down the car window and tossed Kate's wedding band out. Maybe some hapless hobo will find it and believe in God again. His thoughts lingered on the picture of Kate's half-eaten body at the bottom of the ocean. "Hey, Poe," he said, evoking his favorite poet, "I bet you never thought of doing it this way," as Jimmy Hendrix's "Hey Joe" roared out of the radio.

When he reached his well-tended half-acre in Columbia he immediately showered to wash away the memory of his body reacting to another man's. He had a strong nightcap, and fell into bed to a night unencumbered with dreams.

Waking up the next morning, the house felt different.

He made himself a cup of coffee. Strong and black like Deirdra Jackson, the woman he had been seeing for the past two years. He had first seen her at an office party at his wife's job. She was part of the catering team, and he was quite aroused by the way she strutted around in her blue maid's uniform with the white frilly apron. She had dark chocolate skin, full breasts and hips and pouty lips, which he soon found she knew how to use. She was a far cry from what he found to be attractive back in his college days.

Colin grinned at the thought of Deirdra—so young and so luscious. Now that he was free of Kate, he could spend his evenings with her, sprawled on the couch with a drink in his hand. In the shower, he let the steaming water wash over him. By ten o'clock, he was saying hello to his secretary Suellen.

CHAPTER SEVEN

Windward

The morning was covered in gray, but the sun was doing its best to dissolve the haze. Already the house was thick with tropical heat, which made Abigail appreciate her new cotton shift with buttons down the front. She cheerfully put it on and fanned her chest with her hand.

She went to the window and looked out at the morning. A few chickens were scratching in the dirt, looking for a worm or a forgotten grain of corn. Someone's dog sat under the sapodilla tree with his tongue drooping out of the side of his mouth. There was not a person in sight. She wondered how long she'd have to wait until someone came peeping. No sooner had the thought entered her head than she saw her.

The woman wore a pink flowered skirt and an orange plaid shirt. She had two thick braids that stuck out from under an old fedora. Her feet were bare. On top of the battered fedora, she balanced a large bucket with the precision of a gymnast. She was heading towards the house. She walked briskly, making Abi wonder how she managed not to spill more of the water she was carrying. The woman slowed down as she approached the front steps, stooped down and removed the bucket from her head and placed it on the ground.

"All you home? I have some water here," she called out shrilly.

No one had asked for water to be delivered. Breed had his own running water in the pipe behind the house. So Abi knew that the bucket of water was an excuse. Sure enough, the woman walked around cautiously, checking things out so that she could tell the others what she had found. Everybody knew that if she saw nothing, she would make up a story anyway.

Hiding behind the curtain, Abi watched the woman meticulously inspect the clothes on the line for any evidence of a feminine presence and then peep through the bedroom window. She then picked up her bucket and reluctantly shuffled away. Abigail giggled to herself as she stuck her head out the window hoping a wayward breeze would happen by. She was dripping in sweat.

The table in the front room was littered with paper. She sifted through the pile to find a sheet thick enough to serve as a fan when something else caught her eye. On the wall above the table was a small black and white photograph framed with worn out passé partout. Age had made it brown and yellow at the edges. The photograph was of a man and woman on their wedding day. The man had a flat head and broad African features and was squeezed into an ill-fitting suit. The woman was tall and slender. She wore a long shapeless frock, originally white but now faded into a pale yellow, with a wide band around her waist. She looked happy next to the man harnessed in the unforgiving suit. Abi recognized the woman at once. The features were unmistakable. The proud eyes, full mouth and a prominent nose. Popo was a handsome bride.

Abi reached out to straighten the photo when she heard a blood-curdling yelp. It took her a second to realize that it came from her. Something had crawled out from behind the photograph on the wall. It was the ugliest thing she had ever seen. Sporting the square body of a deformed lizard and a short, stubby tail, the mud-brown creature looked like a miniature crocodilish dinosaur. It was the first time since she landed on Windward that she wished she were back in Maryland.

After she collected herself, she carefully put the photograph that had fallen to the table back on the wall. God's mishap nonchalantly crawled back under the frame. Not wishing to witness any more of its kind, she went into the bedroom and lay on the sheets. When Breed returned, she was fast asleep.

Abigail opened her eyes as Breed gently smoothed her furrowed brow. The morning sun had brought the fish to the surface early, giving him a day's catch long before evening. "Plus," he said slyly, "Ma Po not coming today."

Abigail urgently grasped his hand and told him about the awful mini-dinosaur.

"Is only a woodslave, Green Eyes. It ugly but it won't hurt you."

She tried to protest some more, but her mouth was smothered with his kisses. He removed her cotton dress and she disappeared under his body. She wrapped her legs around his back and drew him closer and closer so he could penetrate the very core of her being.

Later, wrapped in towels, they went outside and sat on the bricks that served as steps. A steady breeze washed over them. Everything was quiet except for two green parrots squawking overhead and Patsy Cline singing in the radio.

"Patsy is not the only crazy one," Breed said, giving her a sweet eye. "I am crazy too. For you."

The night swept swiftly across the sky—black violet and peppered with stars. They speckled the sky like a kaleidoscopic canopy and twinkled at the crescent moon. Suddenly one of them darted across the vast bowl of space.

Abi poked Breed hard in his chest with her elbow. "I've seen my first shooting star," she squealed with delight.

"Ha," Breed nodded. "You ain't see nottin' yet. Dat sky is a real carnival when it ready."

Somebody's dog let out a sharp yelp as if something had suddenly stung him. Down the foothills, dogs picked up the chorus and started a symphony of howls and yelps. Even Gershwin would be charmed by this canine rhapsody, she thought as she snuggled closer to Breed.

They sat silently enjoying the night for what seemed like hours. Hungry, they finally dragged themselves indoors to feast on mangoes. After her revelation at the market, Abigail couldn't get enough of them. Breed soon realized that he'd have to wrestle her to the ground to get a bite of any of them, a task he did not mind at all. Tonight she reached into the basket and pulled out a plump red and yellow one.

"Sea Lawn," she said proudly.

Amused by her studious pronunciation, he undertook a quick tutorial. "It's Ceylon," he chuckled. "Like the country now known as Sri Lanka. It was renamed in 1972."

"Well, what do you know," she said, as she pursed her lips in anticipation.

She did not cut her prized possession into neat little squares like they did in America. She instead sank her teeth into the fruit like Dracula finding a virgin neck in the night and then sucked the pulp and juice noisily into her mouth. She groaned as the sweetness coated her throat and the excess liquid ran down her chin. She continued slurping until there was no evidence of fruit left. When she was done, she saw Breed staring at her in awe. Yes, he concluded, she was a vampire.

"We have a name for people like you," he finally said. "We call them 'mango police.' But you in a class by yourself. You kill that mango. What you is, is a mango head."

"Come," he leaned forward speaking in a low hoarse voice as he pulled her into the bedroom. Falling on the mattress, he groaned, "I have something for you."

"It wouldn't be attached to you, would it?" she whispered seductively as her mango stained lips caressed his face.

"It is," he moaned, "and I pray it remains attached but suffers the same fate of that mango."

Early the next morning, Abigail woke up with a start. There was a thunderous racket overhead. It sounded like bullets were hitting the roof. She was about to dive under the bed to save herself when she noticed that Breed was not at all concerned.

"Is only the rain, Green Eyes," he assured her.

"Why on earth is it so loud?" Abigail shouted so that she could be heard above the ruckus. "I thought we were being bombed."

"By whom?" Breed smiled broadly. "That would never happen on dis little island. We not in the world's crosshairs."

"The roof make with galvanize," he continued. "When the rain come suddenly and hard like it just did, bucket a drop, it makes a bacchanal over your head. It soon stop with the same speed it start. That's our rain. Let's go outside and see if we can catch some."

They dressed quickly and went outdoors. Breed adjusted the spout that fed the rain water into a large steel drum at the side of the house. The drum rapidly filled with water.

"Dat is good water to wash clothes with," he told Abi. "Sometimes when there is no rain at all, we will be happy to have dis."

"Dat is right, mon," Abigail yipped back, cupping her hands in the barrel and sending a spray of water his way.

It was the first time she had ever let rain just pour down on her. She threw her head back with delight, stretched her arms upward and let the raincloud have its way. When she was a little girl she did the same thing when it snowed in Baltimore.

"Are you going to stay in the rain all day?" Breed asked, looking at the little girl trying to inhale the rain.

Abigail never expected rain to be so comforting. It had always been too cold to enjoy. She could hear the nearby squeals of some village children running around nearby. She would have been happy to join them.

Breed wrapped her up in his arms. Time was off-duty and it took them a while to realize that the sun was back out. It was as if the rain suddenly remembered it had somewhere else to fall. What it left behind was the smell of perfumed wet grass, a muddy roadway and a group of children staring at them wide-eyed with their hands over their mouths.

"What unu watching?" snapped Breed good-humoredly. The children ran away giggling and poking at each other. "What did I tell you?" he whispered in Abi's wet ear. "A nation of peepers."

What he knew for sure was that everyone who did not already know now knew that Breed LeGrande and a white woman were "hugging up in broad, broad daylight." The rest of the story would be richly seasoned, cooked up and made into a spicy pelau.

Breed reluctantly left Abi alone so he could go work his land in the next village of Mayaro and collect what provisions there were. Abi sat down with the weekly newspaper. She read with interest about the conflicts between the prime minister and the "radicals" over education, sometimes with raised eyebrows and audible sighs. A large percentage of the people on the island were struggling to make ends meet, the opposition party charged at protest rallies. The poor had to pay for educating their children and because they couldn't afford the cost, their children wound up in the same situation as their parents and grandparents.

She saw a letter in the paper that had Breed's name typed on it. She was eager to read what he had to say. It was a letter addressed to the Prime Minister.

"As a fisherman," it began, "I am finding it impossible to gain access to the sea in order to fish. With new buildings being erected constantly and more and more land sold to foreigners who desire property on or near the water, we fisherman are finding it increasingly difficult to get to the ocean. Some of us have been warned and threatened for passing through private property in order to work. Fish is our livelihood. If we cannot fish, we cannot eat nor can we provide for our families. We are being made to feel invisible as foreigners become more visible."

Abi put the letter back in the newspaper and went outside to sit. She thought about how no one in America could guess what's really going on in Windward. She herself had assumed on her first day that such a beautiful island had to have happy people.

Walking towards the house, Popo got knowing glances from the women she passed. They all knew that Debbie, Breed's ex-woman, had just charged up the road a few minutes earlier. Counting on a confrontation, the women left their children behind instructing them to behave themselves, then formed a procession behind Popo, and marched to Breed's house. They expected this to be more fun than carnival. No one wanted to miss what surely would happen next. Who would win the fight? The white woman or Debbie? Everyone put what money they had on Debbie.

Debbie walked ahead of the crowd lost in her own thoughts. She really did not want to fight anyone. Least of all some American woman she did not know. But she could not lose face. It was unheard of to let another woman take your man without a fight. Debbie knew that Breed kept her only for his sexual pleasure and nothing more. But because of her pride she would fight for him knowing that even when she beat the hell out of the woman, Breed would never marry her.

Hearing someone approaching, Abigail walked out of the house thinking it was Breed returning with food. What she encountered instead was a striking young Amazon standing belligerently in the yard. She was dressed in a rainbow colored sarong tied just above her breasts. Her hair was newly braided, and thick plaits stuck out at various angles from her head. She wanted to attract Breed while she cussed him out and slapped his new woman around.

She kicked off her sandals and approached Abigail aggressively.

"You have my man?" she demanded. "I come for he. Where he is, eh?"

Even in her anger, Debbie's voice was so musical that it took Abigail by surprise. She did not see Debbie's right hand whip towards her face, but she felt the sting a second later.

Abigail Fisherman had been hit before. Memories of middle-school brawls flashed through her mind. Every girl in The Valley knew how to fight. Not the hair-pulling fighting like the well-bred girls in Roland Park, but down and dirty like the boys in Hampden. You either fought hard or you became a victim. Instinctively, she lunged for Debbie and wrestled her down to the ground, tearing off the startled woman's sarong in the process.

They were thrashing about in the dirt when Popo and the women arrived. Debbie was naked except for her panties and Abigail was on top of her, one hand around her neck and the other punching her in the stomach. The village women laughed hysterically.

"Woi," screamed Sasu, jumping up and down and clapping her hands. "Dat white lady can fight, oui. She bussin' Debbie tail."

Unamused, Popo went to fetch a pail of water. As Abigail tried to get up, Debbie clutched her between her thighs. Debbie's thighs were strong. Every man in Windward could attest to that (even if they had not personally experienced their grip). Abi toppled back to the ground but managed to land a punch to Debbie's chin. Popo returned with the water and threw it on the women. Squealing with surprise, both women scrambled to their feet to a robust round of applause. This fight would be remembered and embroidered for years to come.

Breed ran up after hearing all of the commotion. He was met by the spectacle of the two women splattered in mud, both in various states of undress. Popo covered Debbie in her wet sarong and walked her back down the hill before Abigail, who was rearing for a second round, got to her. Debbie was the victim of all of the pent-up anger that Abigail had stored away for years. A lockbox of frustration had busted open.

"Well, well," said Breed, impressed. "Now I recognize you. You are that dirty white woman I picked up in town last week, right?"

Abigail peered at him with a look of befuddlement through her mud mask. Who had she become in such a short space of time? She used to be a respectable, professional married woman. What was becoming of her? What had this island done to her, and what else might it do?

"You don't have to fight for me, Abigail Fisherman," Breed said as he gently touched her bruised cheek. "I am all yours. But is good to know you can fend for yourself, girl. I better watch out in case you decide to put a lickin' on me one day. Come to think of it, I was just tinkin' bout getting a guard dog. But I could just sit you down by the door instead."

Abi lunged at him, but he escaped into the house. She chased after him and slammed the door before any more curious neighbors came peeping.

Meanwhile, a freshly washed and cleanly clad Debbie was already making plans to go to town and find herself another man. Losing the fight with this American woman did not bother her. She was proud of herself for not having lost face. She walked with her head held high knowing that she would be respected in the village for fighting for her man, win or lose. She wasn't worried. It wouldn't take her long to replace Breed. The line was long and, like Charles Dickens' character, Barkis, they were willing.

CHAPTER EIGHT

Windward

Abigail idly contemplated how days turned into weeks and weeks into months on this remote island. Being so close to the equator, there were no summers or winters. The sun rose and set only a few minutes apart in June and January. The tradewinds that sprung across the ocean from Africa kept the heat down, while the liquefied clouds pushed by the winds replenished the gardens, small farms, plantations and cisterns with life-giving rainwater. She had no plans for the future. "Tomorrow come soon enough" was what she had heard Breed say.

When the two of them lay together at night, they shared their stories. They laughed through the funny bits and held each other through the sad memories. Once they talked until the big red rooster, Chantycleer, asserting his authority over the rest of the chickens, started a cacophony of cockadoodledoos in the face of the morning sky.

"Tell me about dem O'Neils," Breed asked her. "Were they good people?"

"Good people?" Abi pursed her lips like she was trying to make up her mind. "I never thought of them as being good or bad," she finally said. "They were just there."

Her parents had met each other at an orphanage in County Cork, Ireland, and moved to America when she was an infant. She had no siblings and there were no relatives—at least none that she knew of. Mr. O'Neill was employed at a raincoat factory in The Valley, but he drank for a living. Mrs. O'Neil, a slightly built woman with a retreating spirit, had gotten a good whipping from life. By the time she was thirty-five her skin was leathery and her eyes had sunk into dark round sockets. Her eyebrows, always raised in suspicion, made her look like she was perpetually expecting the worst. Kate lived with Mr. Malcontent and Mrs. Disapproval, as she secretely called them until she left home for the University of Baltimore, only a mile away but a world apart from that ramshackle rowhouse by the river.

Breed nodded and squeezed her hand tighter when she shared her life with Colin Carrington and the unhappiness of the union.

"Dats over with now," Breed sympathized, caressing her brow with his fingertips. "You never have to experience being ignored again. I will take care of you. You will never see him again. Unless he come here looking for you, and I promise you, he not doing dat."

"How do you know that?' she looked at him quizzically.

"Bim Bim," he said. "She know everyting."

"What of your family?" Abi snuggled close to him. "Can't be worse than mine."

"Dat's what you tink," Breed laughed. "But you probably right. I grew up surrounded by enough love from my grandmother to last me a lifetime. What I know is what my grandmother told me. But I am happy enough. Besides, now that you in my life, we can make our own story."

He told her how his grandparents met in Jamaica, where they were both born. How his grandfather's name was really Jeremiah Wellington, but people changed it to JW because "it was too blasted long to remember." JW had inherited some land in Windward from his mother, Bernadette Alexis, and when she died, he moved with his young wife. They had one child, a girl named Christine. Breed's mother.

Breed sighed softly and more than once when he recounted what Popo told him about his mother. She was a dreamer. She dreamed of bridges that could take her to Trafalgar Square or Westminster Abbey. She read Shakespeare and loved the Bronte sisters. She wanted to be a writer but doubted if anyone would ever read what she wrote about life on a little island.

Totally out of character, Christine went and fell in love with Hari Singh. Saga boy Hari, who had sex with any woman who stayed put long enough to give him time to take off his pants. It didn't take long for Hari to disappear into the cold of Brooklyn, New York, where he would certainly need his pants. Christine was 16 when she gave birth to Breed.

When Breed was two, Christine left him with her mother, picked up what was left of her self-esteem, stuck it in her suitcase along with the fried red snapper, guava cheese and tamarind balls that her mother had packed for her, and left with a boat-load of hopefuls headed to what they were mistakenly told was the "mother country". England. They shared that belief with the Windrush generation who had left the West Indies in 1948, traveling thousands of miles across the Atlantic ocean in search of a better life.

The British government had encouraged mass immigration back then to fill the shortages in the labour market caused by the Second World War. The ship was called the *Empire Windrush* and that was the first time so many Caribbean people including children, arrived in Britain at once. They were invited to live in England as British citizens and help in the rebuilding of the "mother country", but when they got there, most of them faced unequal treatment and prejudices that continue today.

"As far as I know," Breed continued, "she studied journalism in London and eventually got a job with a newspaper. Her letters were sporadic at first, then non-existent. Maybe she followed the example of some people from these islands that go overseas. At first they write and send money back. Their families wait in vain for that ticket to join them overseas. But they sometimes embrace their new country and start new families. Some of them are never heard from again," he concluded soberly. "Time for us to sleep."

The next morning they made their standard breakfast together. Hot cocoa made from the seeds Abi had pounded for him, fried bakes and codfish. When Breed went to the ocean in Vinvel to fish, his grandmother would come to check that her boy had enough food and that his house was clean.

Popo Le Grande was proud of her grandson. He was very much like her husband. JW was always concerned about the "community" as he called it, when he explained to Popo that he had to organize in the town so that people had enough to eat and children could afford schoolbooks and uniforms. Popo did not care much for his philosophy back then. She was content to wrap herself around him and "smell him up all day." But he always had to leave too soon because Mr. McIntosh up the road or Miss LaTouche in the valley had an issue worthy of his atention.

A constant stream of neighbors flowed to the house to air their differences and ask for his advice. JW settled disputes for miles around. He helped people "see reason", a sight that surprised and unsettled some of them. An elusive concept.

Not long after Christine left for England, JW was murdered. Who did it was never determined, but why was readily apparent. He vocally opposed the government and was trying to implement change. He was especially concerned that only the families with money could send send their children to study in places like England and America to become doctors and lawyers and other noteworthy professionals. The poor were left behind. He wanted to see the government build institutions on Windward so that everyone who wanted to, could afford a higher education.

Popo missed JW dearly, but Breed filled the hole in her heart. He became the focus of her life. A life that Popo thought until now was pretty uncomplicated. She was used to living with a revolutionary. She was used to hearing lectures on Marxism and imperialism. She knew about social conflict and government corruption and a failed federation in the West Indies. What she didn't know was what to do with the white woman in her grandson's bed.

CHAPTER NINE

Baltimore

It didn't take Colin long to grow accustomed to his life as a single man. He quickly got rid of Kate's belongings. The Salvation Army was happy to get her expensive clothing. He tossed the photographs of his wife into the garbage and sold off her jewelry, which afforded him a tidy sum of cash.

As Kate Carrington became a memory, Colin's thoughts were increasingly fixed on Deirdra. He sometimes wondered why this black woman aroused such passion in him. Growing up in suburban Towson, he had never interacted with black people. Working for the city, he found those not laying dead in the morgue to be quite tiresome.

He paid for all of Deirdra's expenses, including a house in Charles Village so that she'd be just minutes away from his office.

"There is something about that woman that makes me go wild," Colin muttered happily to himself as he drove home to his half acre in Columbia, sated after another evening with her.

It was one o'clock in the morning when the telephone jolted him out of a deep slumber.

"Hello," he muttered.

"Remember me?"

The voice got Colin's immediate attention. This was a call he did not want.

"Of course," Colin said sternly.

"We need to talk," Ross hissed.

"There's nothing we need to talk about. You promised never to contact me again. I am surprised you are not a man of your word," Colin snapped.

"Wrong. We need to meet. I need some more money, my friend."

Colin rubbed his face with his free hand. He was at a loss for words. He knew there could be no good end to this.

"I will not be blackmailed. Got that?" he shouted into the phone.

"Wednesday. Same place at 8 pm with 10K, or your cover is blown," Ross replied calmly.

Colin hung up the telephone and went into the kitchen. He fixed himself a stiff drink and sat down to think. There would be no more sleep for him tonight. He knew he could withdraw the money from the bank, but he also knew that would not be the end of it. He would have to keep shelling out more and more as time went by. The Rosses of the world cannot be satisfied. Colin had money, but not enough to pay off a Ross.

Two days later he came face to face with Ross Winter again. The hired gun was a bit less dapper than Colin remembered. There was an air of desperation about him.

His blood-shot eyes darted back and forth as he looked at Colin.

"For your own good, I hope you have all of it," Ross said uneasily, meeting Colin's hard stare.

There was an unpleasant odor to Ross, not dissimilar to the smell of bodies Colin encountered at the morgue. How could he possibly hand over this much money to a druggie, he wondered. Here was a guy bound to be pinched by the police and who would quickly snitch on him for a more lenient sentence.

"Let's talk," said Colin, with feigned sympathy.

"Just hand over the money," muttered Ross, nervously looking around the room. "I need it or I'm a dead man."

"There's no more where that came from," Colin replied sharply, as he handed over the large manila envelope.

Ross grabbed the loot and bolted out of the bar. By the time Colin reached the door to follow him, he was lost in a crowd of partygoers. "Who do you get to kill a killer?" Colin asked himself.

Concentration eluded him the next morning at work. He was lost in thought as he looked at the bullet-ridden body in front of him and wondered who had done the deed. "Snap out of it," he told himself. "Get a grip."

Colin's job was to discover what a dead body revealed about the time, cause and manner of its demise. His expertise was in ballistics. He analyzed the impact of bullets and other projectiles on the muscles and tissues. He enjoyed the responsibility of collecting evidence, then writing a report on his findings. It gave him a feeling of ridiculous importance to know that his reports could put a criminal behind bars or set an innocent person free. He had friends high up in the police department, and he worked closely with prosecutors and detectives. Dr. Colin Carrington knew the ins and outs of crime, but now it was on a personal level.

With gloves covered in coagulated blood, he shoved his hand into the groin of the body on the slab, suddenly thinking that the body belonged to Ross Winter.

"Dr. Carrington," the attendant on duty looked at him, aghast.

"Uh, I'm sorry," he stammered. "I thought there was a bullet fragment lodged in the uhhhh, corpus spongiosum. Never mind, I need to clean up so I can write my report."

Ms. Shafer walked out of the room confused. She had worked beside the medical examiner for six years. What had gotten into the normally mild-mannered doctor today, she wondered.

Yes, Ross would have to be dealt with, Colin thought while scrubbing his hands in the washroom. But how? And when? He returned to his office with lurid thoughts swirling in his head.

Two days later, the dead body of Ross Winter was found slumped next to a dumpster on Wicomico Street in Pigtown. He was dressed in women's clothing and wearing a straw hat with a blue polka-dotted headband.

CHAPTER TEN

Windward

A bigail had both of her hands in the belly of the kingfish. She had become an expert at pulling out entrails and gills. After washing the fish under the tap, she picked up a sharp knife and cut the fish into slices. Then she rubbed chive, garlic, tumeric and chadon beni into the flesh.

After her legendary fight with Debbie, the women in the village had warmed up to her and now she had friends among them. They taught her how to cook Breed's catch and the importance of preparation. As she looked at the slices of fish in front of her, she could not help but stew over Colin. She closed her eyes and for a moment imagined that he was on the counter, all sliced up. She felt a strange stir in her stomach maybe brought on by the eggs she had removed from the dead fish. Roe, the women called it. She put the eggs aside to prepare for Breed. He liked fish eggs cooked up with big thyme, seasoning peppers and lots of garlic.

She patted her teary eyes with the corner of the kitchen towel and remembered the old days when she would take prepared slices of frozen fish out of the wrapper, pass them under the water, sprinkle on some salt and pepper and pop them in the oven. She smiled as she let this one languish in a spa of curried flavor until it was ready for frying later.

Popo came by to help Abi with the washing every Monday morning.

"Where is the laudromat?" Abi joked, the first time Popo showed up to help her wash.

"Here it is." Popo chuckled as she handed Abi a big tin bucket in one hand and a wooden scrubbing board in the other. "Let's get going before the sun get too hot. Is dis or the river, and I too tired to walk down there today."

Popo showed her how to spread the scrubbed and soapy clothes on a table-top made of wire mesh to allow the sun to bleach them white. She taught her how to rinse the clothes and hang them on the clothesline behind the house to dry. So much for soft, smooth hands, Abi thought.

After years of promises by the government, electricity had finally reached the village. Some of the villagers could now press their clothes with an electric iron, but most of the families still relied on the obligatory coal pot and flat irons. Even with electricity, it was always a guess and a gamble as to when it would work and when it would flicker off.

Abi's thoughts often wandered back to Colin. Surely Madge had told him that she never got back on the cruise ship before it had returned to Miami. So why hadn't he come looking for her? Or at least sent one of his police buddies to find his missing wife. Obviously, he was glad she had stayed, yet it all felt peculiar—unsettling. She vowed to write to the person who would keep her whereabouts a secret while providing her with the latest intelligence about Baltimore and Colin. It was Hanna Gamble, her co-worker at Johns Hopkins Hospital who knew her probably better than anyone did.

Fortunately for Abi, a new Hanna had materialized down the road. One day there was a big commotion outside as a boisterous group of men brought long pieces of wood, galvanize and bricks to a clearing.

"Is a maroon dey having," Breed explained to Abi before he left to join the group. "People get together and help each other to build their house and the family cook plenty food to feed everybody."

"Like the Amish people in America," exclaimed Abi. "What a great idea. But why do you call it a maroon?" she added.

"I don't know, my dear." Breed twisted up his face quizzically to imitate hers. "It was either that or crimson. I guess dey prefer the color maroon."

Abi knew when she was being made fun of. "Very funny. People who don't know the answer to things always resort to humor," she replied with an exaggerted shrug of her shoulders, "This will be fun to watch," she added, eager to follow Breed to the event.

And that's how Abi met Jenny Robinson. A very pregnant Jenny moved into the new house with her son, Alister, and her common-law husband, Peter. Not a week later, Alister pounded on Breed and Abi's door after midnight, screaming at the top of his lungs.

Jenny was in labor early and the midwife was across the island helping another mother.

"Where my underpants is?" Breed mumbled drugged with sleep.

Had they ever slept in pajamas, they could have run out to help Jenny. But Breed always insisted that they sleep in their birthday apparel and here they were: Breed wearing pink lacy panties and she wearing nothing at all. They stopped to hold on to each other and laugh at themselves when another high-pitched scream burst into the window.

"Grab some towels and follow me," Abigail instructed Breed as she darted out into the night. She bumped headlong into Peter, the father of the baby, who was running around in circles. Abigail rushed into the room to Jenny, gave orders for the men to get hot water in basins, string, cold water for drinking, rum for disinfecting, and went to work. Abigail Fisherman had immediately reconnected with her true self. Two hours later, she pulled a little girl out of her mother that possessed the same set of lungs her mother had displayed. She wrapped the baby up and put it down on the bed next to Jenny.

An hour later, Abigail left a comfortable mother, a contented baby, a sleeping older brother and a very happy father. She walked back to her house with Breed's arm loosely wrapped around her.

"I hope you can hold up when it's my turn," she whispered in his ear. He did not hear her and she did not know why she said it.

At night when they lay together before sleep claimed them, Abi peppered Breed with her latest burning questions about the island and its people. Tonight the subject was Bim Bim. How come everybody refers to her? Why is she so respected? How come nobody ever says Bim Bim told them something, but they know she said it?

"Lord, have mercy," Breed said sleepily. "Bim Bim is in touch with our ancestors. They tell her everything. As a matter of fact, if wasn't for her, I might not have brought you home dat day."

"What?" Abi shrieked. All the sleep had gone from her eyes. "What are you saying?"

"Well," said Breed, sitting up with her. "She tell me dat I will meet a green-eyed beauty dat will be my mate for life. Otherwise, I might not have had the nerve to pursue you,"

Abi fell back on her pillow and screamed out, "Thank you, Bim Bim."

"And," Breed continued, after removing his fingers from inside his ears, "I hear dem say in the village dat she have a twin sister somewhere in America. Some place named Merryland. I'm guessing dat people dere are very happy. But nobody know for sure. What we know is dat dey born in Haiti. One twin come here and one went dere."

The next morning after Breed left, Abi sat down at the kitchen table and wrote a letter to Hanna. She told her about her new home, her new man, her contentment. She told her about delivering a baby and the many medical needs of the village. She talked about the lack of drugs and the absence of basic equipment to help mothers and children in Windward's rural districts. "I never thought about how fortunate we are to live in the U.S. where so many services are readily available. It makes me angry to see such great inequalities in the world."

Abi began to understand and sympathize with the people on the island who were protesting and calling for new leadership. Her eyes had opened to a world she had known little about and she started to think of how she might make a difference. She felt a great sense of relief in unburdening her heart to a trusted friend. She read the letter over before she sealed it not because she was unsure of Hanna keeping a confidence, but because she felt that she was stepping away from the shadow that had pursued her the minute she left Baltimore.

Later that day when she and Popo sat down together, she felt unburdened. Popo was sipping her rum and grimacing with every sip.

"Why do you keep drinking rum if it causes you to make those ridiculous faces?" Abi asked.

"Because I like rum. Dats why," Popo answered while briskly fanning her open mouth with her hand.

"It doesn't make you drunk," Abi insisted, not content with the explanation. "Because I've never seen you even wobble. So maybe you just like getting high."

"Lordy," exclaimed Popo. "You want an explanation for everyting. O.K. I don't get drunk because I don't like vomiting on people. And if I wanted to get high, I would sit in a comfortable chair and read Toni Morrison or Shakespeare. Right? I drink rum because I like rum. Good?"

"Good," Abi answered quietly, making a mental note to not bring up that particular subject again.

"One more thing, though," Abi started up again, trying to ignore Popo's patronizing look. "With all the rum-drinking all over the island, how come Windward does not have an Alcoholics Anonymous chapter like in the United States? I think that would be of great help to these guys before they fall down permanently or their livers quit on them."

"Look here, Florence Nightingale," Popo laughed, wiping her mouth with the sleeve of her shirt. "We don't need any damn Alcoholics Anonymous in Windward. We know who drinking. Everybody. Nothing anonymous about we."

CHAPTER ELEVEN

Windward

It did not take long for everyone in the village to figure out that the white lady in Breed LeGrande house, "de one dat put a lickin' on Debbie," was a nurse from America. No sooner had Abigail sealed her letter to Hanna than she heard someone in a singsong voice call out to her from the front yard.

"Miss, you could look at my sore foot, please?" The woman had the ruddy face and broad shoulders of a plantation hand.

"OK, let's take a look," said Abi happily. Smoothing her blouse of wrinkles and assuming an officious look, she stepped outside to assume her new role.

"I have dis sore foot a long time now," the woman confided, hiking up her brightly flowered skirt to reveal an oozing red sore below her knee. Abi had come to know that island people tended to call any part of the body south of the hips, the foot.

"Morning," Abi said cheerfully. Pointing to a nearby rock, she said, "Please have a seat. I will be right back." She stepped indoors to fetch bandages and a bottle of white rum.

She cleaned up the sore as best she could with the rum acting as an antiseptic. Then she wrapped up the wound and told the woman what salve she should get from the chemist and how to set it on the sore. She realized she was humming to herself as the woman said softly, "Tank you, Miss."

Standing later under the cold water in the shower, she thought again of Colin and her life in Baltimore. She did not miss it. Nor did she miss the hot baths or warm showers. She let the cold water run down from her freshly washed hair to her toes. She ran her fingers along a scar that started under her navel and continued to her pubic hair. She recalled the worst experience of her life. The doctors at Johns Hopkins Hospital had performed an emergency operation to remove a daughter from her womb. The infant girl died in an incubator a week later, leaving Abi with a broken heart and a husband who cruelly called her "deformed." At a time when she would have appreciated a little support from him, Colin not only insulted her but was oblivious to her pain. After that horrific time, her self-esteem sank so low, she never let him see her completely naked again. She scuttled in and out of the bathroom always wrapped and furtive, and never let the bedroom lights go on without dimmers.

She blushed when she thought of how Breed had gently touched the scar on their first night together and then run his lips down the length of it. Although she was convinced that she had conceived on their first night together, she kept the information to herself. What if Breed did not want a child? There weren't many marriages taking place in the village, yet babies kept showing up. She chuckled at how the news would spread like a wild fire across the village: "Abigail Fisherman, de white woman dat make a chile for Popo Le Grande grandson."

She decided to tell Breed when he came home later on that day. It was time, especially since he had been making remarks lately about how fat she was getting "in de place."

As careful as Abi was to keep her pregnancy a secret, someone else knew. Popo kept quiet out of respect for Abi's privacy. She knew Abi had her reasons. As much as Abi had come to love and depend on Popo, she did not tell her about the baby for fear she would tell Breed. But she did share with Popo what she had run away from—a cold and cruel husband.

"Dat man is a real jumbie," Popo exclaimed. "You had to be in hell for you to meet him," she concluded with finality. Popo listened in befuddlement, then amusement, as Abi talked about how she tried to hide her unhappiness by shopping at the extravagantly opulent new mall in Columbia.

"What anybody want wid all those clothes and jewelry and taylaylay?"

Popo's questions came one after the other. "Dats just more tings to keep track of. If a person unhappy, no amount of ring and tiara could make a difference. And no matter how shiny your kitchen was, and how full you refrigerator stay, can dat bring you happiness?"

When Abi told Popo about her decision not to get back on the ship that day, Popo complimented her for "jumping with both feet into unfamiliar water."

It was Popo herself who made arrangements to prevent Abi from being "kidnapped" by the American Embassy or by Colin himself. The women in the village were instructed to keep an eye out for anything foreign showing up in their midst. Boysie's rum shop acted as the center for surveillance and, if necessary, Abi's hiding place. Popo took pains to assure Abi that Colin had moved on with his life. She got this intelligence from Bim Bim, who knows all things.

"I'm happy I'm here, and so well protected," Abi sighed. "But tell me how come Breed never left the island?"

"Hmmm," Popo began. "Because his head too hard. He was supposed to go and study law in England and find his mother. I save up meh money for de boy to do something with his life. But no, he stay here and study fish instead. But I still proud of him. He involve wid the people dat working for change."

"I'm glad he stayed to help, too," Abi interjected. She had never been involved in politics in America, but she realized that in Windward everything was political.

"I will go with you when the opposition leader comes to speak next week," Abi said with determination while attempting to put her wannabe dreadlocks into a bun.

"Good," said Popo. "That man have people excited. But before you go anywhere wid me, we have to fix up these dreadlocks you trying to grow wid straight hair."

Later that evening Abi and Popo sat picking rice on the front step. They placed a large bowl between them and were separating the chaff from the rice before washing it. On the ground, was another big bowl of peas waiting to be shelled. Shelling peas was not one of Abi's favorite pastimes, ever since she opened one to find a fat green worm crawling out.

"I din know white people could bawl so loud," giggled Popo as she squeezed Abi's arm. "Is only a worm, chile. He has to eat, too. All you have to do is make sure he don't get in the pot and sit down in the soup. Even so, what won't kill, will fatten."

As Popo crinkled up her face in laughter, her eyes almost disappeared. When they reappeared, they sparkled in merriment. "I do crack myself up, oui!" she giggled.

Abi's new island home seemed wild, untamed and beautiful to her. There were mountains and streams and a hundred shades of green. With all its beauty and majestic trees that bore all kinds of amazing fruits, and flowers from yellows to scarlet, she expected to see fairies flitting about waving tiny wands that made streams and berries appear. But instead she saw hardworking people with no time for berry picking. And if they ever imagined such a pastime, would hastily rush to Bim Bim to complain that someone had put a spell on them.

On this island everyone seemed to have a different story to tell. Some of them moved to the island from other islands and others came back as children from as far away as Toronto and Bombay. Still others were always travelling somewhere abroad for fortune or to quell the restless blood of their fathers that quickened inside them.

What really fascinated and inspired Abi most was how the islanders made so much out of so little. How they embraced and celebrated life to its fullest, despite the fact that food was sometimes scarce and resources low.

"I never knew so many things were worthy of celebration," she told Breed in one of their late night bedtime talks. "Christenings, funerals, people travelling, people coming back, people who didn't die when they were supposed to and even people who didn't get eaten or worse by a duppy or a soucouyant."

Breed smiled as he heard her observations.

"First and foremost, we are a creative people, Mango Breath," he snuggled in closer to her. "It is an African trait we inherited from our ancestors. We know how to make the best of life. Take the steelpan you like so much. Dat is the only non-electronic instrument invented in the twentieth century you know? The first one was invented around World War II in Trinidad. In case you don't know where Trinidad is," he added jokingly, "it is right off the coast of Venezuela. Anyway, Bim Bim say that when the slave masters throw away the drums we used to make music on, the people get empty oil drums cut them up in half and tune them up to make a symphony. Beethoven and Tchaikovsky must roll in their graves with surprise when they hear de boys and dem playing their music on pan. And without sheet music to boot. We just clever people dat God take His time to make."

"Mango Breath?" she queried with new-found mischief. "Yet another name for me. But this one is actually true. Abi leaned into his face, covered his nose with her mouth and breathed heavily into his nostrils.

Breed did not try to get away. "I have one last question for you," she said. "What would happen when you all have run out of things to celebrate?"

"That's easy, Julie Face. We will celebrate that." He clapped his hands, let out a melodic laugh at his own cleverness and pulled Abi on top of him.

CHAPTER TWELVE

Baltimore

Colin read the news about Ross Winter's murder with detachment. Ever discreet, *The Baltimore Gazette* did not publish a picture of the dead body. Instead there was a photo of Ross, probably supplied by a relative, when he looked a whole lot livelier.

What a way to die—in women's clothing and wearing a silly hat. Opening and closing his mouth mechanically, Colin was lost in thought. Hadn't Kate worn a similar hat when she walked out the door on her way to the cruise ship?

The police speculated that the 35-year-old man was a victim of a robbery gone bad. He was beaten and shot once through the head at point-blank range. The hole the bullet left in the middle of his forehead was almost clean, but the back of the head was shattered open. It was a .38 caliber bullet. Police found it lodged in the dumpster behind the victim, along with an empty wallet and a large empty envelope. Ross's body was already in the morgue, Colin knew. He would review the assistant examiner's report with care, but for now he was content knowing that his .38 caliber was safely locked in the top left drawer of his liquor cabinet.

Unknown to Colin, someone else had read the story closely, only her mouth remained open the entire time. Madge Sorenson had gotten up early to review some real estate listings before making an appointment with the plastic surgeon. She needed to remove some wrinkles that had appeared around her eyes and pull some more of her face up if she was to catch her latest target.

The picture on the local news page stopped her dead in her tracks.

"Holy shit, I know this man," she blurted out. She recognized him from the cruise ship. And now she saw the words "Ross Winter" and "dead."

"Holy shit," she repeated, shaking her head.

What about Kate? Where was she now? Her name was nowhere to be found in the story. Maybe when she found out Ross wasn't what she thought he was, she moved on. Or maybe she was back in Baltimore. Madge's plan had been to give Colin enough time to pretend to grieve at the disappearance of his wife before she snagged him for herself. Now she would have to work fast. She would have to get to Colin before Kate came back into his life. There's no time like the present, she told herself. A woman had to strike while the iron was hot, and Madge's iron was steaming.

Colin placed the newspaper on the living room table and picked up the telephone nearby.

"Good morning. Chief medical examiner's office," said a cheery voice belonging to Suellen, his secretary. "And how may I help you today?" Suellen was perpetually pleasant. Not even Monday mornings thwarted her.

"Good morning, Suellen. No need to ask you how your weekend went," he said as cheerfully as she had answered.

"I know it's Monday and the dead bodies from Bodymore are vying for attention," he bantered casually, "but I won't be in today. Something has come up," he said with a mouth full of cinnamon bun. "Tell Ms. Shafer to please do the honors. I will see you tomorrow morning."

"I trust everything is fine, Dr. C. Have a good day." Suellen hung up the phone with delight. It was going to be a great day for doing nothing.

Next door, Madge sprang out of the shower and headed for her wardrobe, flicking on the small TV on her nightstand.

There he was again. The same head shot of Ross that was in the paper, staring out of the television at her. Then she heard the reporter's saying, "The victim's body was found early Sunday morning near a dumpster. He was wearing a woman's hat with a polka dotted headband. He was pronounced dead on the scene. A .38 caliber bullet had gone through his forehead, but a police source tells us that a puncture wound was also found in his stomach. It seems that the victim was kicked with some force with a shoe that had a pointed tip."

Madge stared at the television as the reporter ended his story by noting that the police had recently interrogated Ross Winter in regard to the death of a young socialite from Suitland, Maryland. Her body was found in the engine room of a cruise ship in Puerto Rico. The woman had left a sizable insurance policy from which her husband would benefit.

Madge was getting woozy. Who was this Ross guy? Why was he on the cruise ship? Wild thoughts raced through her brain. She grabbed her now-cold coffee and sat down by the TV. She played back in her mind the reporter's story as she started concocting her own. A gigolo suspected of murder. A man who frequented cruise ships to pick up women. A man she thought she saw in Miami, but who turned up dead in Baltimore. A hat with a polka dotted headband found at the crime scene. Could it possibly be the same hat that she saw disappear into a cab in Miami?

Her heart began to beat faster. Was Ross a hired gun? Did he do something to Kate?

"Were I a praying woman," Madge murmured to herself, "now would be a good time to offer one up."

"Damn you Kate," she shouted out loud. "Are you dead or are you coming back to screw me?" Realizing that she was shaking uncontrollably, Madge took a few of the deep breaths she learned in yoga. Her plans wouldn't change. She got up and finished dressing.

Colin had also watched the morning news. He, however, was nonplussed by the reporter's account. He had always been a gambler. Knowing that he'd have final say at any police inquest into the circumstances of Ross' death, he figured the odds were in his favor. "I got this," he reassurred himself.

The doorbell had been ringing for a while before he realized it. An impatient person had kept a finger on the button so that the bell shrilled nonstop in his head.

"Hang on," Colin yelled from the living room.

He tightened the belt on his robe and ran his fingers through his hair as he looked at himself in the front hallway mirror. He liked what he saw except for the bit of cinnamon icing that he swiftly licked off his well-tended moustache.

"Madge," he stammered as he opened the door. "Well, for God's sake, woman. What brings you here at this time of day?"

Colin was not so distracted that he did not smell the Chanel No. 5 wafting its way from between her breasts.

Madge heaved a loud sigh to make them jiggle inside her low-cut blouse.

"May I come in? I know it has been a while. Have you been well?" Madge asked, thrusting the upper part of her body forward before he had a chance to reply. She was as tall as Colin and very well toned. She wore a skirt that had no problem accentuating her legs and rounded bottom. She had the pronounced features of the Greek Jews that migrated to Baltimore after World War II, a strong jaw line, not too large nose and dark almond-shaped eyes. Her jet black hair had been cropped by her hairdresser to fall over her face at 30-second intervals. She would take a well-manicured finger and push the hair back behind her ear seductively. The hair would again fall towards her face, giving her an opportunity to start the process all over. Today she wore a hat. A wide-brimmed soft straw that touched her shoulders on both sides when she leaned her head back.

"Do come in," Colin said, angry at himself for being so affected by her presence. "Yes, it's been a while. I haven't seen you since, uhhhh. I guess you must miss your shopping buddy, aye?" he added, trying to ease the tension that accompanied her into the house.

Madge removed her hat carefully and placed it on the rack in the hallway just as she did when she used to visit Kate. The house looked pretty much the same as she remembered it. Except for some clothes thrown over the back of the sofa and a somewhat cluttered center table. The living room, which she swiftly entered uninvited, was well taken care of. Maybe a woman came in now and then to keep things in check.

"I don't miss Kate, to tell the truth," she purred in a soft voice as she picked up the newspaper and settled herself in the middle of the sofa.

"Did you read this morning's headlines?" she asked Colin.

"Yes, as a matter of fact I did. Why would you ask?" he said with a slight tremor in his voice.

"Do you know this man?" Madge continued in little more than a whisper, pointing to Ross' picture.

"Can't say I've ever seen the gentleman before," he said, glancing down at the picture. "Pretty gruesome story, don't you think?"

Colin darted off to the kitchen, leaving Madge with the paper in her hand.

"Would you like a cup of coffee, my dear? If it weren't so early, I would offer you a drink," he added with a self-conscious chuckle.

"I'll take that drink." Her smile was merry, but her eyes were wary. "I'm pretty sure it's happy hour in Mozambique."

"That's the spirit," Colin replied jovially. He came back into the living room with two of Kate's favorite crystal glasses and placed them on the table as far away from the newspaper as possible.

"Straight up?" he asked, looking deeply into her dark eyes, straining to see if he could read her thoughts.

"Straight up is how I like my whiskey," Madge replied. She took a cigarette out of her purse and slowly licked her lips before lighting it, so that he could see her pink tongue slip in and out between her brightly painted lips.

"Cheers," they said to each other as if on cue. They took equally long gulps from their glasses and then Colin sat down on the sofa next to her.

"Well," he sputtered. "How goes it?" Their eyes met again.

"Good," said Madge. "How is single life treating you? Or have you already taken care of that?" she laughed, looking around the room with one eyebrow raised.

"It's not all that it's cracked up to be. But I am more interested in how you've been getting on," he added quickly. "What have you been up to? I have been meaning to get in touch with you to see if you were missing her." Colin leaned in closer.

"Me missing her?" countered Madge. "Shouldn't I be the one calling you to see if you were missing her? After all, she was your wife, Colin. Or have you forgotten that already?"

Madge brushed back her hair and pushed her empty glass forward. What the hell, getting drunk in the morning wasn't a cardinal sin, she told herself. Besides she liked the bravado the whiskey gave her. Arm in arm with Johnnie, she could move in for the kill.

She got up from the sofa and walked toward the sideboard where Colin was refilling her glass and his own. She kicked off her shoes and snapped open her blouse just enough to let the Chanel continue it's magic.

"This man," she said, pointing to the picture of Ross Winter and speaking with a softness that made her words seem matter of fact. "I know this man," she paused to let the information sink in, "and so did your wife."

Colin blanched.

"Whatever do you mean?" he snapped. "That's not possible."

"Think what you choose, Colin, but this Ross Winter character was on that cruise ship to the Caribbean. Both Kate and I were acquainted with him. Although, I'd wager, she was more acquainted with him than I was."

Colin's glass slipped from his fingers and shattered to pieces on the tiled floor.

CHAPTER THIRTEEN

Windward

The sun was showing off more than usual. It flung flashes of heat everywhere, causing the buttercups to climb up the walls, the hibiscus to wilt on their stems and the chickens to seek shelter in the crawlspace under the house. The women ignored the enveloping ball of fire. Armed with paper fans and wet rags around their necks, they sat contented under the breadfruit tree. Abi had a jug of water next to her and Popo had a glass of cold coconut water.

Popo tucked her dress between her knees and pulled out a yellowed photograph from a manila envelope. It was a picture of three white men. Each one looked more battered and bruised than the other. They were barefoot and their clothing hung like rags from their gaunt bodies. What was visible of the terrain behind them suggested a place pretty much like the one in which Abi and Popo now sat.

Popo pointed at the missing spaces in the men's mouths.

"Look," she told Abi, cackling with laughter. "Dey teeth like houses in the village. One here, one over dere."

Abi did not think that was funny. She hadn't gotten quite used to island humor. Calling a person "no foot" because his leg was cut off in an accident, or "nosegay" because his nose was unusually broad, seemed more cruel than comical. Not to speak of several men in the village, all of whom answered to the name: "Big Head."

Popo leaned forward and pointed to the man with the least amount of teeth. "Dis man," she said, "was my grandfather. His name was Dean Mackenzie. Scottish. The Scots were among the first indentured servants to come down to the West Indies. Later on, some Irish came down, too. About fifty thousand Irish were sold to Caribbean plantation owners. Come to think of it, you and I could be related. You certainly good-looking enough to be family."

"Really," Abi interrupted. "What did you put in the coconut water?"

"Nothing," Popo said. "The so-called New World was built from the labor of both black and white slaves. But white slaves were the first to be brought to the colonies. Most of dem landed in Barbados, den they transport some to the other islands. That is how Dean Mackenzie's people come here. They had to work long hours in the hot sun. The sun showed them no mercy and they burned fast—especially their legs. They were nicknamed 'redlegs' and 'redshanks' because of their burnt legs."

"Oh, my goodness," said Abi, her face animated. "That's interesting because in America we call some white people 'rednecks'. There were a lot of red necks in my old neighborhood. I wonder if it had something to do with their ancestors getting burnt in the neck!"

Popo looked at Abi quizzically, shook her head and continued.

"The slave owners could not get their money's worth from dem white slaves. They got all kinds of gangrene and ringworm and yaws from walking barefoot. They could not work long or hard enough. Dat is when the British looked to Africa for more reliable bodies."

"Did the slaves get along? I mean the black and white ones." Abi asked, taking a sip out of Popo's coconut water.

"You mean like you and Breed?" Popo chortled. "Sometimes they did and sometimes they did not."

Abi sighed.

"You know, Abi," Popo continued thoughtfully. "Maybe all Breed's fighting spirit did not come just from Africa. He is a descendant of Clan Mackenzie from Scotland and those boys and dem knew how to fight for a cause. Dey gave the British hell back in the 1700s. Dey was outnumbered and hungry but dey was fierce and brave. Dey got slaughtered by the Red Coats and many of the bedraggled survivors end up in the West Indies. But the British sent down criminals and derelicts too. Just like dey did in Australia."

"You know what happened over 200 years ago? How come? Bim Bim, right?"

"Very funny. But dats an easy one. One generation tell the next one and so on and so on. Just like in Africa. Dean Mckenzie father told him, he tell his child, his child tell me, I tell Breed and he will tell his child. Den his child will tell his children. I just hope he find a good-looking woman, because I don't fancy ugly great, great, grand children. Not me."

Coming into the yard, Breed found the two women laughing uproariously. "Ma Po, you will make Abi have dat child before it time," he said good-naturedly. Popo got to her feet and wrapped her arms around her grandson kissing him on the cheek. "I going home now, dahlin. All you take care of one another, Mr. Black and Miss White."

"I love you," said Breed.

"I love you, too," Abi chorused.

Abigail stared at Breed. How did he know about the baby?

"I've known all along," he said, reading her thoughts. "I knew from the first week you were here. Every time we made love, I knew. I was just waiting for you to know, too."

"Ahhh," stuttered Abi. "I was afraid to say anything in case you were disappointed. Then I didn't know when to tell you and kept waiting for the right time. Are you happy?"

"Me? Happy?" he whooped. "I am the happiest man in the world. My wife is making a baby." It was the first time he had called her his wife.

Breed and Abi went indoors arm in arm. It was Breed's turn to cook dinner. He had brought home some fresh lambi from the bay. Abi prepared the vegetables and Breed started the stew.

Every time she cut up onions, her eyes burned. Popo had shown her how to rub them on someone's hair to relieve the burning. She grabbed a handful of Breed's locks. To her surprise, it always worked.

"Today when I went to the bakery in John John, there were some people marching down the road singing," Abi told Breed.

Before Breed could launch into a diatribe about what she was doing in John John with "dose kinda people," she went on hurriedly. "I dropped by to say hello to Marva. They were singing something about stopping anyone who wanted to change things and that they were willing to fight, fight, fight. Apparently the man they were singing about was some kind of saviour in their eyes, and also a relative to all of them."

Breed looked at Abi and said, "My lovely Green Eyes. The man isn't a relative, but they do love him and want to send a warning to those of us in opposition."

"Oh," said a flustered Abi. "What do I know?"

What she did know was that sometimes a few of Breed's comrades would gather in the kitchen for long debates about who would be the best person to replace the prime minister. During these discussions Abi stayed out of the room, but always listened in.

"We need unity to make progress," she heard Breed say. "We need people to speak their minds in an effort to shape their own and their children's futures. The fact that so many people around the world are ready and willing to risk their lives for this way of life is testimony to its appeal."

She laid the table for dinner, placing the salad she made in the middle of the table and the candle that she always lit when they ate.

"OK," Breed said, spooning the stewed lambi into a large bowl that he placed on the table. The rich aroma filled the room. Abi sat down partly because she was tired on her feet, but mostly because the fragrance of the food demanded that she sit.

"When did you become so political?" she asked as they sat down to eat.

"After reading 'Das Kapital' and studying Leninism." He closed his eyes to fully savor the spoonful of stew he was chewing.

"Me and dis prime minister have one thing in common. We are both disciples of Tubal Uriah Butler. Butler was born back in 1897 and served in the British West Indian Regiment. After the war, he moved to Trinidad in 1921 or somewhere dere. He was a working-class man, like myself, and joined the Labor Party. Pass the roti, please. He started his own party in 1936 and called it the British Empire Workers and Citizens

Home Rule Party. A long name dat had more letters in it dan it had members at first."

Breed laughed at his spontaneous humour. "Anyway, 'Buzz' could organize a strike at the drop of a hat. There was a riot one time after which he was sentenced to two years in prison. But he kept fighting for the cause. He make another jail from 1941 to 1945 because the government say he was a threat to the British war effort. Imagine that, a leader of the working class, a threat to Her Majesty's' war effort. Hmmm. The man was charismatic. That's something he and dis Prime Minister have in common, charisma."

"You know, Abi," Breed knitted his brow thoughtfully. "Charisma would be a good name for we baby if is a girl."

"Yes, Breed," Abi said with a smirk. "And if it's a boy, we can call him Charismo."

Breed forced a piece of lettuce into her mouth to keep her quiet.

"Before I was rudely interrupted," he cleared his throat with authority. "Butler was a praying man. He was like a martyr to the people, and he was very popular. He kept on fighting till he couldn't anymore. It's good I am telling you dis, Abi, so I can refresh my memory to tell it all again one day to Charismo."

Breed ducked to miss the imaginary bowl that Abi had thrown at him.

"You call my child Charismo and you're a dead man, Breed LeGrande," Abi said. "But do tell me how the prime minister fell out of favor with the people."

"You not listening. White people don't like to listen." This time Breed ducked from a real plastic bowl that had materialized in the air.

"Anyway," he continued good-naturedly, "dis prime minister is like a disciple of Butler. He is charismatic as well as controversial."

By the time he finished talking, Abi said she was tired. She pulled Breed up from his chair so that they could wash the wares together.

When they were through cleaning up, they headed for the bedroom. They had only made a few steps when Abi slipped from his arms and fell heavily unto the hard plank floor. Breed dropped to his knees is panic. "Abi," he shouted, his hands shaking her shoulders. "Abi, wake up."

There was no response.

He tried to pick her up to place her on the bed, but as strong as he was, he couldn't move her. He got up and hightailed it out of the house to get help.

CHAPTER FOURTEEN

Baltimore

"Whatever do you mean, Madge?"

Colin spoke as casually as he could as he swept up the broken pieces of glass. He leaned over to Madge not only to get a better look at the picture of Ross Winter but more strategically to brush against her breast.

"In adversity comes clarity," Colin thought to himself. He had never been especially fond of Madge. She was too flamboyant for his taste. He found her pushy and a bit crass. He did, however, admire her lust for real estate. Madge could sell sand to a Saudi.

Madge Sorenson was well known in the neighborhood for her business prowess. She could cut deals and get people into new homes fast. She was not a millionaire, but had plans to marry one.

There were three things that stopped her from snagging Colin Carrington in the past. One: He was married to her friend. Two: She was not certain about his net worth. And Three: He never made a move on her. But Madge was tired of working to support herself and was eager to place that responsibility on someone else's shoulder. She had recently lost a pretty penny on a bad investment with a slick real estate mogul who was supposed to be building mega condominiums in the county. So what if Colin was involved in Kate's disappearance? She was willing to take her chances.

"How on earth would Kate know a character like this?" asked Colin with what he hoped was a question mark on his face. It was hard to tell with Johnnie Walker hanging around in his head.

"Remember that cruise?" Madge began coyly. "He was on the *Tropical Sea*. Well, they met." She did not want to imply anything more at this point. After all, what good would it do to tell him that his wife had slept with a sleaze bucket. On the other hand, she might need to whip out that bit of information later on.

"Madge, are you sure? You must be mistaken," Colin interjected. Realizing his voice had gotten too shrill, he took a deep breath. "Maybe they just said hello to each other," he continued slowly. "People tend to do that on cruises." Colin felt better now that he had explained it to himself.

He fixed himself another drink. What on earth did Madge know? He steadied himself, took another swig and allowed his bathrobe to loosen just a bit. Circling back, he sat close to Madge and exposed his left thigh. Men can play this game too, he said to himself.

Colin whispered in her ear, "So what if she met him? There's no harm in that."

"She did more than just meet him," Madge persisted. "They had drinks together."

In spite of the alcohol, Colin was sobering up. "I see," he said in a somewhat agitated voice. "And were you with them the whole time? How often are we talking about here? The drinking together, I mean."

"As far as I know, he put his moves on her from the first day of the cruise," Madge purred, lightly touching his thigh.

She did not want to divulge too much information too soon. She wanted to pull Colin in with her words and body to the point of no return. She would feed him only bits. Besides she couldn't be sure that what she suspected was accurate. Surely this respectable medical doctor could not have hired Ross to kill his wife. Kate must have run off with Ross because she had finally accepted that her marriage was over. Kate had left with Ross that day in Miami, when she saw her with her own two eyes get into the cab and speed off. The hat with the polka dotted headband is what gave her away.

Or was it Ross wearing the hat, she thought as she recalled the morning news. Kate had moved on when she found out that her Atlas had a penchant for panties and is probably doing just fine whereever she is.

Whatever had happened, it was Madge's job to make sure Kate did not come back, because if she did, it would be too late. She needed to get Colin to commit to her before that happened. Her purse was getting thinner and her "sell-by" date for snagging a rich husband was fast approaching.

"It's time," she unintentionally said out loud.

"Time for what?" asked Colin, as he reached over and removed a wisp of hair from her cheek.

Colin's mind was racing. What if Madge suspected something? Could she have followed Ross and Kate to the deck and watched him throw her overboard?

"That is crazy," he unintentionally said out loud.

"What's crazy?" asked Madge catching his hand before it left her cheek.

Colin wondered, and not for the first time, why Madge hadn't come to his house sooner. Why hadn't she come over to ask questions about Kate's disappearance? She seemed to have bought the story hook, line and sinker that Kate had just disappeared. What did she know? The two women had spent so much time together it was a bit hard to swallow that she really believed his story. But then again, he reassured himself, she was Madge and prone to be very self-involved. A faint smile crossed his lips when a picture of a headless Madge floated in front of him.

"What's so funny?" she wanted to know.

"Nothing," he said. "Nothing at all."

"I'll tell you what else is crazy," Madge continued nonplussed. "This Ross guy was not shot just for his money or a drug deal gone bad. I'm no detective, but if that were the case, the single bullet wound in his head would have been sufficient."

"Do continue, Sergeant," said Colin, trying to look uninterested.

"Sure," she said, sitting up straight to relay her conclusion. "The fact that he was kicked with so much force in his lower abdomen, enough to damage his insides, suggests to me that the person who killed him was a very angry man and probably one of his own kind. Why else would he be wearing pointy tipped shoes?"

Colin got up unsteadily from the sofa and allowed his robe to open fully. He had nothing to lose. Luckily, he was wearing briefs and not boxers this morning. This allowed Madge a full view of what could be in store. She was impressed.

Madge circled behind him and wrapped her arms around his chest. This was so much easier than she had imagined. Her hands dropped down his torso, her fingertips massaging his crotch.

By the time Colin had separated Madge from her clothing, he was panting. Too late to make it up the stairs to the bedroom, he bent her over the kitchen table, kicking aside a chair. They pounded against the table as several dishes rattled and dropped to the floor around them. Grabbing hold of each other, they picked their way hurriedly through the dicey terrain and headed for the sofa.

Colin was the first to move after the sexfest. He nudged Madge who was sprawled out on the sofa with her arms hanging to the floor. She gave him a surprised look and then grinned smugly when she realized where she was.

"Come on, dearie," Colin croaked. "We might as well make the most of the day. Let's go out, have a big lunch, some more drinks and enjoy the sunshine. Heck, we could even take a ride out into the country. Any where in particular you would like to go today?" He was feeling like he just won the lottery.

"A shower is on the top of my list," Madge said as she pinched his backside. Rolling herself off the sofa, she smiled seductively at Colin and sprinted up the stairs, very satisfied with herself.

Colin whistled as he busied himself cleaning up the room. He should call Deirdra at some point today, he idly thought, before she started calling him. Then it suddenly struck him: What do I do with two women? He ran his hand nervously through his hair. "I just might have to kill one of them," he laughed out crazily. "But which one?"

When he got upstairs, Madge was on her way out of the shower wrapped in a large towel.

"Your clothes are on the bed, my dear," said Colin, pecking her on the cheek.

In all the years that Madge had known Kate and Colin she had never been in their bedroom. She looked around it now. It was expensively decorated. The bed was big and inviting. That was good because she knew she would be spending a lot of time in it. She checked the closets to find that Kate's side was empty. That would soon change. There was no apparent evidence that he had female company.

Out of curiosity she looked inside Colin's closet. Expensive suits and ties. The man made good money. She checked out his shoes—Oxford wingtips in a Van Dyke & Bacon box. "Classy," she murmured to herelf. Then she noticed, pushed far into the back of the closet, a pair of cowboy boots with pointed silver tips.

"How unusual," she thought. Reaching to pick them up, her face flushed red when she noticed a brownish color smudged at the tip of the right boot. The morning news report flashed in front of her.

CHAPTER FIFTEEN

Windward

When Abi opened her eyes, her vision was blurred. Popo's face came into focus a few seconds later. The visiting nurse, Mavis, was also in the room, putting damp washcloths on Abi's forehead and an extra pillow under her knees.

"What happened?" Abi asked, her brows furled in alarm. "Where's Breed?"

"I'm right here, my love. You just fainted and scared me to death."

Breed brushed the hair from her damp forehead and adjusted the washcloth. "You'll be OK now." He kissed her gently on both cheeks. "She alright, right?" Breed turned to Mavis for assurance.

"Yes, of course," replied the nurse soothingly. "Is only faint she faint. That not uncommon with women at this point, especially if she is too tired and stayed on her feet too long. Dis look like a big baby she making."

"What you was doing to make de girl faint, Breed?" Popo demanded of her grandson.

When Popo and the nurse had arrived, Abi was still lying on the floor. Breed was afraid to move her in case it made matters worse. At first, Popo thought Abi was dead. She screamed so loudly that the nurse had to pacify her at the same time she helped Breed carry Abi to the bed.

"What you did to make Abigail faint, I ask you?" Popo had Breed by the neck in a half Nelson.

Struggling to catch his breath and unclasp his grandmother's determined fingers from his throat, he gasped. "We were just talking about politics. I was telling her about the prime minister."

"Well no wonder de poor chile faint. You can't go telling people about the prime minister dis time of the night. You crazy? Dat's enough to kill anybody. Talk about de prime minister in the afternoon when she sitting down and have plenty of water to sap she head and enough rum to drink."

"Now don't be getting sick, Abi," said Mavis turning to leave. "I need you down at the visiting station. As soon as you make dis child, we putting you on the payroll, so hurry up. I hear about all the good work you doing in the village. We need you."

Popo and Mavis walked outside satisfied that all was well inside. Abi and Breed were curled up together—Breed clinging to her hips and sobbing softly into her belly. He couldn't begin to imagine a life without Abi. It was as if she had become an extension of himself. The baby shifted to the side to accommodate its father.

The next sound Breed and Abi heard was the dependable crow of Chantycleer. Then came the familiar chorus of the other roosters in the village filling the air with their cockadoodledoos.

Breed got breakfast for Abi and made sure she was comfortable. Then he waited for Popo to come over to stay with her, so he could get his day started. He had to fish far out in the ocean today, sell his catch and then go to town to a political meeting. Members of his party were being arrested for no reason other than they were opposed to the tactics of the prime minister. The meeting would last well into the night. Breed was good at organizing peaceful rallies and keeping everyone in check. He diffused disputes among the opposition party and was a passionate speaker. Even the prime minister's thugs seemed to respect him. Once a couple of them came to visit him at the fishmarket to explain why they had bashed someone's head in.

By the time Abi finished her porridge, Popo bustled in armed with a bag of provisions, some Julie mangoes, her Bible and some house shoes. Popo always wore house shoes. Even Abi had gotten used to the comfort and freedom of her bare feet on the floor and the warm ground outside. But not Popo. Popo liked to say that she born with shoes on and will die with shoes on.

Breed left the women. He would stop at Leland's house and remind him to get the galvanize and wood to start the addition to his house because the baby would be born soon enough. He and Abi would need more space, and it was about time he put a fresh coat of paint on the outside of the house. They had already settled on bright orange with green and blue shutters. The inside toilet and bathroom were almost completed and he even had the men put in a tub should Abi want to have a soak.

Back at the house Popo was watching Abi eat a mango. She had never before seen anyone enjoy a mango like this American woman.

"Girl, I know you like a mango, but I don't think I ever see anybody enjoy one like you do. You eating like you've been in jail for months and didn't get any food. Didn't you just eat that whole bowl of corn meal porridge?"

Abi pulled her face out of the mango, flashed an orange smile and delved back in. Today she and Popo had plans to sew baby clothes to get ready for the child. Right now, her main objective was to eat the last mango in the basket.

"I wonder what our baby will look like, Ma Po. Will it look like me? I hope it looks like Breed, especially if it's a boy," Abi said, looking quizzically at Popo.

"I don't know chile. What I do know is that it will be black, no matter what," answered Popo authoritatively. "That's the power of one drop of black blood," she added, amused at her philosophizing.

Sometimes Popo infuriated Abi, but she'd learned to hold her tongue. "It's food for thought," she said, staring at the half-eaten mango in her hand.

Popo picked up the yellow wool to continue making the little booties for her great grand baby. "Look how you get after eating a mango. You so peaceful now, you listening to me nice, nice and you just smiling away," Popo patted Abi's belly lovingly. "We should give mangoes to all the world leaders and the world might become a much better place."

"You ever wonder what happening in America, doux-doux?" Popo asked as Abi sat down carefully next to her and started unraveling the wool.

Abi always smiled at the word doux-doux. (pronounced doodoo) If anyone were called doux-doux in America, she could just imagine the laughter. On this island it meant "darling." Her thoughts went to her unborn child, and she rubbed her stomach instinctively. Maybe one day her child would go to America to study or something. Who knows what the future held? Only God and Bim Bim.

"Not really," she told Popo. "Now and then, I think about the hours I spent watching television and shopping. Buying things that collect dust. Stuff that made me feel successful. Crystal bowls and stainless steel. Granite countertops. Chippendale furniture. Seems like a totally different world to me now. Did I tell you I wrote to my friend Hanna in Baltimore? I think I should be hearing from her soon. I love you and Breed so much. I can't imagine what I did to be allowed this joy."

Abi leaned over and kissed Popo on the cheek.

Popo patted her gently. "I love you too, doux-doux, and I know my grandson is in heaven when he is with you." The women continued to knit in silence. Away on the horizon a double rainbow promised good luck.

"When we done knitting, I will show you how to cook a nice lambi stew with the catch Breed brought home yesterday," Popo said.

"Good," said Abi. "Let me get pen and paper."

"Lordy. All you Americans always writing things down. We should take a page from your book." Popo mopped the sweat running down her face.

"I don't know what 'some of dis' and 'some of dat' means, so I'm writing it down after I measure it all." Abi was laughing despite herself. "Your 'some' is not my 'some'".

"Okay, get your lead and paper, and let's go sit down outside. I have to get out of this hot house before I get baked."

Despite the sun, the air seemed freshly washed by the morning rain. The long, slim leaves of the breadfruit tree swayed to the soft breeze that blew through. The women sat down in their favorite spot under the tree.

"I will tell you a story about the breadfruit tree. I know you love your oil down when I cook it." Popo looked up at the tree as if to ask for permission to tell its story.

"The breadfruit tree didn't just spring up in the West Indies just like dat. Eh eh. A man named Captain Bligh bring the plants from the South Pacific. It was heavy and dependable and could feed the slaves cheap and keep them full. Not until emancipation was breadfruit accepted in the Caribbean. Now we frying it, stuffing it, mashing it, creaming it, making salad with it or eating it plain with butter. And don't mention oil down, that's the best breadfruit meal. The breadfruit is like the potato in America, oui."

Jenny sauntered into the yard with her baby in her arms and little Alister rolling a bicycle tire behind her. Abi stretched out her arms to cradle the first baby she had delivered on the island.

"Say morning, Alister," said Jenny, prodding her son.

"Morning," said Alister looking down at the ground for something imaginary he had dropped.

Abi was always tickled by the way the local people greeted each other, but never added the word "good" before morning, afternoon or evening. They seemed to say "Good Night," though. This habit would be added to her list of mysteries of the island.

"Morning, Allister," she smiled at the little boy.

"Joan down at the Post Office say to tell you that you have a package waiting for you whenever you ready," Jenny said. "She say you can come for it or just send Breed. It come from America. Is the first time you ever get a package."

Jenny was informing Abi as if she was not aware that it was, indeed, her first package. Everyone in the village knew before Abi did that a fairly large package had arrived for her from Baltimore, USA. Abi's heart leapt within her. It's from

Hanna. Good old Hanna. She knew there would be a long missive within.

"Thanks, Jenny," Abi remembered her manners. "Will you stop and chat a little with us today?"

"No my dear," replied Jenny. "Some of us have to work," she laughed as she prodded Popo in the ribs.

"You can't see is work we working here?" exclaimed Popo. "Somebody have to teach this child about the world because apparently all she learn in America was America. So is up to me to fill in the rest."

"Ma Po, you might be right there. I have learned a lot from just talking with you and Breed. You should have been a teacher, you know."

"Me? I cannot teach these harden children. The rum shop is my school. All who want to hear could come. I just giving you private lessons because Breed don't want you in the rum shop with all dem rangatang people in there."

"I look rangatang to you, Popo?" Jenny tried to look offended.

"OK, rangatang and others," Popo corrected herself as she slapped Jenny playfully on her backside.

Jenny left the two women to enjoy their day and continued into town with Alister and his tire in tow.

Abi followed Popo inside so that they could get on with their meal. Stewed Lambi. She got her pen and paper at the ready and wrote as quickly as she could to catch up with Popo.

"Good, the lambi ready to go because that in itself is too much work. Always try and get it clean and pounded to soften it up. OK?" Popo looked at Abi. "I not laughing with you. When I gone up to meet my husband, you will have to cook and teach your child to do the same. Especially if it is a boy. You don't want him marrying a girl just because she can cook. Teach him how to cook, how to wash, and how to sew for himself. Otherwise he will marry a woman for the wrong reason."

"I hear you," said Abi politely. "Point taken."

"Good," said Popo satisfied that her lecture was going well. "Now write fast.

> *One lime cut in half.*
> *Chop up one onion.*
> *Add some burnt sugar.*
> *A nice amount of curry powder.*
> *Coconut milk, dis much.*
> *A dash of ground cloves, dat much.*
> *Some oil and garlic and black pepper.*
> *Thyme fresh or dry.*
> *And anything else you find that can work."*

Abi was always secretly surprised at how everything Popo put in the pot rallied together to make a delectable meal. She had watched with great interest that morning as Popo washed the lambi with lime and tossed it in with onion, pepper and the other seasonings and left it to soak in its own juices until she was ready. Now Popo heated the large iron pot and put in some oil and sugar. After it browned a bit, she tossed in the lambi. It made a loud screeching sound when it hit the hot syrup.

The kitchen seemed to get 100 degrees hotter in an instant, but the aroma was worth it. Popo stirred and added curry and other seasoning over a medium heat. Abi wrote as fast as she could. Then Popo added the coconut milk, lowered the heat and instructed Abi, "Leave it let it simmer for about 20 minutes or something like that. If the sauce too thick, add water. If it too thin, add cornstarch. Stir. You finish when the lambi soft enough. You got all that down, Shakespeare?"

"I have," Abi answered dutifully. She had been keeping all the recipes and information she had gotten from Popo to share one day with her children. She was going to make sure they knew more of their history than she did of her own.

Popo and Abi ate their lunch under the breadfruit tree. A couple of stray dogs wandered by in the hopes of getting a little something.

"Mash," Popo yelled at the dogs. They scampered away.

"Dis is not America," Popo pointed out to Abi. "Here, dogs stay outside where they belong. They not allowed to lick you all up in your face and you kissing them up. They are not children. Me? I don't want any dog licking my face when I see the amount of time dey spend licking their bamsy."

CHAPTER SIXTEEN

Windward

Abi's favorite time for a walk was after a rainfall, when the air felt warm like human breath. She liked to go barefoot in the succulent red soil and feel the mud slide through her toes and caress her feet. What Breed called 'The Land' was not at all like the soil in Maryland. When she gardened in Columbia, the ground was brittle and unfriendly. This thick, warm, velvet-like mud was more to her liking. She would stoop down and mush it in her hands and dream of opening a clay pot shop one day.

She was at peace on this green island where nature seemed to have an eternal youth. It was a peace so delicious that sometimes she worried that it could end. What if something happened to Breed? What would happen to her?

Popo said Breed knew how to take care of himself even in these times of more and more unrest.

Night came abruptly to Windward. Darkness dropped from the sky like a curtain after a play. Abi was tired after her walk. She must remember, she told herself as sleep tugged at her eyelids, to have Breed run down to the post office to pick up her package from Joan tomorrow. She fell into a deep sleep before Breed came home from another political meeting.

As usual, the first sound she heard in the morning was Chantycleer. Breed then would wrap his arms around her. She moved her body around until she was on her back and the baby had settled in somewhere under her ribcage. There were no arms around her, so with her eyes still closed she reached over for him. His space had not been slept in. Abi jumped up fully awake.

"Breed," she called out. "Where are you?" She climbed out of the bed and went into the other room. He was not there either.

Fear gripped her. "Breed!" she yelled.

She hurriedly got dressed. She would walk down to Popo's house and let her know that Breed did not come home. By the time she got dressed, Popo was knocking at the door accompanied by Marshall, the only neighbor with transportation.

Abi opened the door and bade them morning. By the look on their faces, she knew something was wrong.

Popo was the first to speak. "Now don't worry," she said with reassurance. "Breed OK. He got in some trouble last night."

Marshall interrupted, "He was with some of the men from the party, planning a strike. I hear all of them in a jail cell."

"I am going to town with Marshall to see what is what," Popo continued.

"I am coming, too," Abi replied sharply, her right hand clenched in a fist.

"You not going nowhere, Miss," Marshall interjected. "We can take care of dis. I know Breed, and he not going to want you to come and see him how he is. You carrying a baby and all."

"He right, Abi," said Popo. "You stay here. He is my boy and you know I will take good care of him."

"Well, all you better knock me down now," said Abi defiantly. "Because is go I going wid unu." No one was aware that her language had changed.

"OK, make haste," said Popo, knowing that there was no point in trying to stop her. "Marshall will drive us there. I'll get my cutlass."

Popo went across the yard and picked up her cutlass that was leaning on a tree trunk waiting for action.

Marshall was not happy about having a cutlass in his precious car. He took great pains to take care of his prized possession. It was an old blue Vauxhall he had bought for a song from an older white couple who lived in Windward. The couple had predicted a mad exit by the British from the island and wanted to get away before things got too "hot."

Marshall had taken to the car like a proud father takes to a son. "Marshall car," (as it became known nationally), served as a means of direction in lieu of a map. Since the streets in the village did not have names, it was not uncommon for people to give directions based on houses, trees and Marshall's car. The islanders were prone to say, "If you see Marshall car, you gone too far," or "de place you looking for is before Marshall car."

Once in a while Marshall would give a weary person a ride in his car but not before spreading plastic on the seats and newspaper on the floor. No women bothered him for affection because they all knew that they could not compete with his car.

So when Popo Le Grande jumped into the car with a cutlass, he grimaced.

Seated in the back with Abi, Popo addressed Marshall. "Dat boy better be in one piece or else I chopping up somebody today, so help me Lord. Remember dat time when dem boys and dem kill my husband? All he was doing was trying to block the door of a building where some women and children were hiding, trying to get away from being slaughtered like dogs. Their only crime was they wanted to live the life God give them." Abi wrapped her arms around her.

"Lawd," Popo continued, batting back the tears forming in her eyes. "Let me finish. You know what happen to your baby great grandfather, Abi? They shoot him dead."

Popo fell silent as she recalled that painful time. JW could have joined the government like other men did in order to protect themselves and their families, but he stood his ground. He believed what was happening was wrong. He spoke out about the seizing of properties by the government and the exploitation of women.

"Before he dead," Popo blurted out, turning to Abi, "he told me dat it broke his heart to see dis island he love so much become one full of oppression and lies."

Popo buried her husband in a plain, wooden coffin in the cemetery in John John under a big flamboyant tree. JW did not like the "hot sun", and she wanted to keep him in the shade. He always wore a wide-brimmed straw hat so that his head would not "burn up." Red was his favorite color and the color of his blood when his life was suddenly cut short.

Abi was speechless. How could such things happen in such a beautiful place? Now she truly feared for Breed. She felt her hand grasp the cutlass next to her. For the first time in her life, Abigail Fisherman realized that she was capable of killing someone.

Marshall, not at all happy about Popo bringing a cutlass into his car, turned to an agitated Abi and said, "Miss, please hold on to the cutlass. I don't trust this old lady at all today."

Popo hissed back, "Marshall, speed up or I take the wheel and drive to the jail myself."

Needing no more encouragement, Marshall pressed down on the pedal, and Abi suddenly thought about her trips as a child to the amusement park. This car ride wasn't unlike the famous Cyclone roller coaster. She held on to her seat as Marshall negotiated one hairpin curve after the other. She clasped the cutlass tightly lest it go flying and chop somebody in half.

Once in town, things seemed to calm down a bit. Marshall drove the car up the steep hill to the jail. Before he could park, Popo leapt out of the car, grabbing the cutlass from Abi in the process. Abi followed, holding her stomach with both hands. Marshall had to run to keep up with them.

The guards would not allow Popo entrance to the jail with a cutlass, so she reluctantly had to comply. She handed it over, but not without argument. If her grandson was not looking good, she warned, she was having a chop party right in the jail and then they could put her in the cell next to him.

Abi, who had never been inside a jail and never imagined that she ever would be, followed Popo. She looked up at the inscription above the main door as she walked under it. It read, *Honi soit qui mal y pense.* "May he be shamed who thinks badly of it." She wondered to herself who should be shamed by what and why the sign was placed there.

She smelled the cell before she came upon it. It made her gasp for air. Nothing in her wildest imagination could have prepared her for this experience. Pale yellow light came from a single low-hanging bulb. The place was claustrophobic and dank. Abi channeled her inner Scarlett and repeated to herself, "I will not get sick. I will not get sick." A few guards stood around dressed up in starched red, white and blue uniforms, carrying heavy nightsticks. She could sense them inhaling her presence with disdain. They were obviously not pleased that she was among them and made no move to assist or address her. She inched towards the open cell with all the strength and dignity she could muster.

There were five bodies lying on the concrete floor. They all appeared to have been beaten within an inch of their lives. Breed was among them. His dreadlocks were cut off. Some of them had been yanked out of his head because clumps of dried-up blood and tufts of hair were stuck to his scalp. The rest were scattered on the floor soaked in his blood. Abi looked at the men on the ground and was incensed that a government could treat its people in that manner. Her heart ached for Breed since she knew his hair was his treasure. He had told her that it was not just hair, but a symbol of pride and strength. She thought about how he would laugh when she called him Samson because his hair was so long. Now the Philistines had come upon him. She figured that the freshly dressed guards could not have committed this atrocity judging from their impeccable uniforms. They must have gotten the government's hench men, *le gang du sang rouge,* to do the dirty work.

One of the men was lying lifeless. Two guards came towards the women and pushed them aside. They picked up the man's body by the legs and dragged him out of the cell like he was a sack of discarded coconuts. Abi wondered if his mother knew what had become of her son.

CHAPTER SEVENTEEN

Baltimore

Hanna Gamble was a survivor. She had moved from rural Georgia to Baltimore in the 1960s when moving from the segregated South to the North seemed like a good idea. She quickly found Baltimore to be a lot like the South. While she wasn't faced with the indignity of "colored only" bathrooms, she still felt uncomfortable. She noticed that black people never sat at the front of the bus and the big department stores downtown catered to one color and one color only. There were no longer signs in the windows saying, "Whites Only," but everyone knew it was implied. Hanna didn't give up. There was a reason why she was the only member of her sharecropper family to finish high school. She rented a single room in a crowded rowhouse on North Broadway and enrolled at Morgan

State College. After five years of taking classes by day and waitressing by night, she got a nursing certificate, which she promptly took to Johns Hopkins Hospital, a round-domed edifice of red brick that loomed haughtily above her neighborhood. Given the midnight shift on weekends, cleaning bedpans and rousing drunks in the waiting room, she persisted, calmly and competently, until she was assigned to the children's ward. That's where she met Kate Carrington.

The two women hit it off immediately. They bonded at first over their mutual love of children and then their admiration of each other's honesty. Hanna Gamble, it could be said, was the only person in Baltimore who knew the real Kate Carrington. It was unusual to see an interracial pair so closely knit. They ate lunch together and, whenever possible, took their breaks together.

So when Hanna Gamble pulled out the letter from her mailbox, she was startled. The return address clearly stated West Indies. Hanna knew no one from the Caribbean. What she did know was her friend's handwriting. Hanna hurried up the stairs to her apartment.

She dropped into a chair and, with shaking fingers, tried to open the envelope. She had to put it down more than once because her fingers were too unsteady. She poured herself a glass of water and got a knife from the kitchen. She dug the knife into the fold of the envelope and pulled out three pages of neat, swirly handwriting revealing that her best friend had been reincarnated as one Abigail Fisherman.

Abi gave as much detail as she could about everything that had happened after she left Baltimore. "I miss you terribly, but there's no way I'm ever coming back to Baltimore." Hanna read with her mouth wide open. When she got to the bits that were unfathomable and there were many, she slapped the letter down on the table and called on God for assistance. She cried and she exclaimed and she laughed.

There was a P.S. to the letter where Abi asked Hanna to withdraw the money in the bank account she had set up in Hanna's name after finding out about Colin's body parts sideline. Hanna was instructed to send the money to Tsekani LeGrande at the Windward Post Office. Hanna was happy that Abi had entrusted her with the money—a tidy $8,000.00—after Colin had become more erratic and unfamiliar.

"Abigail Fisherman?" Hanna said out loud, rolling the name around in her mouth and holding the letter to her breast. She had found her friend at last. She always knew that Kate would never have forgotten her.

What concerned her a bit was the account that Abigail gave in the letter about the political unrest on the island. But Abigail certainly seemed happy. She had found a piece of paradise and was in love for the first time in her life. She had a family that loved her back. She found a mother in Popo, a soul mate in Breed, and an unbridled passion for the life that was growing inside her.

Abi wrote that she was amazed to find out how little a person really needed to survive in the world. "I can't imagine why I needed all that Wedgewood and Crystal. And I really don't care what becomes of all the stuff I left behind, including my unfortunate marriage."

Hanna couldn't help but think back to when she first met Colin Carrington. It was at a Christmas party at the hospital. She noticed that he had hardly uttered a word to his wife, and instead focused intently at a young black waitress across the room.

"Haven't I seen you before?" Hanna had sidled over to the woman and introduced herself.

"I don't remember meeting you," the woman answered with a quizzical look. "My name is Deirdra."

Hanna thought for a moment, then exclaimed, "I know where I've seen you, Deirdra. You work at the Uptown Supermarket in Charles Village, right?"

"Yup, I sure do," Deirdra replied. "But can't say that I remember seeing you there. It ain't easy to remember folks that come in and out of that damn place."

With Kate's letter grasped in her hand, she remembered that she had seen Colin at that supermarket on more than one occasion. She'd seen him go up to Deirdra's checkout register at the supermarket with just a tangerine in his hand and lust in his eyes. Kate had told her by then that Colin was having an affair, but that she had no idea who the woman might be.

Hanna noticed that every Wednesday afternoon Colin showed up at the supermarket parking lot and sat in his car reading a newspaper. Wednesday then became the day that Hanna did her shopping. At around 5:30 p.m., she'd watch Deirdra saunter out of the supermarket like she was coming down the runway of a fashion show. She'd swing her hips this way and that, watching Colin as he watched her.

Hanna was saddened for Kate in a way, but she also knew that the marriage had fallen apart and Kate was very unhappy. After Kate vanished into thin air, she worried that perhaps Colin and Deirdra had done something dastardly to her friend. But now that she had this letter in her hand, her heart leapt for joy. She was happy that Kate was safe, even if it meant that she might never see her again.

With brand new energy, Hanna got busy working on the list of things that Kate had requested. She bought cute little baby clothes, toys and booties and whatever else she thought might come in handy. Including Kate's nursing certificate.

Kate had also requested that she send gifts for Popo, Breed, Jenny and even Joan at the Post Office. Other people who got packages from England and the U.S. knew to always give Joan "a little something," otherwise she just might keep your letters tucked away in a special bin.

CHAPTER EIGHTEEN

Baltimore

Madge put the boot back in the closet and continued snooping around the bedroom looking for any evidence of the black woman. The one she had seen Colin follow into a rowhouse in Charles Village. Kate might have put up with it or pretended it did not exist, but not Madge Sorenson. Madge would have Colin all to herself, regardless of what that took. She knew how to buy and she knew how to sell. This woman would be no match for her. She covered every inch of the bedroom in the time it took Colin to shower. She turned over pillows and peeked under rugs looking for forgotten underwear. Nothing. She did everything but dust for fingerprints.

When Colin came into the bedroom to get dressed, she slipped back into the bathroom to look for the ever-elusive hairpin. That's where she saw it.

Madge surprised herself. She did not know that she could scream that loud. Colin ran into the bathroom and found a red-faced, terrified Madge still yelling while pointing to something on the floor. It was black, about the size of a quarter and round with little spritzy tentacles. In between screams she wondered why in the world he kept a broom upside down by the toilet.

"Calm down. It's nothing." Colin tried to console her, but to no avail.

"If you don't kill it, I will." Madge grabbed the broom and started whacking away at the curly black thing on the floor.

When she grabbed the handle of the broom, she felt a distinct shiver run through her body, which she attributed to her fear of the insect. She hit it with the broom, then stamped on it with her feet.

Colin watched the spectacle before him in amusement. When Madge was satisfied that she had killed the thing, she asked Colin to get rid of it. To her surprise, he stooped down and picked it up with his fingers.

"What the hell is it?" Madge asked, keeping a safe distance. "I've never seen one like that before."

"It's nothing, my dear. It's just hair," answered Colin with a grin.

"Hair?" Madge said with growing agitation again. "What hair? How could that be hair?"

"My cleaning lady, who happens to be black, must have combed her hair in the bathroom before she left for the day and forgotten to pick this up," said Colin. "It obviously came from her comb and fell on the floor without her knowing. She is usually very careful." Colin tossed the ball of hair into the bin, cleared his throat and walked out of the room.

Once Madge had recovered from the revelation that black people have very interesting hair, she realized that she had never heard Kate talk about having a cleaning lady.

"It was that woman, of course. She's been here," she said, louder than she had planned to.

"What dear?" Colin asked from the hallway.

"Nothing," answered Madge.

Striding into the bathroom and wrapping his arm around Madge, Colin said, "Let's do lunch and toast our new relationship."

Madge was not naïve enough to think that Colin had any feelings for her. But she was more than ready to rest on her laurels for the rest of her life. He had better put a ring on her finger before Kate came back or this black woman reappeared. The two walked out the front door, each deep in thoughts of their own.

Colin knew that he could not get away with keeping Deirdra on the side if he married Madge. It hadn't been more than a month before he had Kate legally presumed dead and it seemed much too early to jump into another marriage. But if Madge suspected that he knew Ross Winter, or that he might have had a hand in orchestrating the killing of his wife, then the only way he could keep her quiet was to marry her. A wife cannot testify against her husband. Besides, judging from her earlier performance, she was not at all shy in the bedroom. Yes, he would have to give up Deirdra.

Madge on the other hand, knew what she knew. She had read the newspaper article about the pointed shoe that had caused Ross' kidney to be punctured. She also knew that the police were convinced that the shoe was a women's stiletto worn by another cross dresser. No witnesses had shown up to prove them wrong. Besides, she thought, what cop particularly cared what happened to a druggie on a Saturday night in Baltimore. The death of Ross Winter would join the files of cold cases.

She'd seen Exhibit A in Colin's closet. But Colin would be no good to her in jail, so she linked her arm in his as they walked to a nearby restaurant on a beautiful spring afternoon in Columbia.

"When we get back home, I will clean the blood off the boot," she thought to herself. "Then I will take care of that woman with the buggy hair."

"I'll have a steak. Very rare," she told the waitress, between bursts of giddy laughter.

"And I'll have the same," said Colin, slowly and deliberately. "And please bring a bottle of your best champagne for me and my future wife."

Madge's eyes lit up when she heard his words but not bright enough to notice the coldness in his.

CHAPTER NINETEEN

Windward

After an extraordinary amount of secret deliberations, the authorities let the families of the imprisoned men take them home. Two of the men were too badly beaten to go home. Breed was one of them.

Abi held back her tears and helped Popo pick up Breed's hair from where it was strewn around the floor of the jail cell. Someone handed them a plastic bag, and they put in the pieces of dreadlocks that he had grown for 20 years to become a part of his very soul.

Popo and Abi took Breed to the hospital in Seaview in Marshall's car. With his head leaning on Abi's shoulder and his body held up by his grandmother, Breed quietly moaned with every bump in the road. For the first time since he owned his car, Marshall did not mind the blood stains that it inherited.

Breed was given a bed in a packed wing in the hospital. People sick from various maladies or injured from fights, vomited and howled together. Abi had always assumed that most hospitals were like Johns Hopkins Hospital in Baltimore. She had visited some inner-city hospitals during nursing school, but nothing remotely resembled the squalor in this one. The hospital staff, although very polite, did not have adequate medical supplies or drugs to help the sick and injured. The bed on which they placed Breed had no sheets on it, and the bare mattress sagged from overuse.

Water did not always flow freely, so there was a filled basin near his bed. Electricity flickered erratically from an overhead bulb. Abi and Popo cleaned up Breed the best they could and got fresh bandages for his head from a helpful nurse. Both wanted to spend the night with him, but they were not allowed to. For the next two weeks one or the other of them rode to Seaview with Marshall to care for Breed. They brought their own linens, towels and toiletries.

"Do you suppose there is a separate hospital for the wealthy people?" Abi asked Popo after one of their trips back from Seaview. "I can't imagine they are subject to the same treatment that the average person on the island receives."

"Look what you asking me. I don't know," answered Popo. "I never heard of it. Come to think, I never thought of it. We have a way on this island of getting used to tings the way they are."

The women continued to take care of Breed at the hospital until he was healed enough to travel to the village.

Back home, the healing process was slow and painful. Breed could not stay outdoors too long or do any heavy lifting. Abi tied a cloth loosely around his head so that the sun would not tighten the scars that were forming and cause him more agony. If his scalp itched, he had to endure the discomfort. With every onslaught of pain, Breed thought about the experience of his comrades. He especially thought about the ones who hadn't survived. Abi washed and tended his broken scalp until it had mended enough for him to wear a hat.

When he was finally strong enough, he and Abi washed his locks, removing the pieces of dead scalp and clotted dried blood from the roots. They left them to dry in the sun with the day's washing and then placed them in a clean plastic bag.

When he had enough hair to comb, he made a ball with the palms of his hands with the dead strands left in the comb and placed it on the sink in the bathroom. Later on when Abi came into the bathroom, she yelped. She had seen her share of curious things on the island, but this thing was something new. She picked up the broom.

Hearing the commotion in the bathroom, Breed strode in to see what the noise was all about.

"Kill it Breed. Kill it," Abi shrieked. She whacked the thing with the broom frantically.

"It's only my hair, Green Eyes," said Breed, amused.

"How could that be?" asked Abi, perplexed.

Breed picked up the ball of hair and threw it into the bin.

"I did not know that black people had such strange hair," Abi said in mild shock.

"We don't," said Breed laughing. "White people are afraid of anything they do not understand."

The baby in Abigail's stomach was making its presence felt more often. Breed said he knew it was a little revolutionary. It thumped inside of its mother like it was leading a rally. Once in a while, a little lump would appear on Abi's stomach.

"That's his foot," his mother said to his father.

"No," his father replied, "That's his little fist. His arm is raised in defiance of all that is evil and unjust."

"Let's call him Thumper," said his mother with a laugh. "That would be in keeping with his African ancestors that name their children after they see a personality trait. We don't have to wait, he has already told us what to call him. Thumper LeGrande."

Breed took Abi's hand in his and pressed his lips into her palm. Something magical seemed to leave his body and rush into hers, causing them both to shudder. His lips left her palm and moved to her mouth, causing her heart to skip a beat.

"I'll be gentle," he whispered hoarsely as he lifted her up effortlessly and carried her to their bedroom.

"I have a name for our boy," he said after their lovemaking. "We will call him Ernesto Patrice LeGrande. His nickname will be Che. He deserves the name of great revolutionaries. Ernesto after Che Guervera and Patrice after Patrice Lumumba."

They were a happy pair. Sitting on the verandah, Breed was wearing a new shirt that Hanna Gamble had sent from Baltimore, and Abi was clad in a very comfortable cotton shift with brand new sandals. She leaned on Breed and he cradled their unborn child. They felt blessed in the face of all the disarray around them. Breed was now well enough to go back to fishing and, of course continuing the struggle for change.

"You know Abi," Breed turned to look her. Neither of them could remember the exact time they believed that they were husband and wife. Breed thought it was when they had first made love. Abi knew it was when he had turned the fishing boat around in the harbor and brought her back to the island.

"You asked me earlier how a little place like this could suffer so much turmoil," said Breed, stretching his legs beyond the edge of the railing. "Who's to say that because a country is in the Caribbean and supposed to be a lovely place to vacation and drink and party, as the foreigners tell it, that all has to be well? Look at what some countries in Africa had to suffer. Women carried broken bits of their dead children in their pockets as they ran to escape the brutality of their own governments. And the Jewish women had to choose which child to give up to be burned in the gas chambers. The world is full of grief and injustice. Is it because we live in a pretty tropical island that we should escape the atrocities of the people that rule? Who escapes, Abi? Do any of us, regardless of where we live, escape?" Breed sighed reflectively. "To endure pain," he continued, "is damaging, but to be aware of the pain of others and do nothing, is truly damning."

A lizard dressed up with no regard for what color-matching meant, flitted about in the dirt looking for flies while keeping its eyes on Abi. Fortunately for him, Abigail was far too weighted down to pick up a stone to throw at him.

"Che Guevara?" asked Abi, a tinge of alarm in her voice. "I remember reading once in college about him. From what I can recall, he was not a particularly nice sort. I am not sure I want our baby named after such a radical."

"Of course Che would be called a radical in America!" said Breed, animated again. "Settle yourself on me let me tell you about Che. I know the baby listening because he done hear his name call already. A lot of people don't know that Che Guevara was an educated man. He was a doctor, author and a military theorist. He born in Argentina in 1928. I have a friend right now whose son studying medicine at Indiana University in America. Papi could tell you the kind of discipline, compassion and perseverance you need to stay the course. You would know that, being a nurse yourself."

"Anyway," Breed repeated, "Che was a doctor. He was in Guatemala around 1954, if my memory serve me right, when he witnessed the socialist government of President Jacobo Arbenz overthrown by an American-backed military coup. Che decided to hang up his stetescope to become a revolutionary in the Fidel Castro movement."

Breed paused and drank some water from the jug that Abi had placed on the table in front of them. "Do you remember reading anything about the July 26 movement in school?" he asked Abi, not expecting an answer. "Well," he said, "that was mid 1950s when Fidel Castro and about 80 men and women came to Cuba to try and overthrow the government of General Batista."

"Did they do it?" asked Abi, swatting a huge horsefly that had come to rest on her nose.

"Hold on, Doux Doux. Hold on," he said. "Nah, they didn't succeed," he continued, shaking his head. "Before they could even start anything, the government troops attacked them. After the attack, only 16 men were left with only 12 weapons between them. Imagine dat! Remember when we talked about the suffering in the world? Well, many innocent people were pulled in for questioning around that time because the so-called peasants were helping the guerrillas. Dese people were tortured and some, including children, were publicly executed. Their bodies were left hanging in the streets as an example to anyone trying to upset the status quo. But the struggle continued and is alive and well. Che died at 39, fighting to the very end."

"Who is we to escape suffering. Tell me dat."

CHAPTER TWENTY

Windward

With the addition to the house finished, Abi was enjoying hanging new curtains in the windows and decorating the baby's nursery. Hanna, who was appointed godmother by proxy, spared no expense when it came to Che.

Under no circumstances, Abi had instructed Hanna, was she to send a stroller since there was practically nowhere in the neighborhood flat enough for her to push it. Other prohibitions included:

- NO walkers because the babies just crawled until they walked.
- NO pacifiers because it made their teeth crooked.

- NO bottles and formulas because that is why God gave women breasts with milk in them.
- NO teething toys because their mothers had fingers to dip in rum to soothe their sore gums.
- NO disposable diapers because she would be showing off when the other mothers could not afford them.
- NO Johnson's Baby Lotion because they had coconut oil that was pure and much better for the baby's skin.

Despite the many prohibitions, Hanna managed to squeeze in some of the unwanted things. She knew that disposable diapers would come in handy, as would the teething toys and lotion. Che's little part of the house was stocked so amply that women from the village would bring Abi ground provisions just to see the baby's room. If ever a child was spoiled before he arrived on the planet, it was Ernesto Patrice LeGrande, aka Che.

Jenny's boy Alister, waited anxiously to see the baby. Before Abi's belly began to swell, Alister would be over all the time and ask Abi to tell him about life in America. But when her belly got bigger, he got concerned. He finally asked his mother what was in Miss Abi's belly and was told it was a little boy. Following that conversation Alister kept his distance until Jenny told him that no, Miss Abi did not eat little boys.

Alister loved making up poems and calypsos. He cherished the book that Abi gave him, saying it was from her American friend, Hanna Gamble. It was a collection of poems by Langston Hughes. He was happy to discover that Hughes looked like him because the writers he read about in school were very seldom black. He memorized his favorite poem so that he could recite it to Miss Hanna when she visited the island.

The night is beautiful
So the faces of my people
The stars are beautiful
So the eyes of my people
Beautiful, also, is the sun
Beautiful, also, are the souls of my people

After just two barrels of clothing, food and other goodies had been sent to the island, Hanna Gamble had become Hanna Claus to the villagers. Popo had always wanted a fancy pipe and good tobacco. Soon she was blowing tobacco smoke everywhere and on everyone, spitting out bits of tobacco on the ground for effect.

For Abi, Hanna sent some wind chimes that she found in a speciality store on Madison Street. Hanna thought that when the wind blew, somewhere in the "dings" that the chimes made, there would be a sound that would keep her friend comforted. She wrapped the chimes in soft tissue paper and then to protect them further, folded in a section of the *Sunday Sun Times*. Abi hung the chimes on the breadfruit tree for the wind to play with. Seemed like the wind blew more often now, just so she could hear the tintinnabulation.

As she was about to throw out the newspaper, something caught her eye. It was a photo of a man under the headline, "POLKA DOT MURDER REMAINS UNSOLVED." Could it be? The past suddenly flooded back, almost knocking her to the floor: The trip down to the islands on the cruise ship. Madge Sorenson. The good-looking man who had asked her to have a drink with him. The very bad sex. The abject shame she felt the next morning, and her lurid thoughts of throwing herself overboard.

She gasped. Che tossed this way and that, then kicked with disapproval.

Abi read the article with blurred vision: The deceased, Ross Winter, was a suspect in the killing of a woman from Virginia, one year ago. The woman was allegedly killed at the order of her husband. Mrs. Wilkins was found murdered on the cruise ship, *Star of the Ocean.* Mr. Winter, who was also a passenger traveling alone on the ship, was fingered because of reports of loud, raucous behavior in his cabin the evening before the murder. One passenger reported that she had seen Mrs. Wilkins go into his cabin before the melee, but had never seen her leave. She later recanted her story. There was not enough evidence gathered to arrest Ross Winter, but he was the only person of interest in that crime. Now he was dead. Shot in the head.

Abi stared at the paper. Could it be that Colin hired Ross to...no, it couldn't be. She sat down with the paper in her hands as her mind did cartwheels. She recalled Colin's last world to her, "I hope you drop dead, Kate." Was Madge involved? Abi got to her feet unsteadily, dropped the newspaper and let her body slide down the wall to the floor.

Hearing the thud, Breed called out to his mother who was outside feeding the chickens.

"Is it time to call the midwife?" he yelled out.

"No, this is not the time," Popo shushed him. "This is something else. Something I have been expecting all along. Lawd, Lawd, Lawd."

"What is it, Doux Doux?" Breed asked Abi, gently cupping her head in his hands.

Abi silently handed him the newspaper and pointed to the story. Breed and Popo, heads pressed together, read the story in front of them and looked at the picture.

"Do you know this man, Abi?" Popo dried the tears from Abi's eyes with the edge of her skirt. "Is he your husband?"

Abi shook her head back and forth, and through her tears told her story to them. When she got to the part where she had sex with Ross in his cabin, Breed tightened his grip around her shoulders, and Popo raised her hands and called on the Lord again. Relief poured out of her as she spilled out her secret. Now with the floodgates open, nothing was left unsaid. She told them about the miscarriage of her daughter, her despondency and Colin's callous reaction to the situation. The smell of arrogance and disdain that came out of his pores. And finally, the curse he leveled at her the last time she walked out of the house wearing her new polka dotted hat.

Popo's pipe flew out of her mouth and went sailing through the air when she read the part of the story that said the dead man was wearing the very hat that Abi had just described. Breed fetched a bottle of rum and started sapping his mother's head with it. Popo grabbed the bottle and tipped it into her mouth.

"My head is alright on the outside boy, it's the inside that need the rum," Popo declared.

Turning to Abi, she said, "Dem clothes he was wearing must have been yours. He took your suitcase. Lawdy, it looks like Colin was trying to kill you in truth. No wonder you were scared to go to town all this time."

"Calm down," said Breed urgently. "Abi is the one in crisis, not you."

"Let's make some sense out of this," he gulped, trying hard to swallow the lump that had formed in his throat. "There is a strong possibility that Colin was trying to kill you for true. That bastard, I will go up to America and fix his tail, today self."

"Now look who excited," cried Popo, "We will get Bim Bim, the Obeah woman, to kill him from down here, and we won't have to go flying all the way to America for dat. Besides I never been on no plane and I still believe that if God wanted me to fly He would have made me a cockroach."

"Cool yourself, nah," said Breed. "Leh me tink what is the best ting to do. Obviously Colin tink you dead, Abi. And somebody kill Ross because he found out Ross kill he daughter for her husband and now somebody obviously going and kill Colin. Ma, you and me don't have to go to America after all." Breed sighed with relief.

Abi stared at both of them and broke out laughing. Pretty soon all three of them were holding on to each other and howling uncontrollably.

When a certain amount of composure returned to the room, Breed folded up the paper. They went outside and put a match to it. "He thinks you're dead, my love. Now you're really free."

"And now I know why I could not get out of your boat, Breed," she told him. "It was as if something held me down. I tried to get up, but my feet turned to lead and would not move. I let you take me back to the shore all the while wondering what had gotten into me. Yet I wasn't afraid. I just followed you home."

"Dats the Holy Spirit," exclaimed Popo, jumping up and down like a Jab Jab in a J'Ouvert band.

"Your guardian angel knew that if you got back on that cruise ship that day, is dead you dead. It hold you down," Popo said knowingly. "That man was waiting to kill you dead and throw your body over board for the sharks and dem to eat. Big shark dat just tear people limb from limb and eat them up, clothes and everything. That man was a demon. Or maybe he would have shove you overboard while you was still alive and trying to hold on to the railing for dear life and bawling. Papa God, have mercy!"

Breed and Abi grimaced at the gory details. Breed raised his hand and placed it over his grandmother's mouth to quiet her.

Supper was late that night because of all the excitement. Abi had no more secrets to reveal. But she made a mental note to write to Hanna as soon as possible to ask her to try and find more information regarding the death of Ross Winter. She wanted to know if there was any link between Ross and Colin. And between Madge Sorenson and Colin for that matter.

Long after Popo had gone home for the night, Abi found sleep elusive. Her thoughts went to her earlier conversations with Breed about injustice and brutality in the world. It occurred to her that cruelty had no boundaries. It was bold. It had attitude. There were people dying from disease and war. Others were put to death by corrupt governments. Some made an untimely exit because another failed to decline that last drink. And others were murdered by their husbands because it was, well, convenient.

"Come, Chunkaloonks, let me cuddle you so you can sleep," murmured Breed.

"Is that my new name? What does it mean?" she whispered, snuggling up close to him.

"My chunk of sweetness," he answered.

CHAPTER TWENTY-ONE

Baltimore

<p style="text-indent:0">

Deirdra Anne Jackson did not like her new status. She had concocted elaborate plans for herself and Colin Carrington after the disappearance of his wife. And now, when they should be spending all of their spare time together, Colin had become a disappearing act.

The last time she snuck into his house she did not have time to work her ju-ju. There was barely enough time to leave her scent. All she could manage to do was to leave a ball of hair in the bathroom. She peed on it first, of course.

"What's the point of leaving the hair without the pee," her mama had told her years before. "Leave something for somebody to find. And just to be safe, girl chile, always turn the broom upside down. That never fails. He got to touch it at some time. If a woman comes in there, she got to touch it. After that you just wait."

Colin's visits had dwindled down to drive-bys at the grocery store, where he'd bring her an expensive box of candy and tell her to be patient. His excuse was that he was working longer hours and doing more out-of-town seminars to bring in the big bucks. Deirda did not come cheap. Colin had bought her that house in Charles Village six months ago. She rented out the top floor along with the basement. He bought her jewelry and perfumes as his taste for chocolate-covered skin grew. Deirdra, under her mama's guidance, opened a bank account that increased quickly with the monthly rent checks. She sold off most of the jewelry. She attended night classes to get her GED and took a course in accounting. Her plans included opening a beauty salon on a much-traveled strip in Baltimore City. She got her driver's license and requested a car. She was amazed that Colin took her to the dealership the very next day and she left in a fire-engine red Chevrolet. She did not expect so fast a response, but when she thought about it now, it was after that purchase that he had stopped coming by regularly.

She had no other option than to spy. She drove to his house in Columbia at around the time he would leave for work and parked her car across the street out of his direct sight and waited. After a few minutes, Colin emerged from his front door with a woman clinging to his arm. Deirdra grimaced. She watched as they exhanged a furtive kiss and went to their respective cars and drove off.

If there was one thing her old friend Ross Winter had taught her, it was how to break and enter. She retrieved the For Sale sign she had earlier stolen from someone's lawn and walked towards the house. Ross would have suggested she stick the sign in the grass on the front lawn in case there were nosy neighbors wondering what a black woman was doing in the neighborhood. When one is propelled by passion, the brain thinks up all kinds of convoluted contingencies.

She expertly jimmied the front door lock, walked in and found what she expected. Evidence that she had been replaced by another woman. The woman's clothes were everywhere. There was even a piece of wispy underwear hanging on the Tiffany table lamp. Deirdra picked it up carefully with her fingertips and put it in her purse. She would use it later for revenge.

She sprinted up to his bedroom and headed for his closet. Shoes were Colin's fettish. When they made love, he wore his shoes and sometimes he made her wear hers. He liked to buy her shoes especially for those occasions. She scrambled through the metal rack looking for his favorite aphrodisiac, the kinky cowboy boots with the pointed silver tips. That's what he called them, especially when they played cowboy.

The boots were nowhere to be found. She knew they were somewhere in the house because they were a big part of their games. He often told her that all he had to do when he missed her was hold the boots to his heart and lick them to pacify himself. Deirdra sighed.

She looked down at the unmade bed. Colin always slept on the right side when he was with her. She smelled his cologne on the pillow and knew that he still slept on the right. She closed her eyes. If Ross were alive, she would ask him to kill this new woman who had stolen her place.

She was so lost in her thoughts that she did not hear the keys in the front door. The sound she did hear was Madge Sorenson coming up the stairs. Deirdra dived into the closet.

"Where is that damn folder?" Madge said out loud.

Peeking from between the louvres of the closet door, Deirdra watched Madge grab something from on top of the dresser then look around the room suspiciously. Madge wrinkled her nose as if it had detected an unusual scent. Maybe Colin changed his aftershave, she thought. She muttered something under her breath then walked out of the room.

After the front door slammed, Deirdra peered out of the bedroom window. Madge was staring at the For Sale sign in front of the house. She shook her head and got back into her car. Maybe one of the agents was playing a prank on her.

Deirdra sat down on the bed and thought again about Ross Winter. She missed him. She and Ross had few secrets between them. Back at Eastern High School, she was one of the few kids who accepted him for what he was. She helped him shop for women's clothes and showed him how to apply mascara and rouge. She knew that everyone considered him a sleazeball and that he had a drug problem, but he was her friend. She had told him about Colin. She wanted him to know about the man she loved. Now someone had gone and killed him.

She jumped off the bed and dried the tears that were falling down her cheeks. She set about determined to find a souvenir to keep Colin alive in her life. She headed for the laundry room. It was the one room in the house that she had not gone through. Behind a crate of discarded magazines she found a plastic bag.

Deirdra squeezed its contents to make sure it was what she was looking for. She quickly stuffed the souvenir into her oversized pocketbook and left the house. On the way to her car, she grabbed the For Sale sign and disappeared in a red flash.

What Deirdra did not know was how long Madge had been searching for those boots since finding them in Colin's closet. The man of the house, wary of his new companion, had hidden them out of sight in the laundry room.

Madge had looked all over the house for the boots, but they were nowhere to be found. She did not think to check the dim corners of the laundry room because she made as few trips there as she possibly could. The boots were soon forgotten and never spoken of again. Madge assumed they were misplaced, and Colin figured they were where he put them.

Back in Baltimore, Hanna Gamble had her own theory about Colin and his women. She knew about the affair between Colin and Deirdra. She also knew that the story Colin told about Kate's disappearance was an out-and-out lie. A breakthrough in her sleuthing came when she read in the society page that Baltimore's chief medical examiner had become engaged to a top-selling real estate agent.

Colin, Hanna knew, was a man afraid of nothing and no one. A trait that came with position and the color of his skin.

Hanna was too absorbed in her own thoughts to notice the quizzical stares she was getting at the supermarket. She stood in the produce aisle with a large ripe tomato in her hand. She did not realize she had squeezed the life out of the fruit until the pulpy juice was running down from between her fingers onto the front of her dress.

"Ma'am are you alright?" asked the perplexed store clerk. Everyone else had pivoted around their carts should the crazy black lady in Aisle 6 go berserk.

"I'm so sorry." Hanna took the rag from his hand and cleaned her fingers and dress. As if on cue, a young man rolled up with a mop and pail to wipe away the spillage and place a Wet Floor sign.

"I'm OK," Hanna said apologetically to the young man. "I'll be happy to pay for the tomato."

"That won't be necessary ma'am. I see you here all the time. Have a good day." The man went back to his post of spying on would-be shoplifters, especially the ones who tried to stuff whole packages of frozen chicken into their pants.

Hanna strided up to the checkout counter. Her game plan was to chat up Colin's ex-girlfriend and see what she could discover.

"Is Deirdra in today?" Hanna asked the cashier whose distant eyes suggested that she'd much rather be on a beach in Jamaica.

"Deirdra?" the woman said, jumping back to her sad reality.

"Deirdra did what most of us wish we could, hon. She done left." The woman looked blankly at the conveyor belt and began ringing up Hanna's purchases.

"Would you happen to know where she went?"

"Girlfriend opened a hair salon on Charles and 25th Street. You can't miss it. It's called Kinky Hair and there's this big neon sign with a cowboy boot flashing on and off. Deirdra was a funny woman. I miss her. Next."

The woman dismissed Hanna and looked vaguely at her next customer who was getting antsy. Hanna, meanwhile, hurried out of the supermarket. Had she not bought so many items, she would have walked straight down to Charles and 25th Street, but she was too burdened.

"Taxi," she called out, anxious to get out of the afternoon rain. She climbed into the back seat of a yellow cab unpleasantly scented with stale tobacco. "Broadway, please." Tomorrow was another day. There was no hurry. Hanna would find Deirdra and sort things out soon enough.

The taxi sped down North Avenue past a group of homeless people pressing their bodies against a storefront trying to stay dry. She offered up a quick prayer for the one lying face up in the middle of the sidewalk. Maybe he was asleep. She hoped that was the case.

Back at her apartment, Hanna slipped off her shoes and pondered the news about Deirdra and her ability to scrape up enough money to open a hair salon. Kinky

Hair? What does kinky hair have to do with cowboys, she wondered.

She re-read Abi's last letter, where Abi specifically asked her for information about the murder of a man named Ross Winter. Why would Abi want this information, Hanna wondered again. Did she know someone connected to him? Hanna was unable to find anything more than a few paragraphs on the murder even after checking the local library's newspaper room. She guessed she'd learn more about what was going on when she made her much-anticipated trip to Windward. For now, she'd better get over to the post office to see about acquiring a passport. If 8 hours on three different planes was the only way to see Abi, then that was what she would do.

Three months later, Colin and Madge became husband and wife in a simple ceremony before the magistrate in Columbia. The only witness was the lady who cleaned the courthouse. They each knew something that the other did not and decided to keep things that way.

Ross Winter was never mentioned again. As Madge had predicted, his murder case joined the countless other cold cases in Baltimore City and was put in a file to collect dust. There were no suspects. No witnesses had showed up except for a homeless man who always confessed to crimes in the hopes of going to jail where he could get three square meals and a mediocre bed.

The newly weds settled down to a life of drink, debauchery and deceit.

CHAPTER TWENTY-TWO

Windward

Abi hung the two nursing outfits that Hanna had mailed down in her closet. She had given her nursing certificate to the head nurse at the Visiting Station, and was immediately hired as a nurse, a position she would take up after she gave birth and was back on her feet. She was now eight months along and every day was a lesson in patience.

As a prominent member of the party opposing the government, Breed was constantly away from home. He had meetings to attend and rallies to organize. His hair never grew back the way he would have liked so he kept it shaved. There were deep scars on parts of his scalp where hair would not grow. He took to wearing a large straw hat like his grandfather did to deflect the discomfort of the sun. He also wore colorful bandanas courtesy of Hanna.

As the time for the baby's delivery came closer, he opted to hold his meetings on the front verandah to give his comrades escape from the blazing sun. Abi liked to sit in on the political discussions. She particularly liked listening to Malik, a walking history book who invariably got the others "hot" with his need to battle it out with the group's pessimist, Tallboy. Some of the local men who had nothing to add to these discussions just came along to lime. This was an opportunity to just hang out and pass the time and maybe learn something they did not know.

"I don't know why so many people have to die in order for things to get better," Tallboy began in his raspy voice. Despite the inroads made by the oppostion, Tallboy always came back to the whys and wherefores of rebellion. "I hope nothing happen to our leader and he don't get kill."

"Besides," he went on, "If all you think we making progress, think again. Just because we have Texaco and Coca Cola don't mean progress. Dat mean foreign occupation. Is backwards we going."

Malik held up his forefinger in warning to Tallboy, who abruptly stopped talking. "Our leader will be as safe as leaders can be," he said solemly. "We cannot worry about that. Remember Michael Collins? He was an Irishman who was killed at the age of 31 fighting the British. That man was a real genius."

"What I want to know, is," Lester jumped in, "is why we can't go to a country like the United States with our cause. Michael Collins went to London with the other plenipotentiaries to negotiate the Anglo-Irish Treaty."

"Woi, pleni what? Dat's a big word even for a man with a big nose." said Malik as the group convulsed with laughter.

"Never you mind my nose," said Lester, unamused. "I is a African man and some of we nose big."

"Governments," said Malik, furrowing his brows for effect, "do not like revolutionaries. Michael Collins became Britain's number one enemy. He was a 'bad John' right up there with Napoleon."

Whenever the conversation involved Ireland, Abi's ears would perk up.

Now she heard Breed chant, "Power to the people," as the others joined in chorus.

Malik had been studying wars and revolutions since he was in primary school. The fact that the Irish spent 800 years trying to be rid of the British always fascinated him. Collins was in his early twenties when he started fighting for the freedom of his country. He was not convinced that shooting and killing solved problems, but he knew that shooting and killing was sometimes necessary. He had lived through the Easter Rising in 1916, where there was an extraordinary amount of bloodshed.

"What kind of man," Malik inquired, "stands up to a government, risks his life and the life of his comrades when they are facing death. I wonder if dey ever ask themselves, was it worth it?"

"Don't forget," Lester interjected, "dat when Collins' army didn't have enough weapons, he held his ground and refused to back down. He tell the British dat his only weapon was his refusal. And what did his refusal get him? A shot in the head. Is this what we want?"

There was an uneasy silence until Breed's baritone voice was heard.

"Patrice Lumumba was the first African Prime Minister of the Democratic Republic of the Congo. He got independence for his country from Belgium in 1960. But Belgium double-crossed him and backed the rebels to his government. Dey put de man in prison and then execute him by firing squad. Some people believe they got help from the U.S. Now comrades, do you think we have to worry about the Americans coming for we?"

"Nah," the men chorused back. "We is a little country. What America want with we?" But doubt was in the air, hovering around their heads like giant jungle mosquitos.

They talked into the night, long after the local mosquitoes had retreated to the rainforest and the village dogs had quit their wearisome whining. They talked about Papillon, who kept trying to escape from prison and finally did so as an old man. Are we not all born with the same desire to be free? They asked questions that were picked up by the night wind and scattered over the land. Not even Bim Bim, the Obeah woman, had answers for them.

"Is easy to criticize another man while we sit down and watch," said Breed. "I believe that those who are willing to put their lives on the line deserve respect."

"When I was a little boy," he continued, laughing. "I got up on the stage in class to sing a calypso. The teacher said if you had a talent and you wanted to share, here was your chance. Well, there I was strumming away on my imaginary guitar and singing my heart out. Not singing any old stupid calypso, pardner. I make up my own ting. When I done singing, I realize all the children were laughing at me. I was so shame. But the teacher said at least I had the courage to come up in front of the class and sing my song. She challenged any of the other children to do the same. Everybody stop pointing and laughing one time. I couldn't sing well, but I believed in my song."

Applause rang out. "What makes a man continue to struggle when he has the choice to do nothing or run? Even if the struggle fails and the fight is lost, one still has to respect the men that dare to stand up and fight," Breed concluded.

Civil war, they decided, is what is sometimes needed to gain independence and freedom.

Breed absentmindedly scratched his head and winced at the pain. "We, my comrades, will change the situation in this little country for the better."

"Time for me to say something," said Popo, getting to her feet. "I quiet long enough. Let me tell unu what I know."

"Wait. Before you start talking, you mean what the obeah woman tell you, right?" asked Lester, ducking from the sandal that came flying from Bim Bim's hand.

"Be quiet, and you might learn something," Popo snapped. "So you head big, so it empty. I'll tell all you something interesting. Watch how many revolutionay men whose name start with the letter M. Malcolm X, Medgar Evers, Martin Luther King, Bob Marley, Nelson Mandela. You could even include that Michael Collins we was talking about a few minutes ago. Five of dem dead before they reach 40. I just pray to God that is not a sign and our leader make it. Because you know, his name start with M, too." The group was quiet.

"Hear, hear," said Malik. "All you know what else is interesting? The Messiah. He dead at 33. "

He raised both fists in the air and hooted. He was impressed with his brilliance. No one paid any attention. He continued in a more subdued tone. "On a brighter note, isn't it interesting that despite all the strife, struggle and blood shed in de world, out comes great art and talent? Look at the great novels that came out of Russia, the doctors and scientists out of India, and the poets out of Ireland. Let's go home, brethren. I have a book to write."

No one moved. They were all deep in thought. A revolution can be thwarted, Abi said to herself, but what cannot be killed is the revolutionary spirit. With her Irish blood and Breed's embrace of Marxism, would their baby follow the same path? Abi made the sign of the cross and shuddered.

It was way after 10 o'clock when the group bade each other good night and started walking to their respective homes to get there before the Jumbies, Ting Tings, Bakoos, Soucouyants and other creatures of the night stopped them in their tracks. Everyone in Windward knew that the night belonged to mysterious creatures. Some of them forgetting that you could walk right through them if you chose. Arrogant minions. Popo, who feared no man, was afraid of the night. Not wishing to be eaten by anything untoward, she sprinted ahead of everyone.

When Breed and Abi lay down for the night, wrapped up in each other with Che snuggled between them, Abi asked Breed a question that was burning inside her for weeks.

"Breed," she murmured anxiously in his ear. "How come so many women on the island cannot swim?"

"Maybe they 'fraid the water, my love," He was asleep before he heard Abi's own explanation.

CHAPTER TWENTY-THREE

Windward

Before going out fishing or to his meetings, Breed would make sure his wife was sitting comfortably with her legs elevated. He always waited until Popo or a woman from the village came over before he left her. This morning, however, was different. They had a ceremony to attend. A burial. It would be held under the breadfruit tree.

Breed held Abi steadily as they both walked into the yard holding a plastic bag. He placed the bag with its contents on the ground beside them and picked up the large digging fork that was laying against the tree. With a sigh, he started digging. The ground was soft and malleable after the morning rain. It was time to bury his dreadlocks. He kept one in his clothes drawer to give to Che in a year or two.

Breed tenderly poured the locks into the hole, then sprinkled flower seeds on top of it. He filled up the hole with soil and they sat quietly for a minute. They got up to greet Popo who was ambling up the hill. Breed kissed Abi goodbye.

"You know if you were in America, they done take out that baby whether you ready or not," said Popo who mysteriously knew everything that happened in America. Sitting down near to Abi, she added, "I hear those doctors up there, if they have to go and play golf at the time you due, they will give you a time to come in, and out comes the baby before tee time."

She patted Abi on her stomach and addressed Che directly, "Time for you to come out of there and take a stand. I am getting too old to chase chickens and chop them up for lunch. What you waiting for?"

That morning Popo had run almost half a mile after a nice fat hen before she caught up with it. Before chopping off the head of a chicken, she always gave it the name of one of Henry VIII's wives.

"I done season up Anne Boleyn already," Popo told Abi. "All we have to do is cook her up. Today I will show you how to make a nice curry chicken. Come on, let me help you go inside."

Abi struggling on her feet waddled along beside Popo. One foot today. One foot tomorrow. Popo figured that at this pace they would get to the kitchen by Christmas.

"I swear white people does have more trouble carrying children than black people," Popo declared. "One of you should take some notes and write a book about how to make childbirth easier."

"Very funny, but I don't hear anybody laughing," Abi said with a smirk.

"That is because they laughing on the inside," Po Po shot back. "Anyway, waddle inside the bedroom and get paper and pencil, so you can write down how to cook Miss Boleyn," Popo said. "And look sharp."

Abi arrived back in the kitchen equipped and ready before the holidays.

"OK, let's get cooking," Popo said animatedly, "Make sure, darling, dat before you even season up the chicken, you clean it good. None of this taking chicken out of the package, passing it under the water and flinging it in the pot. You always have to wash the chicken with lime. Just like you do with the lambi and fish. Squeeze some lime juice on the meat and rub the chicken down with the pith. Dat makes it fresh for cooking and also gets rid of any slime between the skin and the flesh. Now start writing, Shakespeare."

> *Limes two/three*
> *Rum (some to drink and some to put in the food)*
> *Some sugar*
> *A whole chicken*
> *Half cup or so of coconut milk*
> *Half a pumpkin, cut up*
> *Christophene (and don't forget to add Christophene to your salt fish cakes, too)*
> *One hot pepper*
> *Onion, garlic, black pepper, chives and thyme and such*
> *2 tablespoon curry powder*
> *Cut up the hot pepper fine or it will burn your backside up*
> *Throw in some oil*

"After you cut up the chicken," Popo instructed, "rub it down with the limes and dem. Heat the oil in the large iron skillet and put a little sugar in until it get brown and start sizzling. Throw in the chicken pieces and brown them up.

Take out the pieces and set them aside. Now fry up the onions and garlic and hot peppers and seasonings for two or three minutes, then add the curry powder. Never stop stirring. You could put in vegetables here if you want—pumpkin chunks, carrots and some green pawpaw for your blood pressure. Add the coconut milk, stir it up and then throw the chicken pieces back in the pot. Sprinkle some of dis and some of dat. Don't make the fire too hot. Cover down the pot and let it cook slowly. After about half hour you could throw in a tip of the lemon juice."

"And then," Popo added with a flourish of her hand. "Get the rum. Drink some and pour the rest in the pot."

Abi looked up from her sheet of paper. "I don't think Breed would want me to put rum in the food since the baby will absorb it, too."

"What does Breed know about rum and babies?" Popo chortled.

"Next time your lesson will be coocoo. Or like the Italian people call it, polenta. We will call it Caribbean Polenta. Write dat down, so we don't forget."

The kitchen had grown too hot by the time the women had finished cooking. Popo took Abi back outside to sit under the tree. They contentedly watched the afternoon drift by to make room for the evening.

"Popo, we not seeing you these days in the rum shop. As Marvin Gaye would say, 'What's going on?'" laughed Boysie, as he and Malik walked up to the women. The men were going door-to-door delivering flyers to keep the people in touch with the progress of the movement.

"I'm waiting for my great-grandchild to born, you can't see that, Big Heads?" answered Popo, happy to see the young men. It had been a while since she had caught up on things political. These days she was never very far away from Abi and the baby.

"Morning, Miss Fisherman," said Malik politely. "I see is any day now."

"Let's hope so, Mr. Morrisette," smiled Abi. She was determined to give people a "handle" if they gave her one. They respected her because of her association with Breed and her legendary thrashing of Debbie.

"We have some flyers for you. Things are heating up." Boysie removed some sheets from the cardboard box he was carrying on his head and handed a few of them to Popo. He took a seat on the box. He was wearing his favourite tee shirt. The one with a solemn Bob Marley painted on the front and the quotation, "The greatness of a man is not in how much wealth he acquires, but in his integrity and his ability to affect those around him positively." Every chance he got, he turned around so the people around him could read it and nod their heads in agreement.

Malik was edgy. He had just come from a meeting in the southern part of the island and told them a horrific story about protesters getting beaten, branded with hot irons and chopped.

"It seem like when men get power, they form a thick new skin," Malik said mournfully.

"Dis is going to be a peaceful place again," Boysie told Popo. "We will go back to where we not afraid to walk the streets and wonder if we safe. We can say what we have to say without starting confusion."

"Peace is a dream," Popo replied authoritatively.

"That is a very prophetic statement for a old lady who don't know nothing," laughed Boysie, smart enough to say his piece while moving a safe distance away. "You make dat up or what?"

"No, you chupidee, your mother make it up," Popo countered, moving towards him with mock menace.

The men stapled a flyer on a nearby tree before making a hasty retreat down the hill.

"What's the matter, child?" Popo put an arm around a pale Abi.

"When is this baby coming?" Abi moaned.

"I don't know, chile," said Popo. "Only two people know. God and Bim Bim. Veni mange. Let's go inside and eat."

Popo straightened herself up from the bench and reached back to pull Abi up. But Abi was glued to the spot. Her right hand clutched her stomach and her legs spread open of their own accord. The cloth tied around her body to keep cool came loose and fell behind her. There she was again, the half-naked white woman that Popo had encountered nine months earlier, only now a lot bigger.

Before Popo could say anything, a blood-curdling scream whizzed past her and headed down the hill. She quickly wrapped Abi back in the cloth and held her close. She had nothing else to do because she knew as soon as someone heard the scream, someone else would hightail it to John John and let Breed know he was about to become a father.

Before Popo got Abi fully to her feet, there was a group of women coming up the hill in full force. Debbie, Abi's former punching bag, led the pack, carrying a bed sheet and a bottle of Clark's Court white rum. Following closely behind her was Jenny and Alister. Next came Joan from the post office. Behind her was Pinx, one of Malik's outside women. Bim Bim followed with a nanny goat in tow, then Mavis the Midwife and Doreen, her assistant. They were joined by a half dozen men from Boysie's rum shop who came along for the lime. All that was needed was a couple of powder-flinging Short Knees and it would have been Carnival.

Outside the house, the women squatted and waited. Only Popo, Mavis and Doreen were allowed inside with the mother-to-be. With every moan coming out of the window, the women bowed their heads, slapped each other on the back and screamed with laughter. Then they sighed loudly and called on the Lord for assistance. After that dislay they straightened up slowly, wiping their wet faces with the backs of their hand, and waited for Abi's next wail to start the process all over again.

Deaf to the commotion outside, Abi crossed her legs with each spasm and refused to obey Mavis' calls to push. She wanted to wait for Breed. She was determined to keep the baby inside of her until its father came home.

Fortunately, Marshall was with Breed when the news hit. At breakneck speed they headed back from John John to Marabel. The goats that usually wandered into the road seemed to know that this was not the time for idle crossings. Marshall kept his hand on the horn for the entire trip as Breed pressed his palms to the dashboard and tried to deflect any damage to his person that might occur while Marshall defied the laws of gravity around the hairpin curves.

Hearing a loud cheer coming in through the bedroom window, Abi exhaled and spread her legs for the midwife.

Breed catapulted into the room with Marshall at his heels.

"And where you think you going, Mr. Man?" Popo asked Marshall. "Go back outside," she instructed, "and keep them women quiet."

Doreen slapped Marshall on his backside as he walked out on the verandah looking dejected. "Give Marshall a drink. He look like a jumbie."

"What drink?" said Jenny as she grabbed Marshall. "Just give him some coconut water."

Breed went straight to Abi and held her hand tightly. He mopped her brow with the wet rag that Mavis gave him and kissed her face over and over. With her man by her side, Abi felt she could give birth to a horse. The air was thick with anticipation. Then came a high-pitched shriek. Ernesto

Patrice LeGrande, aka Che, had squirmed his way into the world.

Breed was overwhelmed with happiness. He had waited a long time to make a child and had even wondered whether he would ever become a father. He got down on his knees and thanked God for the blessing that was Che. Breed then helped his grandmother off her knees, wiping tears of joy from her eyes.

Outside the men were leaving with the women, satisfied that the birth of Che LeGrande had been worth the lime.

The exhausted mother was cleaned up and left to rest in the capable hands of Popo. Mavis, Doreen and Bim Bim headed towards the door. "Now that you make the baby Abi, we expect you at the clinic as soon as you on your feet," Mavis said playfully.

"I am looking forward to it," answered the new mother, grinning from ear to ear. Popo got busy taking charge, starting off by holding up and admiring her great-grandson.

"He looks like your mother," she said, turning to Breed. "We will have to find a way to get in touch with Christine and let her know about her grandchild. But for now, let's just be happy. This house will never be the same again." she sighed contently.

Breed crawled into the bed with Abi, and the two lay looking at each other as if for the first time.

CHAPTER TWENTY-FOUR

Windward

"Why can't we christen the baby in the Catholic church?" Abi wanted to know. It was not the first time that she tried to talk to Breed about Che's options where religion was concerned.

"Any place but the Catholic Church," he scowled. "I know you are Roman Catholic, but I have no religion. I pray to my God directly. What can the Virgin Mary do for me?"

"It's only a formality," pleaded a crestfallen Abi. "I don't see the harm it could do."

"That's my point exactly," said Breed. Pausing to gather his thoughts, he continued, "If it's only a formality, then why do it in the first place? JW used to say that God does not even go to the Catholic Church. It have too much taylaylay. These bishops and cardinals wanting us to bend down and kiss their rings. Dress up like mas in carnival. Are they trying to emulate Christ? A poor man on a donkey?"

Breed paused for effect. "Tell me dat, Miss Abi Fisherwoman!" He tickled her ribs and crinkled up his nose at the word fisherwoman. "Besides, I don't want him buying no rosary beads when he get big."

"Now what on earth do you have against rosary beads?" Abi asked mockingly. "When I was a little girl, I had a set that glowed in the dark. I used to take them to bed with me. One night I broke them absentmindedly, swinging them around in the air and the beads flew everywhere. They looked like little fireflies in the dark."

"What I believe is that your Virgin Mary must be deaf," Breed replied. "Why else would you have to keep repeating the Hail Mary over and over again?"

Smiling at his own wit, he added, "Woman, where you hide that Julie mango? You know I will wrestle you for it and eat it in front of you, right?" Breed picked Abi up and swung her around their kitchen.

Abi had no intention of conceding to his stubbornness. "OK, let's go Baptist then," she countered. "Either that or it's Bim Bim."

Abi closed her eyes tight lest she get dizzy from the carousel ride. Little did he know, that she had already eaten the last mango.

He let her down gently and got busy cooking the wahoo he had caught earlier in the day. In about an hour, night would begin its sojourn. Tomorrow they would doubtless continue the discussion over Che's religious upbringing.

Che slept in the little swinging bassinet that Breed had built. It was painted in the callaloo green and lemon yellow of the bus that ran into town every day.

Abi sat on the rocker that Marshall had made. The soft cushions were a gift from Jenny. She looked down on her baby as he fussed at her nipple, trying to get the entire breast into his little mouth. By the sounds he made in his quest, one would think he was a baby tiger drinking at the Nile.

Abi went into shock the first time she saw Jenny nurse her baby in the rum shop in front of everybody. But when she saw that nobody seemed to notice or care, her heart stopped palpitating.

Still chomping away at her breast, Che brought her back to reality as he drank until his head fell back and his eyes closed. A contented smile played around his lips. A trail of pale bluish milk escaped from the corner of his puffy little mouth and trickled across his cheek. Abi caught it with her finger before it found refuge in his ear.

It had been a year since Abi had come to the island. Gone were the manicures, pedicures and beauty shops. No eyebrow tweezing. No massages. She sighed happily, as she returned Che to his gaudy little bassinet. These days she settled for Breed's strong hands to ease her tired shoulders and legs. She clipped her fingernails and toes with Popo's sewing scissors. A year ago, she would have spent a fortune trying to get a tan from a bottle or lying in the sand at Rehoboth Beach, hoping she did not get sunburned in the process. Her pale white skin now had a deep radiance that made her glow. She had put on some weight around the breasts, thighs and middle. Her face had filled out with all the rich food that Popo cooked. Breed was very happy. Abi realized that skinny women were not admired as they were back in Baltimore. Windward men liked meaty women. Abi ate to her heart's content.

She liked what she saw in the mirror for the first time in her life. She gave away the stack of panty hose and high-heeled shoes that Hanna had insisted on putting in the barrel. It was much too hot for hose in Windward. But Debbie and her friends were happy strutting around town in the nylon stockings and high-heeled shoes, wobbling precariously with every step to the delight of the local men.

If there was one thing that she missed and just a little, was Christmas. Windward celebrated the holiday but there were no Christmas trees and lights, no fantastic decorations in the neighbours yards, no caroling with people dressed up in long-ago garb singing in the malls and above all, no presents to count. What they did was sing and dance to celebrate the season. Bands of people would go from house to house on Christmas morning singing and playing instruments. The owner of the house would usually come out and join in the singing and provide drinks and food for everyone, then join them as they danced to the next house. This was repeated until everyone of them was spent. For gifts, the children usually received books, or small toys, maybe a balloon or two and an American apple. Above all, it was about family and love and celebration of the saviour, Christ.

Popo came over on a daily basis and stayed with Che so his mother could go to the clinic to work. Nurse Abi, she was called. With all the political unrest on the island, the women were busy sewing up lacerations and tending to broken bones. Abi loved caring for the children best. They came to her house to have prickles pulled out from their elbows and from under their feet. They had scraped knees that needed tending and sores that needed healing. They got worm medicine every so often to get rid of intestinal worms. Whatever lay in the future, Abi knew where she belonged. She felt blessesd to be in this place so far away from her past in Baltimore.

CHAPTER TWENTY-FIVE

Windward

The minister at the Baptist church agreed to baptize the baby. He wanted the family to join the church first and become a part of the church family, but he miraculously changed his mind and decided to do the ceremony for free and at their convenience.

"I wonder what made the minister change his mind, Ma Po?" Breed eyed his grandmother with his right eyebrow raised in suspicion.

"What you asking me? I should know?"

Popo busied herself soaking soiled diapers in a battered enamel pail in the shade of the breadfruit tree. A family of horse flies, delighted by the pungent odor, tried to get in the pail for a swim. "I only ask the man to have the christening in his church, and he said yes."

"Ma Po," Breed exhaled loudly. "Why was the cutlass missing from under de tree when you left? Don't tell me you threaten the man with a chopping. He is a man of the cloth, and God don't take kindly to people threatening His flock."

"I didn't threaten His flock, I threaten him."

Popo straightened up from her washing. She wiped her brow with her forearm and puffed out a stream of hot air in her grandson's direction. "I took the cutlass in case some dog try to eat me or worse. Sometimes a woman's best defense against a beast or a priest is a cutlass."

She stopped suddenly when she realized that she had let the cat out of the bag. "I know de man not Catholic, but I did not want to take any chances."

"Anyway," she continued nonplussed, "the bakery in town making a cake for Che. They decorating it and all. I tell dem to put flowers. Roses."

"Ma Po, ah telling you now." Breed said vehemently. "Is my son. Not my daughter. I don't want flowers on his cake. Flowers? You bazodee or what? You will turn him into a girl if I don't watch."

"Then don't watch," Popo replied. "All it take to turn a boy into a girl is flowers? Don't worry yourself. If you give a girl a cutlass dat mean she will turn into a boy? Tell me dat."

"Is not the same ting, Ma," said Breed, pouring fresh water into the pail for Popo to start rinsing the diapers. The chickens following their mother across the yard, sprinted out of the way of the smelly water that made an impromptu river in front of them.

"I always had a cutlass, and I am a woman. To de bone." Popo laughed as she threw a handful of water at Breed, missing his face by an inch.

"No flowers on de boy cake, just the same." Breed insisted. "I not taking any chances."

"I putting flowers on my great grandson cake and dat's dat." Popo glared at her grandson with arms akimbo.

Breed threw his hands in the air. He knew when a conversation was over with Popo. There will be roses on Che's christening cake. Breed vowed to watch his son carefully as he grew older in order to detect any fanciful habits that arose as a result of the flowery icing.

With the additions to the house, Popo was able to secure a separate bedroom for herself. When the sale of her own house was final, she gave Breed half of the money to do more improvements on his own property. The rest she took into town and put in the Penny Bank for Che. Popo was proud of him. All he had to do was make one little squeak and she'd fly to his bassinet and pick him up.

"Ma Po," said Abi one day as she witnessed such a flight in progress. "You don't always have to pick up the baby when he cries, you know." Channeling her own mother's child-rearing philosophy, she continued, "You're spoiling him. He will begin to think that's the way the world is. We have to let him cry now and then."

"You just as kookoo as Breed." Popo countered, rocking the baby back and forth on her shoulder as he gurgled with delight. "The way I see it, spoiling a baby is just loving him and not wanting him to be fretful. So the more you spoil him, the more you love him. Can you love a baby too much?"

Abi knew what Breed had always known. There was a time to not argue with Popo because it was fruitless. Let Popo have her way with Che. After all, she had raised Breed and he turned out just fine. Abigail exhaled.

She had realized that there was never a dull moment at the house with Popo around. Women from the nearby villages constantly came to speak with her. More often than not, they stayed under the breadfruit tree to have their discussions.

Popo sat on the bench while the women gathered around Popo on the grass. If it rained they were confined to the verandah. Breed did not want any rangatang people in his house putting anything in their pockets that did not belong to them.

The women came for Popo's unforgiving advice about what to do with their men.

"Run," was more often than not her solution for any man problem. This is not what the women wanted to hear. They thanked her, but stayed with their men to endure another beating or infidelity and then wound their way back to the breadfruit tree for the same sermon ending with the word "run."

Now that she lived in the house with her grandson and his woman, Popo was privy to occasional snippets of discord between them. "How tings between you and Breed going?" she aked Abi. "I couldn't help but hear raised voices when I went to Che's room to pick him up last night—and don't you ask me if he was crying."

"Things are fine," Ai replied. "We disagree on some things, and I am still adjusting to this new life in a way, although I am as comfortable as a body can get." Abi searched Popo's eyes for understanding. "But one thing we promise to do is to never go to sleep angry. We kiss each other good night, every night and that seems to work for us."

"Well, what I think is that plenty row start because of misunderstandings."

"What is a row?" asked Abi. "You use the strangest words."

· "Row?" Popo shook her head. "Nothing strange about the word. Look it up. It means altercation. You didn't go to school or what? Wait, I forget. You went to school in America."

Popo laughed so hard she almost fell out of her chair. "Watch me, all the way in the 'Third World' have to teach you English. Anyway, let me finish before you try and turn me into a thesaurus. You know what dat is?"

"No need for sarcasm." Abi poked her elbow into Popo's ribs while valiantly trying to tuck up her dreadlocks with her other hand. It didn't work. The hair came cascading down again and framed her face trying to channel Medusa.

"It's not my fault that you use English words in all the wrong places. But why should that surprise me? You also drive on the wrong side of the street. Of course on this island there is no wrong and right side. Its all one bumpy, crooked track, so you be quiet. Now what is it you telling me about rows starting because of misunderstandings?"

"Oh, Lawd," Popo's words tumbled out. "Have you ever heard the phrase, 'it's the answer that brings the row? That means no matter what someone tells you, you should pause a little bit first before you answer. Dat keeps you from saying the wrong ting and then the confusion start. It's not what you tell somebody, it's what they hear."

Popo sprang up to check on the baby. Che was fast asleep in his crib, but she picked him up anyway and proceeded to shush him as he sleepily objected to the disturbance.

CHAPTER TWENTY-SIX

Windward

Hanna Gamble was seated at the terminal of the Baltimore-Washington Airport waiting for her flight to be called. It was the second time she would actually leave the ground. The previous time was when she was a child and she had played jump rope with her friends.

She had packed carefully and paid the overweight charge in order to bring every conceivable thing she thought Abigail might need in order to live so far away from civilization. Her knees were pressed tightly together and her fingers clutched her handbag firmly.

She was amazed at the steady stream of people going back and forth. Women pushing strollers and toddlers running alongside. Sunburned couples coming back from someplace warm. Grey-haired business-men returning home to their wives after a business convention or a tryst. Pert air-hostesses stepping lively in their high-heeled shoes that echoed down the long corridors, pulling their overnight luggage behind them. Pilots clad in starched uniforms with uniformly white faces going this way or that.

"Lord," Hanna prayed softly, "couldn't you at least send me one Tuskegee airman?" mentally noting that while the flight crews were not black, the men pushing the brooms and emptying the garbage cans were.

As soon as she was seated on the plane, she ordered a double whiskey straight up and did not regain her senses until it landed in Puerto Rico. Facing a long layover, she took a bus into San Juan and walked through the bustling streets, suprised at the number of black people she encountered speaking Spanish. She realized immediately the importance of travel.

Many hours later, after the propeller plane was replaced by an even smaller one, the island materialized before Hanna. Pressing her forehead against the window, she saw the unfolding tapestry of dense rain forest fringed by majestic palm trees and stretches of white sandy beaches. Colorfully painted houses dotted the hillsides. She at once understood what Abigail had tried to explain to her in her letter. She could not believe the beauty of this place that her friend had found.

The plane swooped down and landed abruptly on a rough field and taxied slowly to a squat cinder block building that served as the terminal. She held on to the exit railing tightly as she walked down the few steps to the ground. Standing still for a moment, she breathed in the salt-scented air with relief. The air was warm but not humid. Behind a chain link fence a few feet away from the plane several small children waved at her. To her amazement she also saw a family of goats, somebody's cow and a donkey looking impassively at her as she made her way to customs. Hanna blew some kisses to the children, which made them giggle. After many questions and several approving looks from the male uniformed officers, she fell into the arms of her friend.

Breed waited patiently in the driver's seat of Marshall's car while the women hugged and wiped away each other's tears and then started crying all over again. The ways of women were a mystery to him. He shook his head in puzzlement and thanked God for making him a man.

Damp with sweat and emotion, the women climbed into the car. Breed piled the many mismatched bags and suitcases in the trunk, on the front seat and on top of the car, thankful that Marshall was not around to witness its new lopsided look.

Not only were Popo and Che waiting at the house, but so was most of the village. Everyone wanted to see the lady from America who had sent them the nice gifts. Children bathed and well dressed, patiently waited with strict orders not to get their clothes dirty. Men and women mulled around, chatting with each other and sipping various drinks from paper cups and coconut shells.

Popo was amused to no end. She sat on the verandah and provided a running history to a gurgling, oblivious Che. "I remember as children, when we had to stand up in the hot sun and wave the Union Jack for Princess Margaret. All morning we line up sweating waiting for she. And after all that waiting, what happen? She drive by with she little gloved hand in the air, trying to wave at a bunch of cunumunus. I hope there isn't anyone in my yard today that own a Union Jack." She directed her last comment to the crowd.

"Popo," said Boysie, hearing the commentary, "cool yourself. Why should the Queen care about we?"

"I will tell you why," Popo replied vehemently. "There was a queen name Charlotte Sophia. The great, great, great, great-grandmother of this Queen Elizabeth II. She was of African descent but born in Germany. The British don't want to acknowledge that, because that would mean that the whole royal family black."

Popo waited so the assembled crowd could frown and shake their heads in disbelief. "Charlotte went and marry crazy George the Third and had 15 children. Can you imagine dat?" Popo paused to remove her ear from Che's mouth. "One of these good days someone in Buckingham Palace will make a black baby, and it will start running around just like King George without his pants yelling what, what."

"Look, the car coming now," someone shouted.

A cheer sailed through the still air for Hanna Gamble. How little it took to be loved. Who knew that the pencils or the pairs of flip-flops that she had mailed could evoke such gratitude? Hanna was overcome with emotion when she met her godson and saw her friend in her new role as mother.

Hanna and Abi opened the suitcases full of gifts under the breadfruit tree. When they were done sharing things out, everyone had something in hand to take back home. The chocolate bars and the pounds of candy, which the children called "sweeties," were the favorite. After many rounds of goodnights, an exhausted 'Hanna Claus' went into the house, had a cold shower and fell into a deep sleep.

On the morning of the christening, Abi wore the orange ruffled summer dress that Hanna had brought for her with the matching strapped sandals. On the side of her head, tucked carefully into her neatly plaited dreadlocks, was a small pale orange linen rose with tiny green leaves. In the middle of the rose was a stone that pretended to be a real pearl. It was her favorite gift from Breed. She was ready for her son's christening.

Hanna was amazed at the brightness of the sun so early in the morning. The warmth felt so lovely and comforting on her skin. She was happy to have left a grey, cold Baltimore behind.

The baby of the hour wore a white gown from which his father had removed all the ruffles or any decorations that might turn him into a girl. On his tiny feet were little plain white booties. For obvious reasons, he wore no bonnet.

Breed and Abi headed the procession to the Baptist church a half-mile away. They were followed by Marshall and Hanna, the godparents. Popo came next holding the baby, whom she refused to let anyone else carry. A happy neighborhood throng followed. By the time the family got to the church, it seemed like the whole village and some were there.

The minister poured holy water on the baby's head and prayed over him, all the while keeping a watchful eye on Popo. Popo stared right back at him. After the ceremony, the congregation walked back to Breed's house where food appeared from everywhere. Chairs and tables were scattered around the yard. The children chased each other around and their clean clothes got dirty.

When the baby woke up from his nap that was cut short by the loud celebrating, he was passed around from one person to the other until everyone in the yard had gotten a chance to hold him. His father then held him up with both hands towards the sky and they all prayed for blessings on his life.

Then the libations began. Breed opened a bottle of rum and poured a little on the ground. The people chanted a prayer for the ancestors and any recently dead. The rum was passed around for anyone who wanted to pour a libation of their own, for an ancestor or a dear one that had departed the world.

The celebration lasted way into the night. The local musicians shook their tambourines and beat their snare drums in a sweet Samba rhythm that caused the people to let loose. The dancers leapt and stomped with exhilaration, their bodies swaying like palm trees in a soft breeze. The drunkenness of the songs and the intoxication of the music made it feel like a heaven right there in the midst of the night. Nobody's feet were silent. They danced away the day and they danced away their blues. Then they laughed and their laughter rang out and caused more merriment.

What fascinated Hanna most were the number of people that looked just like people she knew back in Baltimore. More than once she put her hand across her breast in recognition, only to realize it couldn't possibly be. Breed explained to her that when slaves were brought from Africa, they were sent to many places, not just to the United States. Millions were taken to South America and Mexico in addition to the West Indies. "In fact," he added, "the largest number of slaves were sent to Brazil, which is why Brazil has the largest black population outside of Africa."

"There was a deliberate attempt to separate African tribes by thousands of miles so that they couldn't organize and rebel," Breed added.

"Oh my goodness," Hanna exclaimed indignantly. "I could very well be related to someone here and never be wiser. So much for what they write in history books."

The guests called it a day and dispersed into the night. No one in the LeGrande household awoke until Chanticleer started his morning rant.

When the two friends finally got some downtime together, Abi squired Hanna over to the breadfruit tree and asked cautiously, "How are things in Baltimore?"

"Just as you left them," Hanna chuckled. "What you really want to know, Ms. Kate Abi, is what is going on with Colin, right?"

"Well," she continued with a flourish, "he married your real estate pal, Madge. They came to our office party two weeks ago, and I went up and said hello to him. He introduced her as his wife. She shook my hand like the Queen of England, showing off a large diamond on her ring finger."

Hanna paused when she saw the shock on Abi's face.

"Married?" Abi blurted out, putting her hands over her mouth so as not to draw the attention of Popo who was staring at them from the veranda. "Obviously, he thinks I am dead."

"All I know is, he's married," Hanna exclaimed, before excitedly launching into what her recent sleuthing had revealed.

"His girlfriend, Deirdra, ain't digging it, though. I visited her at her salon to find out what she knew. While I was waiting for the conditioner to take, we got to talking. Apparently Colin paid for the salon and for the red Chevy she drives. She was very forthcoming with the information. I asked her about this dead guy written up in the newspaper. She told me she knew Ross Winter from high school. Very curious, huh? And she said something else that got to me. She said, and I quote, 'It ain't over till the fat lady sings.' Lordy, it sure sounded like a threat to me. Like something she's got planned that ain't too cool."

Abi's mouth was wide open in astonishment.

"If you don't close your mouth, one of these gnats will get in there," Hanna said, swatting the gnats that buzzed around them. "Anyway," she continued more slowly, finishing up her investigative report, "it really doesn't matter because you ain't going back to Baltimore." Hanna paused and looked out at the flowering buttercups and bougainvillea.

"Why would you go back? To snow and ice? Let bygones be bygones, I say."

"It's not easy to digest the fact that someone tried to kill me. Put yourself in my shoes. How would you feel?" asked Abi solemnly.

"Well, it's not like you knew they were trying to kill you. And look at you. Who's happy now?" Hanna said.

"I guess you're right," Abi answered. "I can't imagine a better life anywhere else or with any one else. You know, Breed has asked me to marry him, but I didn't want to because I felt I was committing bigamy. Now that I know what's going on with my ex-husband and my ex-friend, I will happily marry him."

Popo was standing on the porch now and shielding her eyes with her hands. She peered down at the women under the breadfruit tree, making sure Abi was not getting upset by anything Hanna might divulge about Baltimore. When she saw Abi giggling, she relaxed.

"Hanna," Abi held her friend's face in both her hands. "You will come back, won't you? Before Che gets married?"

"You know, I'll be back, girlfriend," said Hanna with a grin. Abi kept her hands on Hanna face and squeezed her cheeks until they puckered into an O and Hanna could barely speak.

"I love you too much to stay away. And the men," she squeaked through the O. "The men are dee-vine. So taut and strong. Maybe when I come back I can find a couple brawny ones to lick the salt off my body."

Hanna pulled Abi's hand from her face and they hugged each other and shrieked.

"Tell me, Ka—I mean Abi," Hanna added earnestly, "are the men really as sweet as the mangoes you gave me?"

"And then some, girl," Abi rolled her eyes towards Heaven.

Hanna's eyes widened. The two howled with laughter. Popo, observing them, knew they were talking about sex and most likely her grandson. A smile played around the corners of her mouth as she remembered her own conversations with her girlfriends of yesteryear.

"So what are you going to do, Abi?" asked Hanna. "About everything."

"Nothing. That's what I will do. Sometimes it's the hardest thing to do. But sometimes its the best thing to do."

"But for now," Abi pulled herself off the ground, and dusted the dried grass off the back of her skirt with her hand, "let's take a walk." She reached down and extended her other hand to Hanna to help her up.

"Where are we going?" asked Hanna, looking around eagerly.

"Do you always have to be going somewhere?" asked Abi. "I have learned in my short time on this island that when you take a walk, you don't have to be going somewhere. If you are intent on getting somewhere, then you sacrifice the pleasure of getting there."

CHAPTER TWENTY-SEVEN

Windward

*A*ttention all! It is imperative that everybody gather and wait for the armed forces of the People's Army to give you instruction. A revolution is in progress. Do not do anything foolish or there will be severe consequences. This is your revolution. We will claim our freedom.

Popo stared at the radio. No sound came out of her mouth—a rare occurrence. She turned around and saw Abi standing in the open doorway of her bedroom. Che, nested in his mother's arms, looked from one woman to the other and wished he knew how to say, 'where is the milk?' He had no time for revolutions.

Grownups around the island, however, were stricken with shock mixed with a strange excitement. For Popo the

175

feeling started in her stomach and worked its way up to her chest, where it increased her heartbeat, causing her eyes to enlarge and her hands to involuntarily cover her mouth.

She walked stiffly over to the side table where the radio insisted that a revolution was in progress. She picked it up and shook it hard as if to bring it to its senses. She placed it back on the table, but as if also in protest, the radio continued with its message. Popo sat down heavily in the rocking chair.

"Did Breed come home last night?" she asked Abi.

By then Che had managed to unclasp his mother's blouse and was nipping away at her exposed breast.

Popo saw that Abi had turned as white as the day she had landed on the island.

"Who knew that's what it takes to lose one's hard-earned tan? A revolution. Think of the money I could make. Revolution in a Bottle—guaranteed to make you white in an instant." Popo laughed crazily.

"No," Abi managed to say. "Breed said he had important business in town and would sleep at the home of one of his comrades. What's going to happen to us? Are we going to die?"

Popo went over and got hold of Che, who had wisely held on to Abi's nipple with clamped gums and was dangling dangerously over the floor.

"Get hold of yourself, child," Popo said, holding the baby to her breast. "First things first. When things blow over, we'll see about putting Che in the circus. He has great ability where gravity is concerned. He will make us all rich."

Shouts could be heard coming up from the streets. They were not sounds of fear. They sounded more like rejoicing, like when a cricket match was won.

"Nothing is going to happen, my darling," Popo said, reassuring herself as much as Abi. "It has already happened."

She managed to speak even though her nasal passages were impeded because Che had gotten hold of her nose with little fingers and was not about to let go. The baby wriggled around in her arms and tried to imitate Chanticleer by making a puckered pout with his milky little mouth.

"So Breed is in this?" asked Abi, looking closely at Popo. "That's what his important meeting last night was about?"

Abi started a loud wailing that impressed Che.

"Come on now," Popo interrupted. "This can't be worse than the Civil War in America. It's only a revolution. After all those stories I've told you about revos, what's to worry about?"

Popo put her arms around Abi, crushing Che in the process.

"What I know about revolutions," Abi replied with some impatience. "is that they've all been bloody."

Before Popo could stop her, Abi rushed out the front door still dressed in her nightgown. The neighbors were out in full force by then. Some answering the call to go to the police stations and other places where members of the former government would be to make citizens arrests or search for weapons. The village had mobilized as if on command.

"Tout moun veni," (everybody come) they shouted. A vibration seemed to pass through the walls of the house when the crowds went by. It was like a rumbling noise like thunder from afar, slowly filling the streets. There was a dull unbroken roar caused by the blowing of lambi shells.

Less than ten minutes after Abi had raced out of the house, she returned stretched across Boysie's shoulder. She kicked and protested, but he held her firmly. Abi did not seem to care if the whole village saw her backside. She was on a mission, and her first task was to get out of the grip of Boysie so that she could go rescue Breed from the jaws of death.

Popo stood impassively on the veranda with the baby and watched. This Abigail Fisherman had a way of getting naked under the most interesting circumstances, she concluded. Popo could not stop herself from chuckling as she remembered the first time they met when Abi had stood in front of her half-naked and then she was naked and covered in mud when she fought with Debbie over Breed and then when she was about to give birth. This must be her encore, she thought.

After Abi was unceremoniously dumped on the veranda, Popo grabbed her tightly around the waist. "Make one more step, madam," Popo warned, "and is me and you today."

Abi sat down.

"A man has to do what a man has to do," said Popo. "Breed will come back soon enough. We have just made history. It was a peaceful takeover, the radio said. Only three soldiers were killed and that was because they were resisting arrest."

Abi composed herself and went indoors to get dressed. When she came back out, Popo held her hand.

"Everything will be alright. I think deep down inside, we were all expecting something like this to happen. Maybe not quite this soon, but this boil had to bust open to let the pus out."

She put Che back in his mother's arms.

"You stay here and keep things under control," warned Popo. "I going and help arrest some people." She grabbed the cutlass leaning against the front steps and headed down the road with Boysie.

Abi looked at her baby and was getting ready to say something like, "What on God's green earth am I doing here?' when she caught herself. There were no revolutions in Baltimore, but they had their share of problems. She hugged her baby and waited.

Many hours later, a very tired Popo walked through the front door with Breed. Abi had cooked up a meal of curried goat, ground provisions, steamed rice with turmeric, stewed pigeon peas and a green salad, anticipating their hunger.

Breed hugged her with one arm and with the other he grasped his son and said excitedly, "It's a new day, Che boy. Change in de air."

The next day, Abi went to the capital with Popo, Breed and Che. They joined thousands of people in a park to celebrate the news that the former prime minister had fled the country. Abi soon realized that something else had happened. Change had not come just to the island, but also to herself and Breed.

"I have been offered a job with the new government," he whispered in her ear as the family returned home after the rally. "I will be the assistant to Dale Joseph, the new minister of agriculture," he said with an air of smugness that she had never before detected.

"Why you?" Abi whispered back. "You are a fisherman, not a politician."

Popo looked away and pretended not to hear their conversation. On the walk up the hill, she went ahead with Che, while the two parents lingered and continued their discussion.

"I know what I am, Miss Fisherman," Breed replied with some heat. "But they need grass-roots people who can work with the masses. I have proven myself and earned this position. So the fish will have to wait."

"I guess you'll have bigger fish to fry, Mr. Fisherman," Abi snapped back and hurried to catch up with Popo and Che.

"I guess I will," Breed muttered to the wind.

When he walked in the front door, tension accompanied him.

Despite all that, he quickly became engrossed in his new job and spent less and less time at home with his family. He discarded his cut-off shorts and sandals and replaced them with a shirt jack, linen slacks, socks, leather shoes and a cotton handkerchief tucked in his shirt pocket. He found that brow-mopping came with high office. It made him look more important when he stopped in the middle of a conversation to mop his brow with an air of exasperation. He no longer wore a bandana because he was now getting treatments from a proper doctor to repair his scalp. To help with the healing, the Ministry of Health gave him a voucher to consult with a specialist in Barbados.

Abi did not ask Popo for advice about how to handle the changes both of them observed in Breed. She knew that Popo would never tell her to "run" like she glibly told other women. Her answer would be "wait, child, wait." So Abi waited. She wrapped herself up in her daily devotion to Che and her duties at the Visiting Station. What most disturbed her, were the similiarities she was beginning to notice between this relationship and her marriage to Colin. The feeling of being ignored or feeling like she was an intruder in the other person's private thoughts. Do good things always come to an end? she wondered sadly.

The head nurse was offered a job at the general hospital and Abi was given the position of head nurse in the village. With that position came a comfortable salary and much more responsibility. Now she not only served as nurse, but also as teacher, psychologist, tutor, marriage counselor, financial advisor, nutritionist and sometimes cleaning lady. Luckily, the hours were reasonable, opening of 8:00 a.m and closing at 2:00 pm, giving her the afternoon to be with Che. She hired Jenny as her assistant, and the two women worked as efficiently as she and Hanna had done back in Baltimore.

One of her favorite things to do in her spare time was to help Alister with his schoolwork. The boy loved coming over to Abi's house to read to Che and have Abi assist him with any lessons he did not understand. Between Abi's academic influence and Popo's philosophical rantings, Alister excelled in school. He was prone to follow people up and down the road in the village sharing information he had gleaned from reading too many books about too many things. He was soon nicknamed 'the road scholar', a moniker he most certainly lived up to.

CHAPTER TWENTY-EIGHT

Baltimore

From its first hair straightening, The Kinky Hair Salon on 25th Street flourished. Deirdra's appointment book was always full. She now employed three stylists skilled at wielding hot combs and slathering on Dark and Lovely to women eager to rid themselves of their natural springy locks. For the unfortunate female who sported a moustache, she even hired a Korean lady who specialized in removing handlebars from women's lips.

While content in her professional life, Deirdra longed for Colin. "I can't live without him, Ma," she lamented to her mother, whose longer tenure on earth made it difficult to feign interest in her daughter's dilemma.

"Of course, you can," Mrs. Jackson said with exasperation. "You need to stop listening to those stupid-ass records you playing. *You make me feel like a natural woman.* What nonsense is that? You are a natural woman all by yo'self."

"I'm serious, Ma." Deirdra's voice rose two octaves higher then the Labelles singing Lady Marmalade. Tears began to swell in her eyes, expecting a sudden call to duty.

"Did I raise an idiot?" her mother muttered, only half in jest. "You'd better learn to be happy by yourself, Missy. That man married."

Mrs. Jackson was sitting awkwardly on a purple velvet sofa that was covered in thick plastic in Deirdra's living room. Aretha Franklin was singing something on the radio about saying a little prayer for some man when she should have been praying for herself.

"What you gonna do, whack his wife? Off him? Kill yo'self?"

Mrs. Jackson lifted her ample butt off the sofa, one cheek at a time, to keep her dress from sticking to the plastic. "Find yo'self another man, Deirdra. And please pick a brother this time. I ain't got nothin against white folks, mind you, but it jess don't feel right."

"Ma, we ain't talking 'bout white folks." Deirdra was up on her feet with rising anger. "We talking 'bout the man I love. His name is Colin, as you well know. If you can't help me here, then get the hell out."

Waiting anxiously for dismissal so she could escape from the unforgiving sofa, Mrs. Jackson sprang to her feet with newfound agility and bolted for the door. She did not like talking with her daughter about this white man. She did not like their relationship.

Deirdra got a mug from the kitchen counter and poured herself a glass of Boone's Farm Wine she had bought from the corner store and sat down on the sofa. She was used to the plastic. It reminded her of her own existence—

uncomfortable and sticky, but necessary to protect what was inside.

She had to get Colin back, and she was going to get him back one way or the other. Her mother had inquired about the neon cowboy boot sign hanging outside her salon. Cowboy boots were not usually associated with black people. But Deirdra Jackson had her reasons. Sooner or later, Colin or his wife would see the boot and assume that she owned the store. While Colin might think the boot was just in memory of their kinky sex, Madge, she knew, would be more suspicious and take the matter further.

A dangerous game it was, but Deirdra thought she had a good hand, so she decided to play. She would keep her best card for last. What would they do if they found out that Ross Winter had confided in her before his death? Kill her?

Deirdra abandoned her drink and climbed the stairs to her bedroom. Reaching into the top shelf of her closet, she took out her secret weapon from its leather pouch. She liked the way the .38 caliber pistol felt in her hand. It was sleek like a man's body and sported a white marble handle. The smooth marble between her dark brown fingers felt downright erotic. What turned her on most, though, was the power it granted her. She took the bullets out of the gun and put them back in, loading and reloading it with growing malice.

Miles away in Columbia, Colin and Madge Carrington continued to live together but apart. The crazy sex that had first connected them had long since ceased to interest Colin, and he felt a sense of foreboding in his wife's presence. Madge occupied herself by getting rid of everything in the house that reminded her of Kate. She bought new crystal, new linens and practically refurnished the house. She was motivated by envy, guilt and a newly acquired insecurity.

Her thoughts often wandered back to the cruise ship when Kate met Ross Winter. Maybe Ross had killed Kate. Could she have intervened instead of encouraging her to sleep with this stranger? Kate was obviously ashamed of herself after she spent the night with him. Try as she might, Madge could not forget the look on Kate's face when she walked past her to disembark on that last island. Now here she was, married to a man that could very well be a murderer. Madge looked at Colin over her glass of wine and wondered if men were known to kill more than one spouse.

As they sat across from each other at the dining room table, Colin broke the silence by chortling over an article he read in *The News American*.

"Well, what do you know?" he said, shaking the paper noisily. "Remember that island you and hmm, Kate visited some time ago? It seems like they are having a revolution. How big is that place—6 miles long?"

Colin laughed contemptuously. "See what you missed? You could have been taken for ransom."

"No such luck," Madge said, staring resentfully at him. She wrapped her jeweled hand around the crystal glass filled with the best Merlot the local wine shop could offer.

"What could those coconuts be revolting about, anyway?" Colin continued cynically. "Not enough mangoes?" He cackled at his own cleverness.

Madge looked at him warily. She had come to realize that Colin was more mask than man. He crafted his image carefully, cloaked in the trappings of a conscientious scientist who commanded a big city morgue. "Always a dead body to keep things merry and bright" he liked to say. Behind that carefully constructed mask, Madge knew nothing of his authenticity and nothing about the dream that he shared with millions of men, to kill a woman he did not love in order to return to a woman he thought he did.

CHAPTER TWENTY-NINE

Windward

In the typical rum shop in the Caribbean, patrons swallowed their liquor straight, then reacted with surprise when the fire engulfed them. With their lips pursed in a scowl, they wiped their burned mouths with the back of their hands, shut then opened their blood-shot eyes, slammed their glasses on the counter and demanded another drink. Sometimes, they leaned precariously to the left or the right. Other times they toppled to the floor before their glasses were refilled.

These emporiums embraced the sweet pungent odor of raw white rum. Neither the rain that came through the holes in the galvanized roof nor the winds blowing in from the Atlantic ocean, nor the hot sun at midday could erase the odor. The clear odiferous concoction called "strong rum" penetrated the ceiling and the concrete floor. It clung to the walls, slithered down the cracks and coated the holes and gaps. The shops acquired the personality of their patrons who, no matter whether they were drinking or not, wore the beaten down and astonished look of the committed alcoholic.

Boysie's rum shop was different. It served politics with the rum. Abi knew she could not take the baby to the shop so that "all kinda people can spew saliva on de boy," according to Breed. But as the new government got into full swing, she would sneak down now and then with Popo when Che was taking his afternoon nap.

The elation of the first year of the revolution was waning, replaced by everyday grumbles. Rumors began circulating about the new government. What they were doing wrong and also what they were not doing right.

"You just can't please people," said Boysie from his soapbox. The politicians without office or information gathered in the rum shop, eager to discuss issues that some of them knew absolutely nothing about.

"They don't know what de hell dey doing," shouted Guido, hopping from his wooden to his good leg. He had gotten his foot chopped off for calling the ex-prime minister a bamsy. "Dat is not how to run a country."

"Well I suppose, you should have been put in power, Guido. Because you would know what to do, right?" countered Ing, who was born on a tiny neighboring island and had to suffer the indignity of everyone telling him to go back there because they were missing an idiot.

"Haul ya'll arse," said Guido, whose only defense was profanity.

"Look, Guido," said Popo, "Don't let me have to chop off your other foot today. Let's have a discussion without all you cussing and name-calling. Stop drinking rum for a minute so we can fix the political woes of the Caribbean diaspora."

"Every government have tings that won't run smoothly. People complain no matter who in office. First, all you didn't like the prime minister because you say he was a dictator. All you hot, hot, hot with the new one. Now that they in power, the complaining start again."

She looked around for disapproval and got none. Instead, there was a lot of head-nodding, throat-clearing and spitting.

"These boys and dem are young. But what unu was doing when you was in you thirties? Don't answer. Drinking rum and skylarking. Anybody here under 40? Raise you hand."

No hands went up, but each person glanced around to see whom she was addressing.

"I thought so," Popo continued. "All you is hard-back man already. If you read history books you will see that it's always the youth that start the revolution. If you know what to do, why didn't you start the revolution yourself, and you wouldn't be complaining about the government now."

"Martin Luther King had a dream in America. And he was right. It was just a dream." Popo paused for breath.

"Dat is not true, Popo," Jenny broke in. "You have to dream before you could do anything else. Without a dream, you don't have nothing."

Everyone seemed happy to catch Popo in what they perceived to be a philosophical pickle.

"You just think that everything you say is law," Jenny blurted out, egged on by the support of the crowd. She continued speaking, not realizing that Popo was watching her and then looking at the cutlass. "You don't know everything, Madam Popo. You just like to talk about tings we don't know about and half the time, you don't know yourself. You too contrary, if you ask me."

"Come here, Jenny, and bring your head with you because I chopping it off today," Popo said as she advanced on the startled woman. All the support Jenny had gotten from the crowd evaporated. Guido and Ing jumped out of the way, giving Popo a clear path to Jenny.

Jenny hightailed it out of the shop. Everyone knew she would come shuffling back in a minute or two.

"What I don't understand is all the fighting that's going on in the government," said Abi calmly. "Why is there so much fighting when people should be agreeing to make things better?"

"We are a fighting people," said Boysie. "And I don't mean just we on dis island. I mean the human race. We always fighting for something. For respect. For money. For recognition."

"Don't forget for other people husband," said Popo, looking warily at Debbie. Debbie stared back at her defiantly and said, "And may the best woman win."

"What Popo mean is…" Guido slurred from his corner of the shop.

"I know what I mean," said Popo. "I don't need an interpreter and especially not a drunk. If you not a politician and you never run a country, how can you tell dem how to run dis one?"

The drunk and the sober were left to ponder this question as Abi and Popo returned to the house. Che had awakened from his nap and was ready to party. Abi sat in the rocking chair, cradled him in her arms and prepared to nurse him. She knew that the boy was ready for a cup because he had begun to unbutton her bodice, pull out her breast and stick it in his mouth himself.

Alister came up the hill, rolling a bicycle tire wih a stick. He parked the tire next to the house as if it was a precious automobile, lay the stick down next to it, dusted off his clothes with his hands and marched into the house. He never wore shoes. The only pair he owned was for going to church. When Abi asked Jenny why Alister went to school barefoot, Jenny had looked at her quizzically and replied, "Shoes? The school right down the road. It's not far."

Alister's mother and Abi had become very close. Wholesome, practical Jenny helped Abi through the rough and difficult spots of living in a foreign country. They shared stories about their families and their men. They took the children to the beach almost every Sunday and helped them collect seashells and run from the tiny blue crabs that patrolled the shore. But the trips to the river were loved best. There Jenny showed her how to wash her clothes, beat them on the rocks to get them clean then spread them out to dry in the sun. Sometimes they just sat and let their feet get caressed in the slow moving water. Abi now and then would pocket a small rock from the thousands that decorated the river.

On Saturday mornings they went together to the open air market to buy ground provisions for the week to do their cooking. Abi's favourite place in the market was the elaborately decorated shed with the name "Magreet's Copious Cakes" painted in bright green on the awning.

Magreet came from the village of Kumasi every Saturday to sell her exotic cakes. The whole of Windward knew Magreet. No one could match her when it came to baking. So people came by bus, car and on foot to buy from her. Abi was never satisfied until she purchased one of Magreet's mango upside down cakes. Magreet believed in using what the island offered, and mangoes were in abundance. Not only did she sell cakes, but she always had words of wisdom for the women and men alike.

"We have to learn to use what we have," she preached from her soapbox in the middle of the marketplace. "We don't always have to go running to the doctor with every little ailment."

Abi and Jenny were always in front of the pack.

"Mango is a good, good fruit full of vitamins, but the mango leaf just as good. Dry them and crush as powder or boil them, steep them and drink as tea. It helps to cure diabetes, lower your blood pressure, help you to sleep when the night come, cure bronchitis, cough and asthma, and relieve anxiety when you don't know where your man gone since Wednesday."

By 10:00 a.m. Magreet was on her way home, satisfied that every one of her cakes were sold and that she was much richer than when she opened her stall that morning.

"You know, Abi," Jenny said during one of their Saturday morning excursions. "I never knew what people was talking about when dey would call somebody their best friend. But now I know. You could be my sister, even."

"I know," said Abi, slipping her arm through Jenny's. "You have become like the sister I never had. I miss my friend Hanna dearly, but she's not here and you are."

CHAPTER THIRTY

Windward

Abi closed the clinic on the day that almost all the people in the village were going to the capital to attend the rally to celebrate the second year of the new government. Jenny had asked her to keep an eye on Alister since she and Peter and their younger child would attend the rally at the stadium.

The day was hot. The clouds above were full of wind and sped across the sky like women headed to market. There was cause for celebration. The air was rent with excitement and pride. They were celebrating heroes and heroism. And the hope of better days to come.

The seats in the stadium were filled to capacity since the early birds had claimed them. Umbrellas of all colors and sizes were opened against the blazing sun. It was a photographer's delight. People greeted each other with enthusiasm and filled up the grounds. It was beyond carnival. This was the future. The voices of the people rose and fell in a continuous melody as everybody waited for the first of many speakers. A steelband played a rhythmic rhapsody and the people cheered.

Then it happened.

A glare as bright as the sun engulfed them. A fraction of a second later an explosion ripped through the area. There was a wave of intense heat, followed by black billows of acrid smoke. Panic immediately set in. People fled in different directions, colliding into each other and frantically trampling over the less agile.

Peter had just left the concession stand with lemonade for his wife and a Heineken for himself when he heard the sound. The drinks fell to the ground as he instinctively threw up his hands in shock. He ran towards the direction of their seats, but could not make any headway. The crowd pushed him back as it bore down on him. He managed to turn his back to them and push himself against the stream of people. Squeezing through the stampede, he stepped over bodies of people injured from flying metal fragments and the soles of other people's feet. He carefully stepped around the bodies on the ground not wishing to find what he feared. Jenny must have run out with the crowd and probably rushed past him on her way out of the chaos. Didn't he just catch a glimpse of a woman fleeing with a baby in her arms?

Why, he asked himself did they sit so close to the stage? So that they wouldn't miss anything, he answered back. The next body he saw on the ground was Jenny's.

He dropped down next to his wife and dared God to have mercy, knowing that it was already too late. He reached over and tenderly lifted the small body of his daughter an arm's length away from her mother and placed her broken body on Jenny's chest. Then he knelt down beside them.

His mouth was open, but no sound was heard because of the loud wailing all around him. His voice had lost its individuality.

"Jenny," he called out her name over and over. He kissed her bloodied face and that of his child, and a flame died inside him.

He very gently removed the wedding ring from his wife's lifeless finger and put it in his mouth. He did not know why or when he swallowed it.

Later that night, he returned shell-shocked to Abi's house to pick up his sleeping son. As soon as Abi saw him coming into the yard, she knew the worst had happened. When Peter cried out to her that his two girls were gone, Abi fell to the floor in shock. Waves of anguish swept over her, but she knew she had to be strong for Alister's sake. Slowly she pulled herself up from the floor to fetch him, then watched sadly as the sleeping boy was carried by his father to their home.

Jenny had been Peter's world. His stage. The reason he woke up in the mornings. He'd known her since she was 12 and had told her then that she would always be his and his alone. With Jenny gone, his audience was gone. He was alone, facing a world with which he was suddenly unfamiliar. He stood on the empty stage, his lines forgotten.

Abi and Breed ate their supper in silence. Neither could speak and both attempted to abate the emptiness in their stomachs with food. There were chunks of sweet potato and dasheen in the oxtail soup that Breed liked so much. Tonight, however, everything tasted like mud.

As she lay with Breed in their bed, she asked, "Does it ever end? Will it always be one thing after the other?"

"I don't have an answer for you, my love," said Breed, caressing his wife's face. "Seems like no matter what happens or who is in power, there will always be that element of surprise."

Abi wept for Jenny and her child. What will become of Alister without Jenny was foremost on her mind.

"He has his father, my love. And he has you," Breed comforted her. "But his life will never be the same. One thing I know for sure," Breed said, sitting upright in the bed. "One thing I know for sure," he repeated, "is that this feels foreign to me. We don't know how to make bombs, let alone one that could cause this much damage. I heard in town today that the bomb was intended to kill our leader, but it went off too soon."

"What are you saying?" Abi asked.

"I'm not saying anything for sure," Breed told her. "Let's get some sleep. We will need it in the days to come. I have a feeling that this is only the beginning."

For the next few days, Breed stayed home to comfort Abi and Alister and to help Peter make arrangements for the funeral. On the day of the funeral there were family members and friends from as far away as London and New York.

Abi saw that despite all the sobbing and gnashing of teeth there was laughter and horsing around. A funeral, she had come to understand, was a social event in Windward. People showed up whether invited or uninvited. Knowing the deceased was not a prerequisite. They came and they commented on everything, from the apparel of the mourners to the quality of the food and alcohol.

The mourners that came from abroad dressed more fancily than the natives. They had to show the ones that stayed on the island that they were better off for having left, even if some of them were not. Others went as far as to adopt the speech patterns of the foreign country in which they now resided, in an effort to impress the untraveled. More often than not, they sounded comical, which delighted the natives to no end and caused the children to speak with American slang and funny English accents at school recess.

At the last wake Abi attended with Breed, people were eating, drinking and playing dominoes all at the same time. At one particular funeral she had to laugh at the sight of the wife of the deceased and two mistresess competing to see which one would throw herself in the hole with the man they claimed was theirs alone. There were blood-curdling shouts of "hold me" from the women in an attempt to get anyone to restrain them from jumping into the hole with the coffin. Abi surmised that they really did not want to jump in at all and they just wanted to show their love for the dead man in this bizarre fashion. They hoped that someone would stop them from jumping in. She wondered what would happen if no one obliged.

After Jenny's burial, Abi returned home with her family to learn again how to live with change. "How interesting it is that one day can make such a difference," she told Popo as they sat together under the breadfruit tree.

Immediately after the burial ceremony, Breed left for the government complex. It was as if he couldn't wait to get away from all the sadness.

"Dat's life," said Popo reflectively. "I guess we will be seeing a lot of Alister from now on. And dat's alright with me. It's not like he wasn't living here already."

No sooner had things started to get back to normal and people were beginning to bring some peace back into their lives than another bomb exploded on a different part of the island. This one was at the yearly cricket match between the northern and the southern parishes. Popo, Breed and Abi just stared blankly at each other when they heard the news. The poor man whose task it was to detonate the bomb, had lost

both his legs and arms. He said he was handed the bomb and
$200 by a man he did not recognize. No was was killed.

A week later, Abi and Popo joined thousands people
on a march through the streets of the capital in solidarity
with the new revolutionary government. She felt she had
to do it especially for Jenny but also to show her support
for the revolution. She wrestled with the notion of staying
anonymous and safe and praying for things to get better, or
going out and trying to become a part of the solution. Besides,
if she didn't go, she knew that Popo would go alone. Breed
would not want his grandmother in the capital by herself.
She was liable to chop somebody if left to her own devices.

This time, Peter opted to stay at home with Alister and
Che. He did not wish to be a part of anything political ever
again. Breed said he understood but staying at home was as
significant as declaring that you will not vote in an election
because you did not like what the candidates stood for. "By
not voting," he told Peter, "you have voted."

Over time, life gradually became normal again. A new
normal. Abi sat with Popo and watched Che chase Alister
around the yard with his bicycle rim and stick. The little boy
was growing like a weed, and he had a full head of bouncy
curls springing all around his head like the sun's rays. He had
glowing cinnamon skin, fat cheeks and long lean legs. And
those legs were fast. Soon Che could almost outrun his father
when it came time for Breed to catch him in anticipation
of some dastardly act like taking a shower. Or when Breed
chastized him for catching lizards and then cutting off their
tails. When Breed asked him why he cut their tails off, Che
said in a little determined voice that it was because he was in
charge.

Was this the making of a revolutionary or a dictator?
Breed wondered.

CHAPTER THIRTY-ONE

Windward

The breadfruit tree was laden. Its pendulous fruit hung like the breasts of a milk-laden cow waiting patiently to be relieved of its burden. Abi had her eye on a particularly plump one to cook for lunch.

Alister and Che rolled up with their bicycle wheels and inquired about the possibility of the grown-ups making ice cream. From his throne in the plum tree, Chantycleer kept a watchful eye in case of mischief.

"We don't have enough rock salt to put in the ice cream can," Popo told the boys. "Wait till later when we get some."

"You know," Abi turned to face Popo with a quizzical look on her face.

"There's something I have been wrestling with since I came to the island. What I don't understand is, how come you put salt in the ice cream can to keep the ice from melting? In the winter months in Baltimore we put salt on the ice to melt it. Isn't salt, salt?"

"Do I look like Socrates to you?" Popo asked. "I know everything except dat one. Dat's my Achilles heel. Salt and its mysteries. Ask me something else."

"OK," Abi began again. "Do you think the United States cares what happens on this little island?" A wave of anxiety clothed her.

"Lawd have mercy," Popo exclaimed. "If they care?" she shot back. "They care more than you can imagine."

"Mind unu don't break unu neck today, "Abi called out to the boys who were getting raucous.

"Well, you is a real West Indian now, or what?" laughed Popo.

Abi smiled to herself often these days when she caught herself speaking in the dialect of everyone around her.

"You know, Abi," Popo continued with some concern in her voice. "I believe whole-heartedly in dis new government. Their ideas are good and they mean to lead us to a better life. But sometimes I tink they bite off more than they can chew. I not so sure about the timing. Everybody does want power. But when they get the power, is something else. But with all that," she continued, "I'll be glad when the new airport is finished. I am just proud something big like this is happening on this island. An international airport, to boot. I am proud of our new government. Well proud." Popo had a satisfied look on her face.

It had rained for a while and the sun was squeezing its rotund self through some clouds, busy drying up things again.

"Breed said we need an educational revolution more than anything else, Ma Po. He said the people still need to get over the residue of colonialism."

"Well, nobody asking him, chile." Popo chuckled. "We need a book in our hands and not a gun, that is what he trying to say. But sometimes people need a gun inside the book. What we know about guns though. But we learning fast. Sometimes I feel like we living in Baltimore with all the violence that going on here."

"And what do you know about Baltimore?" Abi smirked.

"I know enough to tell your president to clean up his own backyard before he come here to clean up ours," said Popo. "Dey doing their own Samba in America. De only difference is that the music is the gunfire and the dance done when the body drop."

"Funny thing about dancing," Abi mused. "You have to know the steps, or things can go awry."

"When I day dreaming, I think about how funny it would be if one day a black man don't turn around and become president of the United States." Popo screeched with laughter at the absurdity of her words.

"I don't see that ever happening," Abi agreed. "But if it did, it had better be Breed that's in the White House. I would make a fine first lady." Abi playfully poked Popo in the stomach.

"You?" Popo laughed. "You forget you don't exist? There is no Abigail Fisherman. Bim Bim say she could make up a birth certificate for you if you want one. But I wouldn't trust Bim Bim, you hear? De last one she make for somebody put dem in big big trouble with the authorities. De man still in jail, God bless him. So just cool yourself and stay right here before Colin come looking for your backside with a machete."

"Popo you ever thought about writing a book?" Abi asked seriously. "You have so much to say about so many different things."

"Me?" Popo held Abi's hands in her own. "Who want to hear what a old black woman have to say?"

"You have some butter for every piece of bread, though," said Abi.

"You is the one with the story to tell," Popo continued. "Abigail Kate O'Neil Carrington Fisherman. The story of a naked white woman. You not registered anywhere. Nobody know who you are. And your life keep changing."

They stopped their conversation to look up as a woman waltzed into the yard, swinging her hips this way and that in case there was a man in the vicinity. She had roasted groundnuts and cocoa balls for sale. She had the merchandise on a large, flat wooden tray, which she balanced with peculiar precision on her head. Under the tray she had a raggedy rag wrapped around her head to protect it from the hard wood.

"All you buying?" she asked distractedly, as if she didn't care whether they bought or not.

"Just one bag today, darlin." Popo dug in her pocket and gave the woman a 25 cent coin, then reached into the tray and helped herself to a bag of neatly wrapped peanuts. The woman pocketed the coin and waltzed away.

Getting up from the bench, Popo reached out an arm to Abi to help her up. It had become her custom ever since Abi was heavy with child so long ago now.

"Today I'm showing you how to make coo coo finally. Its months since I promise you and I tired making it myself everytime. Get your pencil and paper, Shakespeare. Let's away."

The women got busy in the kitchen. Popo sorted out ingredients on the table while Abi waited in anticipation. By now she had acquired a nicely decorated copybook that she'd bought in a little shop in Cascade. Labeled on the front in her nice cursive handwwriting were the words, "Popo's Delectable Dishes."

"Look sharp," Popo instructed. "This is Caribbean Polenta. It came originally from Africa. It tastes real good with salt fish cakes, callaloo soup, stew fish or stew chicken. Day-old coo coo is really good, too, if you slice it up the following morning and fry it for breakfast."

Popo turned to see if Abi was paying attention to her or to Che and Alister, who had come in to the newly scrubbed kitchen floor dragging all kinds of debris between their toes.

A small army of marauding flies came through the open window, settled themselves on the red checkered tablecloth and waited.

"You will need some coconut milk. I don't know how much. Some butter, same ting. Some salt and use yellow cornmeal."

"Now make sure the fire not too high. Throw in the coconut milk and the salt and butter and wait till it boils. Start stirring in the cornmeal. Slowly, not like you have a bus to catch. Make the fire low and stir, stir, stir. Use a wooden palette, not no ordinary spoon. Stir, stir, stir to keep it from sticking to the side of the pot. You hear me? You could add more milk if it gets too thick and hard to stir. Or you add water if you use up all the milk. Right? Grease up one of them nice baking dish Hanna send from Baltimore and pour the coo coo in it. Leave it for a few minutes to cool down. After that, it should be ready to cut into nice big squares."

"Now," Popo paused for emphasis, "you could change it around if you want and add okra. Just throw in some sliced okra with the milk before you add in the coo coo. You got all that?"

Abi was about to close her notebook when Popo added, "By the way, write down in there that you could make christophene bread. Just grate in some christophene with the flour. At least try and make all them carbohydrates a little more healthy for my grandchildren and dem. With the saltfish cakes you like so much, you can sometimes add in some grated christophene too, and grated carrots and onions. OK, lesson finish for the day. Let's wait for the sun to set so we can make a wish."

Later when the sun obliged, it came with a miraculously bright yellow glow then faded into the blue of the sky to lose itself. There was no gloaming.

The women were not expecting Breed on time for dinner. He was seldom home early in the evenings anymore. The elephant in the room found a comfortable seat and settled itself. Neither woman would speak of what might be going on. Abi waited for Popo to say something, and Popo waited for Abi. Truth was, neither one knew what to say. Popo, on nights like these, would retire early and could be heard reading her Bible aloud for what seemed to Abi, like an eternity.

When Abi awoke the following morning, Breed was still asleep. She had to shake him awake, which was unusual. It was the rainy season and the rain poured down mercilessly. When it was satisfied that it had drenched everything thoroughly, it departed without ceremony, and left the sky an uncharacteristic grey.

CHAPTER THIRTY-TWO

Windward

The new government believed in educating its people. Adults who never finished their schooling were given the chance to do so. Some learned how to read and write for the first time in their lives. People who never had marketable skills got the opportunity to attain some. Agriculture was again becoming a viable option for the youth and some of the young people were returning to the soil to make a living. New entrepreneurs were born. Students were encouraged to perform better academically and excel in sports, and others were able to obtain scholarships to study abroad. Some, Breed hoped, would come back to the island to try and make it a better place. Big projects after all needed educated people.

Breed found great satisfaction in his new job. It made him feel a part of something. A government determined to put the country on the world map. He dived so deep into his work that he had less and less time for his family.

When everyone in the office left for the day and he put his feet up on his desk to relax, his thoughts were not always on education and progress. They sometimes strayed to the minister of agriculture. Dale Joseph was an efficient boss who went about her duties with enthusiasm and aplomb. But there was something else, Breed felt. She had taken quite a liking to him. He tried to dispel the notion that someone in her position would notice him—a fisherman in a shirt-jack. But as she became bolder and her "sweet eyes" more pronounced when she looked at him, he knew.

The minister was a married woman, although no one had ever seen Mr. Joseph. Breed was flattered. Dale had big, wide eyes, velvety blue-black skin and curves in all the right places.

Why me? he asked himself. Why jukutu me? Was it, he wondered, that he was fresh meat or was he good enough for her? He chose to believe the latter.

"Call me Dale," she told him one day when he addressed her as Mrs. Joseph. In an environment where everyone in high positions always had a handle to their names, calling her Dale was an open invitation. One Breed found hard to ignore.

"Yes," he stammered. He could not say Dale, because he knew that if he did, it would come out in a croak and she would know that he desired her too.

Breed could have asked to be transferred to another department. He could work in another parish. But in truth, he enjoyed the tension. The possibility of consummation was as erotic to him as the act itself. He took great pains to be professional about this elephant in the room. It appeared that no one in the office suspected anything. The only person that knew was Bim Bim, who knows everything and who in turn told Popo.

When Breed came home in the evenings, Popo thought that he had gone back to his boyhood days. He was light-headed and giddy. Che loved this new daddy because this one was closer to his age.

Breed was determined to let this game of adult hide-and-seek remain just that. But Dale Joseph was a professional. She would get what she wanted, and she wanted Breed. It became a battle of wits. She began scheduling late night meetings for just the two of them and always had a bottle of wine or sherry on the desk for them to drink. Breed liked the flirtation, but he held his ground.

"Boy, watch yourself," was all Popo could offer as the two sat in the veranda one night watching the stars carry on.

"What nonsense you talking about, Ma Po," he protested, glancing at his grandmother, but not looking her straight in the eye.

"Lawd, I have raised a fool," Popo said out loud.

"Let me say just one ting," Popo looked straight into his eyes. "There is an itch called 'wanting more.' Don't scratch it."

Breed got up, shook his head, and walked away.

Inside, Abi lay in bed waiting for him. Over these past few months, he seemed to take as long as he possibly could before he got into bed. The usual talking and long discussions wrapped in each other's arms had all but ceased.

Abi's suspicions gnawed at her. She tried on more than one occasion to bring up the subject with him, but the time was never right. All she had to go on was the feelings she was experiencing that reminded her of Colin when he started his affair with Deirdra. The anguish and subsequent tightening in her chest was familiar. What if she were wrong? She prayed that she was. What if Breed was innocent? She decided to wait and hope that she was mistaken.

Breed continued valiantly to say "no" to the temptress. But when the day came that he and Dale Joseph were alone in the back country, scouting for a site on which to plant a crop of sugar spple trees, he followed her willingly to a quiet spot in a woodsy area.

Unable to restrain himself, he fell down with her onto the soft grass. Dale with the soft curves that made his fingers happy, had a nakedness that caused the sun to blush and scuttle under a cloud. Those months of pent-up desire caused them to abandon self-respect and reason. They thrashed around on the ground like animals in heat, not caring who might come upon them in the broad daylight. Something inside of him asked—what is it? Why am I doing this? Why can't I stop? Why do I not want to stop? Was it the smell of coconut oil on her skin? Maybe it was the ashy elbows and knees that resembled his own. Maybe it was the curly black hair under her arms and elsewhere. Or maybe it was just a craving for chocolate-covered skin.

But when they had totally exhausted each other and lay back on the grass spent, Breed screamed out in disgust, not pleasure. The horrible thought of what he had just done swept over him immediately and his head throbbed as if he were just battered by a ram. They put back on their clothes quickly, not looking at each other. Refusing the minister's pleas to return with her to the office, Breed headed towards the dirt road to thumb a ride back to town.

He sat for a while brooding in the market place, feeling angry with himself for doing something that was not worth what he had to lose. When he finally boarded the bus to Marabel, he sat with his head in his hands thinking about that first trip he and Abi made to the village. How could he tell Abi what he'd done? He knew he would have to. His love for her would not allow him to keep so gory a secret. Breed was a praying man. But in all his years on his knees, he had never thought to pray for restraint.

When he confessed to her, she was unconsolable. Heartbroken. But she already knew. Popo had told her before it even happened. Part of her was happy that he chose to tell her because he did not have to.

"What are you asking me to do, Breed? Forgive you? I can't go through another experience like this again. I shared that pain with you. Or have you forgotten?" Abi stumbled into the verandah where Popo was waiting.

"The choice to love someone not easy," Popo told Abi. "You can't change what happen, but you can try to look at the situation differently. You have to release judgment on Breed, Abi. You don't have a choice."

"Now what are you asking me to do, Ma Po? The impossible?" Abi looked at Popo stricken. "What made him do this?"

"Look what you asking me. He is a man. She is a woman. And they are both human. You have to keep your heart open. Don't let Breed close it down. I can see the pain in your eyes, but I also see the pain in his. Talk with him and you two will find a way to fix this."

"But I love him. How could he do this to me?" Abi insisted.

"He ain't do it to you, he do it to himself." Popo answered. "Look at how much you two have here. Look at Che. My grandson is a good man, but he is flawed like everybody else. Just promise me one ting. If he ever try anyting close to dis again, get the cutlass and chop it off. We will bury it next to his dreadlocks under the breadfruit tree."

"No, Ma Po, I can't chop off his totie. That would be like chopping off my nose." Abi laughed for the first time. "I am very hurt, but I will try and understand."

"That's the way darlin," Popo wiped Abi's wet face with her sleeve. "My mother used to say. 'forgiving somebody is like unlocking the prison cell to set someone free and you realize you was the one locked up de whole time.'"

When Breed told her later that he would rather die than hurt her like that again, Abi believed him. She didn't want to, but she did. He cradled her in his arms and they both sobbed. He with regret, she with disappointment.

"Did you love her?" Abi asked softly.

"No, I didn't," Breed whispered. "Maybe I had a soft spot somewhere but I could never love a woman the way that I love you. You are indispensable to me. One of a kind. I will always love you, Green Eyes."

Other words danced around in his head. None came out of his mouth that he was aware of until he heard her say "yes" and he realized that he must have asked her to be his wife.

"Just to make it official," he added. "This is for you." He put a plump, crimson Julie into her hand. "And you don't have to wrestle me for it."

Abi put the mango up to her nose as she always did before she bit into one. Inhaling its sweet scent, she held it to her breast and closed her eyes.

Popo turned over in her bed, made the sign of the cross and went back to sleep contented. The following morning Breed ignored Chanticleer's rant and made love to Abi. A love he was proud of. A pure feeling of desire spiced with respect and joy.

Later that day, he tendered his resignation from the government and set off to see Marshall about getting his fishing equipment back in order.

CHAPTER THIRTY-THREE

Baltimore

O n the morning of what would turn out to be a day of reckoning, Deirdra parked her car in front of her salon and let in the five customers who were scattered around the doorstep. She disappeared into the shop with them, turned on the lights, the television and a giant multi-colored plastic fountain that graced the middle of the room. She had bought the fountain at a Chinese shop in Dundalk, where the clerk had assured her that it would bring good fortune. Its bulky basin collected the water that cascaded down the sides onto shiny metal rocks and made enough of a racket that the television had to be turned up high for the patrons to hear the morning soaps. A collection of pink plastic flowers floated in the water among some frogs made out of a greenish styrofoam moss.

The stories the patrons shared about who was going to jail and who got out, who shot who, who ought to shoot who and how soon these shootings should take place, made for a very animated shop. There were no white people living anywhere in the neighborhood, so when a middle-aged white woman dressed to the nines walked through the door at high noon, everything stopped.

Madge strode in and positioned herself next to the flamboyant fountain. Every mouth in the shop flew open, including Deirdra's, whose right hand froze in mid air with a curling iron in it.

"We need to talk," said Madge, tossing her hair 4away from her eyes and looking straight at Deirdra. Someone turned off the television and no one spoke. This was an uncommon occurence.

Madge had become wary of married life with Colin. For months she had suspected that something was going on behind her back, so she did what she did best: snoop. Going through his desk one early morning, she came upon the paperwork for the house he had bought for one Deirdra Jackson. Caution was blown away by a jealous wind, and she forgot what her mother had told her about curiosity killing the cat.

When she saw the neon sign in front of the salon, it confirmed her suspicion that Deirdra had the cowboy boots. She would get them from her, one way or the other. She was not about to lose Colin after all her hard work.

"Me? I have nothing to talk with you about," answered Deirdra nonchalantly. The women in the salon slid forward to the edge of their seats, several sitting bolt upright with sudsy water streaming down their faces.

Deirdra sauntered over to Madge, curling iron in hand. "If I were you, Mrs. Carrington," she said with a sneer, "I would leave. You are making a spectacle of yourself."

"I'm standing right here until you give me back what is mine," Madge snapped back, holding her ground. "And that includes my husband."

The women faced each other menacingly.

"Something wrong, Deirdra?" asked Wanda, a large red-haired recidivist who had emerged from under a dryer. "Dis skinny behind woman boddering you, darlin?"

Wanda had just come out of the women's detention center for stabbing her boyfriend multiple times and apparently did not mind going back for a sabbatical. She strolled over and peered down at Madge, close enough for Madge to inhale the texturizer in her hair and allow some of it to seep from the protective cap unto her expensive handbag.

Intimidated, Madge backed slowly out of the salon, but not before hissing to Deirdra, "This isn't over." She hurried to her car, oblivious to the curious glances from the neighborhood's ne'er-do-wells. They assumed she was a junkie from the suburbs coming into the ghetto to collect her drugs. A common enough occurrence.

Madge drove around the corner and parked. Deirdra had to leave the salon at some point, she figured. She would wait here and follow her away from the reach of her curious cronies.

Back at the salon, everyone was talking at the same time. *As The World Turns* was forgotten. This live soap opera was much more to their liking.

"Girl, you know we got yo' back," Wanda said triumphantly after Madge had left. "We scared the shit outta that bitch." She winked slyly at Deirdra.

"True dat," Priscilla said with a grin, "But that sho' nuff is one brave white lady bringing her tail up in here with all that jewelry to boot. I wonder how far she'll get without having to share some of it."

"Honeychile, we can take care of her if you want us to," Wanda rattled on. "I know this guy named Tyrone, who can find anybody in this city and make them disappear. Fast."

"It won't come to that," Deirdra said, amused but feeling loved. "But if it do, amma let you all know."

Wanda grunted and went back to looking at the pictures in *The Enquirer*, and the others went back to their seats to catch up on the antics of Dr. John Dixon.

Normally, Deirdra would take a break at 3 o'clock and head to the White Tower for a cup of coffee and a piece of pecan pie. But today she needed something more. She got in her car and headed for home. A black Mercedes pulled away from the curb and followed her. Deirdra did not recognize the car, so was unconcerned.

A few minutes later, she turned into the alley behind her house and stopped outside her garage. The alley was desolate at that time of day. She climbed out of her car to get her empty trashcan that had been tossed by the sanitation crew into the middle of the alleyway. She assumed that the black Mercedes stopped further back was waiting for her to pick up her can. She stashed the can against the side door and got back into her car. When she pulled into the garage, she noticed the black Mercedes very slowy passing her garage entrance and heard the engine cut off a few feet away.

Deirdra got out of her car and walked toward the car wondering why an expensive model car would be cruising along the back alleys in her neighborhood.

Madge Carrington hopped out of the Mercedes and made a few steps towards Deirdra.

"What the hell do you want?" Deirdra approached Madge defiantly. "Do I have something belonging to you?"

"I want the boot," Madge demanded. "How you managed to get hold of it, I don't know. But I want it and I want it now."

"Oh, really?" Deirdra sneered. She was now only inches away from Madge's face. Poking her on the shoulder, she said, "Come and get it, bitch."

Madge responded by slapping Deirdra hard in the face. Deirdra reared back in shock. With a clenched fist, she cracked Madge with all her strength, square in the jaw. Pain and fear drove Madge headlong across the alley. But Deirdra was not through. Madge had only gotten a few feet away before Deirdra caught up to her and grabbed her around the neck.

What happened next is what happens to humans when they start something and find it difficult to stop. Deirdra grabbed Madge by the throat and banged her head fiercely against a cinder block wall. Madge reached out to stab at Deirdra's eyes with her fingernails, but they missed their mark. Her hands flopped helplessly to her side as Deirdra continued to slam her shoulders and head against the wall.

Suddenly there was a sharp cry. Blood seeped out from Madge's left ear. Only then did Deirdra catch herself. She released Madge's body from her hands. Madge slid down the wall and slumped onto the ground. The floppy hat she was so fashionably wearing, floated in the air for a second before landing in the middle of the alley.

CHAPTER THIRTY-FOUR

Windward

B reed LeGrande was happy to be a fisherman again. While he still attended meetings in the capital and believed in the principles of the revolution, he cherished the time he spent in the open sea. The calming clear water gave him cause to reflect on his life and his family. He felt that the ocean was a gift that God had given him to enjoy. There was so much of it that he thought the phrase should be Planet Ocean instead of Planet Earth. The ocean was a place that he went when he had anxious thoughts and fears about the revolution and his role in it. The sound of the waves drowned everything out in his soul that caused him unease. Its rhythm calmed him and quelched his confusion. The ocean also offered up a wonderful smorgasbord of living food. He relished the feeling of joy that came with the first tug on the line. The thrill when the rod jerks and bends with the weight of the catch. And the victory when he pulled up his prize. Now that Che was strong enough, he started taking him out when he went to his favorite place.

On any given day, a local looking out to sea would see him sitting in his boat, leaning back with this hands clasped behind his head, deep in thought. If the peeper kept on looking, he would see some kind of sea creature pop out of the water a short distance away. A cinnamon-colored thing, glistening in sea salt and golden locks of hair. The thing would bob up and down, and the peeper would sit up straight and stare with wide eyes. Then he would see the thing swim towards the boat. The peeper would hightail it back to the village to report that there is a ting ting under the sea. After a great deal of laughter and liquor at the rum shop, a more experienced peeper would announce, "Don't be a stupidee, man. Dat's only Breed LeGrande and he son."

By playing and spending time with Che, Breed discovered that children could be taught anything. Including how to love and how to hate. Breed created an alphabet of his own for Che. When Che was asked to recite it he would stand in the middle of the drawing room, clasp his little hands in front of his stomach take a bow and say, "A for Africa, B for brethren, C for cause," and so forth, all the way to "R for reason." This recitation impressed the neighors to no end.

"Dat boy is a real sponge, oui," they liked to say. "He soak up everyting."

One night after a particularly good meal of coo coo and lambi accompanied by a bottle of dandelion wine, Abi and Breed sat on the verandah while Popo entertained Che indoors.

"Let's get married tomorrow," Breed said, holding her hand and gently kissing her open palm.

"OK" was all she whispered back, her lips pressed against his ear.

The next day Abi put on her prettiest dress. A pale blue gingham that Hannah had mailed from America. It sported a broad white collar etched in lace and was mid-calf in length. She gathered purple bougainvillea from the garden and stuck them around her wayward dreadlocks to make a sort of crown. She completed her ensemble with white strappy sandals.

She carried a bouquet of bright yellow hibiscus in one hand. The other was wrapped around her husband's waist.

Breed was dressed in a crisp beige shirt jack and long khaki pants and sandals. Together they stood under the mango tree. The chimes tinkled.

Popo and Che followed them into the yard uninvited, knowing that their presence was wanted and welcome.

The couple looked at each other, held hands and spoke the words that came out of their hearts. Each made a solemn promise to the other and their eyes never wavered. They grinned broadly when they said, "I do." Their marriage was as real as anybody's, and the tree with a hundred young Julies clinging on to its branches bore witness. After the bride was kissed, Popo took Che's hand to walk with him down to Alister's house for a sweet treat. The couple dashed laughing into the house, heading for the bedroom.

"Congratulations," Popo called after them.

"Contulation," echoed their son.

If Breed's life had become less hectic, Abi's had become more so. She became the go-to person in her parish who helped with the reconstructuring of the health care delivery system. There were doctors, nurses and dentists who volunteered to refurbish health centers and other facilities to help the nation. She saw the medical care system move from the starched, clean uniforms of nurses and doctors serving the few to health care reaching out to rural communities and visiting stations where people lived. Abi was proud to be a part of the revolution. Her clinic became not only a place to come for healing, but also a training ground for nurse's aides and orderlies.

She helped to organize a demonstration through the streets of the capital to bring health care to the forefront. In past years, a failing hospital system with little equipment, had to share their space with rats, mice and flying cockroaches. Those who could afford it went to Venezuela or Cuba for medical and dental care. Many of the skilled personnel left the island to work abroad in countries where they would be better paid. But things were changing and more young people were beginning to enter the health care field. People were also being taught to practice preventive medicine in the schools and communities. Abi traveled from parish to parish to help implement some of these programs, teaching people to reconsider eating imported foods and going back to "eating local."

"I know why there is so much diabetes and undernutrition in dis country," Popo told Abi while she was accompanying her on one of her trips to a neighboring parish. "They want to eat like dem fat Americans. Juice from a can, frozen chicken, fruit packed with too much sugar. We have everything growing here dat we need."

"Try and not get us arrested for slander, O.K?" Abi chided. "Not all Americans are fat. Only a few. You just don't like the president, that's all. No need to put them all in one basket."

"Hmmmm," grumbled Popo. Despite her wariness, she could not help but marvel at Abi's ability to get things done. She was equally impressed by the humility and kindness that her daughter-in-law possessed and her accomplishments with everything in which she came into contact.

Abi was getting around more. More and more people loved and respected her, including some of the men. Breed became worried.

"Just go and do your work," Popo instructed him. "You have a decent wife. And if you taking care of business," Popo stopped to wink at her grandson and jab him in the ribs, "you don't have anything to worry about, if you know what I mean."

"There is a limit to what I will discuss with you," Breed replied irritably. "Mind your own business and stop embarrassing me today."

The subject was summarily dropped, and Popo slapped her grandson on this backside and went into the kitchen to begin cooking lunch. Che in tow.

Later in the evening, the usual crowd gathered in and around Boysie's rum shop.

"What we drinking today with we rum, Boysie?"

"CLR James," Boysie said with great exuberance. "We drinking CLR."

"Preach bruddah, preach," everyone chorused.

Boysie gave these lectures every once in a while and there was always standing room only when that happened. His head was usually buried in a book whenever he had free time and he shared liberally anything he learned.

"I'm going to read a piece of writing from this book here," he said, holding up a much worn copy of *The Black Jacobins* by CLR James, a Trinidadian historian.

"Alright. All you quiet down and listen hard. We does forget tings we have no business forgetting. Slavery in the Caribbean for one."

Boysie cleared his throat. *"There was no ingenuity that fear or a depraved imagination could devise which has not been employed,"* he began reading. *"Irons on the hands and feet, blocks of wood that the slaves had to drag behind them wherever they went, the tin-plate mask designed to prevent the slaves eating the sugar cane, the iron collar. Whipping was interrupted in order to pass a piece of hot wood on the buttocks of the victim."*

Boysie paused and wiped his brow with his bare hands.

"How people could do tings like dat to other people?" Marshall asked. "The slaves didn't do nothing to dem people for dem to cause so much pain and suffering."

"I can't answer you, Marshall, because it mash up my mind too," said Boysie. "Anyway, let me finish dis while I can still talk."

The crowd was silent. They each carried a mental picture of their grandparents suffering at the hands of the slave masters. Pain and horror formed a partnership in their heads.

Boysie took a deep breath and continued reading.

"Mutilations were common, limbs, ears, and sometimes the private parts, to deprive them of the pleasures which they could indulge in without expense. Their masters poured burning wax on their arms and hands and shoulders, emptied the boiling cane sugar over their heads, burned them alive, roasted them on slow fires, filled them with gunpowder and blew them up with a match; buried them up to the neck and seared their heads with sugar that the flies might devour them; made them eat their excrement, drink their urine, and lick the saliva of other slaves. One colonist was known in moments of anger to throw himself on his slaves and stick his teeth into their flesh."

Boysie closed the book and placed it on the counter.

"That's the reading for today, brothers and sisters. I not doing dis to make all you sick or hateful. I doing it to make all you aware of yesteryear. To help you make sense of what you doing with your life. Anybody have anything to share about what I just read to you?"

No one spoke. No one could.

CHAPTER THIRTY-FIVE

Baltimore

Without waiting to see if Madge was breathing, a panicked Deirdra ran back into her garage, pulled down the overhead door, dashed past a hodgepodge of weeds and climbed two steps at a time, into her house.

No sooner had she closed the back door, than she heard police sirens screeching down the alley followed by an ambulance. She froze. Jail suddenly presented itself as a possibility. Donning an orange jumpsuit every day with dozens of other women was not her idea of fun.

Her thoughts became more jumbled as she heard the commotion outside. "Ain't it something," she thought, "how the 'popo' shows up right away when it's a dead white person? If she had killed me, my ass would be in that alley till Thanksgiving." She collapsed on her beanbag chair in agony.

Across the alley and down the block, a cat burglar scrambled out of a newly refurbished rowhouse from the second-floor bedroom window. He had heard the raised voices of the two women and watched the fight that ensued. He considered it his civic duty to call 911 from the house phone before disappearing the way he had come in. Along with cash and some jewelry, he got a good look at both women.

As the ambulance sped off with Madge's body, two detectives stayed behind to cordon off the crime scene and collect evidence. Deirdra called the salon to tell the other hairdressers that she would not be coming back for the day and that she needed them to close up. The second call she made was to her mother.

Mrs. Jackson got on the next bus to Charles Village. Detecting fear in her daughter's voice, she mentally urged the bus forward, but it paid her no mind. It evidently had all day to get to where it was going. Knowing that her daughter had purchased a gun, Mrs. Jackson worried that Deirdra had found someone in whom to insert some of the bullets. Colin. It had to be him. Deirdra had killed the white man. Or worse, she had killed the white woman. Jail presented itself as a likely outcome.

Mrs. Jackson charged off the bus when she reached her daughter's stop. It took six rings before an ash-faced Deirdra opened the door.

"Did you mean to kill him?" was her mother's first question after they sat down.

"I didn't kill him, Ma," Deirdra wailed. "I killed his wife."

"Oh, for crying out loud, chile. Why didn't you kill him? I woulda killed him if I had to kill one of 'em," Mrs. Jackson said with exasperation.

Deirdra pounded her fist into the beanbag chair. "I got carried away," she sobbed but without tears.

The real wailing started when she conjured up a mental picture of herself in a baggy jumpsuit sharing a cell with an overweight, red-faced woman named Boomer.

"I can't go to jail. I can't! I can't! You have to help me!" She was violently shaking her mother, and Mrs. Jackson was beginning to worry about her own life.

"Tell me what to do, and ah'll do it" was all Mrs. Jackson could say under the circumstances. She was thinking that she was too old to be put in jail as an accessory, and she was not willing to be locked up even for her daughter.

"Go find Colin," Deirdra ordered. "Check the morgue first. If he not there, check his office. If he not there, well, take a taxi to his house." Deirdra pressed a sheet of paper with the Columbia address into her mother's hand. "Find him and bring him back. Don't come back without him."

A confused Mrs. Jackson was unceremoniously pushed out of the living room. She walked blankly out of the front door, down the stairs and into the street, wondering what on earth she should do next when fate stepped in.

"Are you alright, ma'am?" asked a concerned voice. It belonged to an impeccably dressed, middle-aged white man.

The man looked squarely into her face and asked, "Do you know Deirdra Jackson?"

"Me? No!" stammered Mrs. Jackson, fearing he was the police. "I have absolutely no idea who she be."

"I was just wondering since I noticed you come out of her house. My name is Colin Carrington."

Mrs. Jackson's legs buckled beneath her, but he caught her before she hit the ground.

When Deirdra answered her front door, Colin Carrington was standing there holding her mother upright.

CHAPTER THIRTY-SIX

Windward

Abi read Hanna's letter and tried to digest the latest news from Baltimore: namely, that there had been a murder in an alley in Charles Village, and the victim was none other than her former friend, Madge Sorenson.

Watching Abi drop the pages on the ground and turn white as a ghost, Popo jumped into action. "Che, run and catch those papers before the wind take dem to town. Hurry up before your mother pass out."

The boy darted outside and retrieved the sheets of paper and a newspaper clipping that the wind had blown into the buttercups. He brought them back to Popo who was now standing next to Abi with her arm around her. She smoothed out the sheet of newspaper and carefully read the article.

Madge Sorenson Carrington was pronounced dead on arrival at Johns Hopkins Hospital this afternoon, where she was taken after suffering severe lacerations to the back of the head. Her body was found in the alley behind 26th Street and Calvert in Charles Village. There were no witnesses to what appears to be a homicide with police sources saying the victim was "in the wrong place at the wrong time."

The victim's husband was the city's well-known chief medical examiner, Dr. Colin Carrington. Suellen Perlmutt, the doctor's secretary, was quoted as saying, "It is baffling and unconscionable that such a terrible thing could have happened to such a nice man."

A fellow real estate agent, Henrietta de Leon, said that, "Mrs. Carrington will be sorely missed in the business. She was a great inspiration and a very kind person." The mayor of Baltimore City also sent out a statement of sympathy, declaring that there will be zero tolerance for crime in broad daylight in her city. As for the victim's husband, Dr. Carrington was reported to be despondent.

"You really have some mess, oui," Popo exclaimed, shaking her head. "Is one ting after the other with you. But I'm sure is nothing we can't fix. That Colin of yours would have done well to work here with the ex-prime minister, but it too late now, he miss his chance. But maybe dis new government could use him to get rid of some counter-revolutionaries."

"Dis is too much excitement for me here on dis little island of Windward. All dis bacchanal going on in Baltimore, make me want to go and see for myself. Didn't I tell you you should write a book?"

When she had finished fanning Abi, Popo read that Colin Carrington had been questioned by the police, but there was no evidence of his involvement in the tragedy.

"Well, dis man is a real ting ting you marry, Abi. First he try to kill you den he kill his second wife. And God only knows how many other people done dead by his hand. You lucky you didn't go back. All now so you dead. He done chop you up, and Bim Bim alone know where he throw your body. For all we know, he throw your head in a bucket somewhere and your body floating in the Mississippi."

"We don't know he is responsible for this, Ma." Abi said solemnly. "The article didn't say…"

"Forget this article. I know is he. And Bim Bim know is he. She have a sister in Baltimore, you now. So she know by proxy."

"Don't say that," Abi spoke softly. "To think I spent all those years with that man, eating and drinking and talking."

"And don't forget doing the bang bang," Popo interrupted. "Dat very important if you ask me. He could have kill you while he was, you know. I had a man once dat almost kill me with…"

"OK, Ma Po. Right now I really don't want to know about that man."

Abi read the article for the third time. Was Colin guilty? Why did it matter to her? What really made her gag was the paragraph where she was mentioned as Carrington's first wife who had "gone missing during a cruise to the Caribbean."

CHAPTER THIRTY-SEVEN

Baltimore

The robber who had witnessed the death of Madge Carrington, laughed when he read the newspaper's account. What gibberish, he thought, before pondereing his next move. He may be a thief but he was nobody's fool. Like Hanna Gamble, he was well versed in the art of sleuthing. Staking out a person's house required great skill. And great patience. He decided to hold on to his trump card and watch the game unfold.

After reading about Madge's death, Hanna Gamble immediately booked an appointment at the Kinky Hair Salon for a touch-up. She sat down in the only free chair to wait her turn. Picking up a tattered copy of an outdated *Jet* magazine, she opened it on the center page to see what bikini-clad starlet was being featured that month. Hanna glanced at her watch and noted that Deirdra Jackson was taking her time about showing up for work. She waited patiently. An hour passed and still there was no sighting of the salon's madam.

Uninterested in spending an entire afternoon at the emporium, she asked one of the stylists when Deirdra was expected and was told that Miss Jackson was indisposed. Ever the vigilant sleuth, Hanna did not miss the sly smirks and winks that were exchanged among the women after her question was answered. She knew that if the cliche women liked to gossip was true, then beauty shops were reservoirs of rumor. She dived in.

"Can you believe what happened to that woman in that alley in Charles Village?" was all she had to say to open Pandora's box.

What followed was an earful about how the white woman had barged into the shop and started yelling at Deirdra. It was sheer coincidence that the same woman got killed near Deirdra's backyard. The crazed woman had obviously followed Deirdra home to bother her some more, and wouldn't you know, some derelict drug addict socked it to her.

"Would you believe this white popo done come in here asking 'bout Dierdra?" said Wanda, the red-haired recidivist.

"Why would the police come here?" Hanna asked, slouching back in her chair to hide her excitement.

"Well, girlfriend," Wanda began, turning off the dryer. "Some druggie tell the police he was outside the shop the day the white woman was up in here. He told them he knew something was going to go down that was not good, so he hauled ass. He gave them a description of the woman and the car. So them cops bust in here, with their hands on their guns, looking for trouble, and honey, I let them have it."

Raucous laughter burst out in the room as Wanda stood with her gargantuan legs spread apart and her hands on her ample hips. With her face twisted to one side, she was a comical picture with half of her hair in large pink rollers and the other half sticking straight up to the ceiling.

"That white woman never set foot in this shop, I told him. I was here the day the druggie said he saw her and, I can tell you, officer, he lie. Like a rug."

Wanda stopped and looked around at her supporters for encouragement. "I told the popo, a young smart-looking officer like you, should know not to believe anything a junkie say." She batted her eyes as she recalled the cop's words. "Ma'am, I am only doing my job. Are you sure what you are telling me is correct?" "So help me God," I told him.

Wanda had uttered these same words many times in and out of court and had long since given up hope of going anywhere remotely near the Pearly Gates.

"You see officer," she continued, "the sign outside say kinky hair, not white people hair. You wanna touch mine to make sure?"

"That won't be necessary, Ma'am. Thanks for your help." Wanda completed her story with the officer backing out of the shop like one would for royalty when leaving their presence.

So Madge, Hanna deduced from Wanda's long-winded tale, had actually been to the salon. For one reason or another, she must have followed Deirdra to her house and got killed in the back alley. Hanna knew that it had to have something to do with Colin. And she suspected that Deirdra had killed her even if the newspaper said it was a drug addict that did the deed.

She would visit Colin in the pretense of offering her condolences and see what she could find out. She would also return to the salon and talk with Deirdra. She would tell her she knew Madge came to the shop to talk with her and then maybe Deirdra would break and confess to her.

Hanna left the Kinky Hair Salon without getting her hair done but with plenty of thoughts and theories. She would write down everything in a letter titled, "Dear Abi."

CHAPTER THIRTY-EIGHT

Windward

The letter lay on the table before them. Hanna had written in great detail, like she were writing the book that Popo said Abi ought to be writing. She told Abi everything that she knew, heard, witnessed, read and then some.

"If you ask me," Popo began, "my life was alright before you came into it. But I have to say, darlin', dis is more dan I ever expected. Dis is a real movie. Dis better dan all dat damn chupidness it have playing at the cinema in town."

"I don't know what to make of all this," Abi said, looking intensely at the breadfruit tree as if for guidance.

"Dat tree can't help you," Popo laughed. "First, you almost get killed. Den de man who was paid to kill you get killed. Den the second wife get killed. A lot of killers running around in Baltimore. Best dey all move down here and join us in the killing spree we having here. We could have a kill-he-kill-she jamboree. You know what next, right?"

Popo was on a roll. "Hanna will dead. Is kill dey killing she next if she don't stop putting in she ten cents and looking for trouble. If you ask me, you better answer dat letter right now. Tell her you talk to Bim Bim and she say stop before she go and dead."

"You think so? He will kill Hanna?"

"Why stop now?" Popo said authoritatively. "Once killing start, it's hard to stop. Is just like if you steal something from the store. The first time you frighten and you sweating when you think of all the mess that could happen to you. But you get away with it. Dat give you courage to do it again. Next thing you know, you is a born thief. Thiefing goat, donkey and people money right out of dey hand."

"I will write to Hanna. But I wonder what he killed Madge for?"

"You must not end a sentence with a preposition. I always telling your son dat. Dey really didn't teach you anything in America, did they? Mashing up the Queen English."

Popo shielded herself from Abi's raised hand.

"OK," Abi continued, "I wonder what he killed Madge for, you bambam head."

"Because he is a crazy man. Maybe he think his name is Macbeth. And too besides, he want to go back with the woman, Deirdra. Dis bigger dan me and you. Dis bigger dan a book, Lawd."

Popo chortled as another image came flashing into her mind. "Don't be surprised if you see Macdeath Carrington in town one day. With a machete in his hand with your name on it."

"Not funny, Ma Po. You know you not letting nobody kill me. No time."

Popo dried her eyes and pulled herself back onto the bench and put her arms around her daughter. "No way," she said in her ear.

"By the same token," Abi said, leaning comfortably against Popo's shoulder. "It has crossed my mind on more than one occasion how interconnected we all are as humans."

"How so?" asked Popo with renewed interest. "Pray tell."

"Well, look at it this way. If I had stayed in Baltimore and not come on that cruise, Madge, and probably Ross Winter for that matter, would not be dead today."

"Also," Abi plodded on, "if I had gotten back on the ship like I was supposed to, we would not be counting dead bodies right now. It's alarming how what we do can affect other people not only near to us, but across the world as well."

"Ok, Epictetus," Popo said, finding her voice. "You cannot blame yourself for people dying. Sorry to disappoint you, but you are not that powerful. I understand what you are saying, but by the same token, if you stayed in Baltimore with Colin the cowdung, you could have been killed yourself. Your friend and that red-haired man might have lived, but judging from their characters some other jumbie would have claimed them eventually."

"Well," Abi interrupted.

"I not finish yet," Popo said calmly. "If you did not come to the island, or if you had gotten back on that ship that day, there would be no Che. I can't imagine that one. Plus you know you can't live without Breed."

"You always make me feel better, Ma," said Abi lovingly.

"Dat is how God made me, Pandora," Popo beamed.

CHAPTER THIRTY-NINE

Baltimore

Three people sat on Deirdra's uncomfortable sofa and looked at each other awkwardly. Colin was the first to break the silence.

"What happened, Dee?" he whispered in a low voice.

Deirdra relaxed when she heard him address her in that old familiar way.

"Don't be afraid to tell me. Whatever happened, I can make it go away."

"Of course you can," Mrs. Jackson jumped in, fully recovered from her shock of finally laying her eyes on Colin Carrington.

"Deirdra didn't do nothing wrong. But you being a white man and all, I ain't surprised you can make things go away. I ain't never hear no black man say that one. Clout.

That's what it is. Why don't you make yourself go away, Mr. Clout, cause if it wasn't for yo' white ass, none of this shit would have come down in the first damn place."

"Ma," said Deirdra irritably. She bit the inside of her lip had sidled over to Colin. "You need to leave, if you can't be quiet."

"You has got to be out of yo' cotton pickin' mind, Deirdra." Mrs. Jackon was pissed.

Colin had his arm around Deirdra and was studying her face. Deirdra could feel the longing in his body. His grip was taut. She knew that she could tell him anything now, and he would believe it.

"She came in the shop and attacked me," she sobbed, looking at her mother out of the corner of her eye. "She asked me if I still loved you. I told her I did and nothing would ever change that."

Colin tightened his grip on her shoulder and moved his free hand to her knee. Mrs. Jackson sighed loudly and rolled her eyes toward the ceiling.

"I have raised an idiot, Lord," was all she could summon.

"Hmmm," Deirdra cleared her throat. "She said you were her husband and I need to go away. I told her that ain't happening 'cause I can't live without you."

Colin's hand moved up to cup one of her breasts.

"Lord," Mrs. Jackson repeated. But there was no reply.

"She said we will see about that and then she walked out."

Colin was practically on top of Deirdra, having pushed her down on the sofa and into her mother's lap.

Mrs. Jackson sprung up and let Deirdra's head fall back on the arm of the sofa. She placed her hands on her hips and breathed loudly. "OK, I've had enough. I don't need to see this. You two deserve each other."

"Bye, Ma," was all her daughter could manage.

What kind of man would make love to a woman when his wife's corpse was still warm? Crazy thoughts filled her head as Mrs. Jackson hurried down the front steps for the second time that day.

"Now I'm like everyone else in this city," she said to herself. "I know about a murder personally. Only difference is, I gave birth to the killer."

Colin Carrington could not leave Deirdra Jackson's house. Not only did he spend the night with her, but all of the next day. The majority of the time they spent together was in bed.

Colin wanted to know every detail of the killing of his wife at the hands of his lover. "A crime of passion" he called it.

"Did she struggle, Dee?" he licked his lips and panted with a rising excitement that made Deirdra nervous.

"No," Deirdra said, while raising her arms to allow him to snuggle under her armpits.

"I got her around the neck and just banged her head over and over on the wall. I don't know what got into me. I guess I was mad as hell that she was your wife. Next thing I know, she falls on the ground and stops moving."

"God damn," Colin sighed. "I had no idea you were so strong." He threw himself feverishly on top of Deirdra for what seemed to her like the umpteenth time. This time around, however, Deirdra was unresponsive.

Colin Carrington could change anything that crossed his desk. He had friends in City Hall. Money to grease palms. Evidence that could be thrown out. The more they made love, the more the crime faded away.

By the third morning, Deirdra realized that she could walk the streets of Baltimore and not have to worry about being arrested for a crime that some weirdo drug addict had committed. She marveled at the thought that who you knew could make such a difference with what happens to you.

Colin immediately moved in with her and put his suburban house up for sale. They became one of the few inter-racial couples in Baltimore City to publicly flaunt their relationship. Madge Carrington's case joined Ross Winter's in the cold files of the police department. True to his word, Colin knew how to make things vanish—things like evidence and troublesome wives.

CHAPTER FORTY

Windward

Popo had not smoked her pipe for a while. She took it out of its tattered velvet pouch and walked into the yard humming to herself. Upon seeing the pipe, Chanticleer shook his feathers and dipped his head this way and that in disapproval. He did not like smoke.

Popo was out earlier than usual because she could not sleep. She tapped some tobacco into the chamber and looked up into the still dark heaven. She prayed, her lips moving silently and quickly.

People were talking. That feeling of uncertainty was rising up again. Could there be more conflict and bloodshed? Popo mused over what she had heard at Boysie's shop. She took those thoughts, pressed them together with some tobacco, put them into her pipe and smoked it.

She thought of her father and his favorite piece of work written by the Bard, which was kept in her drawer under her night clothes for years. She sat under the mango tree wearily, but had no taste for the fruit today. She did not search the tree to see if any of the Julies were full enough to be picked. She needed to understand why man could strut and fret and cause such torment in so short a time. She took the paper out of her pocket, smoothed it out on her knee, then lifted it up to read:

> *All the world's a stage,*
> *And all the men and women merely players;*
> *They have their exits and their entrances,*
> *And one man in his time plays many parts,*
> *His acts being seven ages.*
> *At first the infant,*
> *Mewling and puking in the nurse's arms;*
> *And then the whining schoolboy, with his satchel*
> *And shining morning face, creeping like a snail*
> *Unwillingly to school.*

She stopped reading to think of Che and pray that the unrest did not change who he would become, fully knowing that it already had.

> *The sixth age shifts*
> *Into the lean and slippered pantaloons*
> *With spectacles on nose and pouch on side;*
> *His youthful hose well saved,....*

She blushed and fidgeted as she remembered JWs youthful hose and the joy it had brought her.
Is second childishness and mere oblivion,
Sans teeth, sans eyes, sans taste, sans everything.

Popo pulled herself up from the bench and, with labored gait, headed into the kitchen to make the morning breakfast for her family. She carefully peeled herself an orange and let the trail of skin fall onto the kitchen counter. When she was done, she hung the trail of peel on a small hook on the cabinet. There the peel will dry up over time and would be used to make the most tasty and sweet smelling tea on earth. She had showed Abi how to put the peel into a small pot with water and let it boil and simmer, then sit back and enjoy with honey or sugar. Popo ate the orange slowly and, as if she had eyes in her back, she reached her arm backward and embraced Che who had wandered in and had headed straight for her skirt.

Codfish cakes and hot bakes was the menu for the morning. No sooner had she started frying up the bakes than Breed and Abi sprung out of bed, pulled by their noses.

"Boy, if you keep eating the bakes as fast as I make them, what will the rest of us eat?" Popo scolded the child, whose mouth was too full to respond. As usual, she knew she had to make more than a normal family could eat.

Because it was Sunday, Breed could linger over breakfast with his family. Lunch was anybody's guess, but in the mornings and nights the Le Grande's ate together, except on the days when Breed had to attend a political meeting.

Che scampered outside to bother Chanticleer and feed the chickens bits of fried bake. Chanticleer grew to expect the small boy to come bounding out of the house and start chasing him around the yard. When the rooster got tired of the game, he would flap his wings and fly to a low branch in the plum tree just out of Che's reach and peer down at him from his throne. One day the boy would learn to climb the tree and the chicken would have to think of a different means of escape.

"Tell me something, Breed," Popo looked into her grandson's dark brown eyes, "because I know you know more than me what going on."

"That would be a rare occasion, Merlin," said Breed, selecting his words carefully. "I don't know if I want to have this conversation."

"Call me what you want, Scaramouch, but I hear tell that things not going too well with the government."

"Oh my goodness." Breed covered his mouth with one hand and opened his eyes as wide as they could get. "What a very unusual occurrence that is, Genghis Khan."

Abi waited patiently for the two to set aside their word weapons so she could hear what was actually happening.

Popo grinned at Abi and said, "Look, Kathryn Howard, tell your husband to stop dancing around the subject like a batty mamselle and answer me."

"Why are you calling me Kathryn Howard? Didn't she get executed by her husband, King Oh....... never mind."

Breed laughed when he saw his wife's face. "Yes," he admitted, "things are getting a bit shaky for real. Seems like the leader and the head of the council are at loggerheads. Things get more difficult when you have two equals. Especially when one is willing to compromise and the other not so much."

Popo stared at her grandson with a mixture of sadness and anger.

"Well dat is why unu should have had the fair elections like unu promise. Nobody telling us jukutu people where to put we foot when we walk. You done hear de American president say dis' is a nice piece of real estate—like he talking about a beach with nobody on it."

"Let dem come, let dem come, we shall bury dem in the sea," sang Breed in his melodic voice.

"But seriously, Ma, watch what you saying, OK? Don't go saying tings, especially in the rum shop. You don't know who is who and who is not your friend. You hear? They will come and get you in the night, chop off your head and we won't even know."

"Let dem come, let dem come, we shall bury dem in the sea," Popo held her head erect and glared at Breed through squinted eyes.

"Go ahead and cause bassa bassa if you want," said her grandson. He was not amused.

Outside in the yard, the chickens were squealing and running for their lives. Che was in hot pursuit with Popo's cutlass slicing the air above his head. He ran through and crushed many of the yellow Jump Up And Kiss Me that Popo had planted so carefully in the front yard.

"Abigail Fisherman, go and stop dat wild chile dat unu make before he kill himself and all my flowers," Popo shouted as Abi giggled at the role reversal of the great grandson wielding Popo's beloved cutlass. Breed went out into the yard to rescue the chickens from their impending doom and Che from his own.

"I am taking my wife for a drive around the island," Breed said to his grandmother, eager to stop the line of conversation. "Watch this boy, OK?"

Now that Breed had transportation, he was able to take his family anywhere they wanted. He and Abi left arm in arm and got into the truck. Che ran off to fetch Alister, while Popo stayed under the tree to keep a watchful eye.

The boys got their Sunday school book and opened it on the ground to read.

"Dese people is the first people dat God made," said Alister to Che, pointing to a picture of a white couple under an apple tree. Che looked at the picture of Adam and Eve, screwed up his little brow and said, "Gran Po say dey not white."

"I know," said Alister. "Because dey in a place with plenty trees and plenty animals. It don't have dat where white people come from. And too besides, dey din have no clothes on." The boys hid their mouths behind their hands and fell about giggling at the thought of two adults running around naked.

"It have to be real hot where Adam and Eve was living."

Alister flipped a few pages and stopped at a picture of a white man standing in front of a boat with a staff in his hand and the wind blowing his long hair about. The animals, all in pairs, were headed into the boat.

"Che," he said looking at his smaller friend. "You see dese animals? Lion and tiger and elephant and ting? Where dey does have dat?"

"Afeeka," shouted Che enthusiastically.

"And you want to know what else chupid?" Alister asked, scratching his head thoughtfully. "Apples does only grow where it cold, my Pa told me. And if it was cold, den Adam and Eve could never be naked," he snickered.

"So I believe," he added proudly, "dat it was a mango dat Eve give Adam to eat."

"Bible wong?" Che demanded to know.

"Boy, I not Bim Bim. I don't know everyting," Alister said, shoving Che playfully. "But Pa say anybody could make a mistake because we all human."

A little green lizard materialized in the grass, and Alister tossed the book aside for a good lizard chase. Che scrambled in his shadow.

Later that night Abi lay with her head on Breed's bare chest. She didn't have a close female friend that could fill the void that Jenny's death left. Some of her womanly stuff was transferred to Popo, but most of it spilled onto Breed when they lay together in bed at night. As a consequence, Breed learned about things he had never thought of before.

Like why yeast infections are torture for women. What really happens in a woman's head when she misses her monthly period. The do's and don't's of douching. Why the size of a man's penis does not really matter.

He stored it all away carefully, waiting for the day when he would have a chance to share all of his new personal knowledge with the boys and dem in the rum shop. He knew a discussion about the size of a man's penis would spark all kinds of taylaylay because every man in Windward knew that size mattered. This revelation though, would be of great comfort to the men that had penises the size of a Jamaican plum.

The opportunity, however, to generate this kind of conversation always seemed elusive. Just when he would be about to explain to Short Man or Ing, why a woman's breasts are tender at certain times of the month, he would lose his nerve and question his sanity. Abi, however, continued to ply him with womanly information, some of which kept him strangely fascinated and some of which colored the contents of his dreams.

CHAPTER FORTY-ONE

Windward

The rumor around the island was that there was even more conflict in the leader's office. Most of the time rumor is just that, but there was something different about this one.

"The Obeah woman say that something dread getting ready to happen," Popo announced to the patrons in the rum shop. It was early evening and they were beginning to fill the shop's small space and spill out into the yard in front. Some sat on makeshift benches made out of discarded tree stumps and others on the packed hard soil where grass refused to grow after years of being trodden down by human feet. Several men leaned against the surrounding trees with one leg bent behind them for support. The most agile just squatted anywhere. These were usually the women who, no matter how ample, could squat with their skirts bunched up between their legs and their bottoms an inch from the ground, and stay in that position as comfortably as if they were sitting on a cushion.

"Bim Bim say something getting ready to happen," Popo repeated, aiming the soggy end of her pipe to the trees in the distance. She blew smoke out of her nose and mouth slowly with her lips bunched together and her face tilted towards heaven. She would not be hurried, so she ignored the looks of impatience in the surrounding eyes.

Squatting next to her was Abi. Not as agile as the others, she considered herself a squatter in training. Her only missing appendage was a bigger bottom, and Breed was trying his best to change that. "Even if this don't work, we would at least have had a lot of fun trying," Mixing comfortably with the best of them, Abigail Fisherman, knocked back her rum with the rest of them.

"The Obeah –"

Popo went for the proverbial hat trick.

"Shit or get your arse off de posie, old lady," said an impatient farmer, who was not afraid of dying.

"Don't take dat tone with my grandmother, boy." Breed immediately jumped in to defend Popo.

"Fight start already and we not even drunk yet," said Marshall, trying to down his rum quickly so he could be inebriated when the blows began to rain.

"De Americans coming for we tail," said Breed. "As sure as Chanticleer know it's day."

"Dey ain't coming for nobody tail. Dey too busy to bother with a little island like Windward. We done had dis conversation a million times already. Dis is not Cambodia." Tall Boy protested.

"Don't listen to Tall Boy, all you," said Fish. "He belong to the CIA. For all we know, it have people right here in dis group dat counter-revolutionary. Dey don't carry a sign and dey look like us but dat is where it end. So talk, Breed, if you name man."

"I agree with de Obeah woman because I can feel it too. Especially when I go to town. As if the time ripe for something dread." Breed pulled out a crumpled piece of paper from his pocket that he shook out and held up.

"Look," he said, "Dis piece of paper have things dat my father write down. 1954—Iran and Guatemala, thousands killed; 1961—Bay of Pigs, to overthrow Cuba's Fidel Castro; 1961—Congo, thousands killed, Lumumba overthrown; 1964—Guyana, Jagan overthrown; 1973—Chile, Allende overthrown, 50,000 killed. It have more I could read to unu about, but dat is enough for now. Who want to add Windward, government overthrown and how many dead. Anybody?"

Breed folded the paper and put it back in his pocket.

"What you saying?" This came from Horsford, who was holding his head in his hands. He had already seen enough blood and was not keen to see any more scarlet streams running out of people's bodies.

"De year don't done yet. We still have four months to frighten," said Breed.

"I don't understand why people want to tell we what to do in we own land," Marshall said. "De first piece of advice we get was back in 1498. Dem Europeans tell us to stop cooking outside half-naked. Dey tell us to go and build a kitchen like civilized people and put on some clothes. Now after all dis time, I hear dat in America dey cooking outside half-naked as soon as de weather get hot. Dey say is a barbecue dey having. When we do it, we uncivilized."

The group shook their heads collectively and someone took the bottle from Marshall's hand.

Abi got up shakily from the ground and dusted off her crumpled dress with her hands. "Whatever happens, we will deal with it," she told the group reassuringly.

"We have to wait and see," Breed nodded in agreement. "We already on the board, so we going to have to play or die."

"Slam," roared Dolphus, as he played his last domino piece.

"Pass me a Heineken and let's talk about carnival instead," said Peter who was legitimately afraid of what could happen. This kind of talk unnerved him especially since he had already lost a wife and child. He still found it difficult to talk about disruption of any sort. Debbie wrapped her arms around him protectively.

"Yes, carnival," said Malik, "but let me make one more point. My brother-in-law in Brooklyn say there are some of us working with the Americans to get rid of dis government down here. Every Judas want his bag of silver, oui."

"Abi, you want to play Jab Jab dis year, girl?" asked Breed, eager to change he subject. He was remembering the first time he laid eyes on his wife. It was during carnival when he had taken her to his house, helped wash her clean of mango and Jab Jab paint, and made love to her. Out of a little battered transistor radio on the ground, Bob Marley started to sing, "*Satisfy My Soul.*" Breed and Abi exchanged knowing looks. They jumped up and bolted at full speed out of the yard and up the hill to their house.

"Look at dose two. What you think dey going home to do?" snickered Old Thief, making obscene gestures with his fingers and grinning stupidly.

"Mind your own damn business, Old Thief," Popo grimaced back at him. "Dem people young still. Dat will soon pass and dey go end up like me so, wid nuttin to run for, because God knows it ain't have one good man on dis island for me."

"Well what am I Popo, a dog?" Old Thief made even more elaborate signs with his fingers and now included his tongue in the effort. This last demonstration got everyone to their feet, ready to go their separate ways.

"Old Thief, you really know how to spoil a party, oui" Popo told him. "Good night."

Breed and Abi shut the door to their bedroom and stood looking at each other. The fierce longing they shared ever since he lifted her into his fishing boat those years ago, had not died. Before his hands could reach over to remove her clothing, her body shuddered with anticipation. By the time his fingers made contact with her skin she was helpless. His lips met hers and the fire burned as brightly as it did their first time together when the chickens ran for cover. She raised her arms to the ceiling and he lifted her dress over her head. She reached over and gently pulled him to their bed.

Popo labored up the hill. She would not hurry tonight. She would give Breed and Abi enough time to carry on before she picked up Che from Alister's house and take him home for supper.

There was hardly a wind this evening. She called out for her great grand son. After the third call, he came running towards her, arms splayed out like an airplane.

Tonight she would fix stew mutton and make a nice rice and peas to go with it. She would add some christophene and vegetables with tomatoes. Breed and Abi would need a good meal after their work out. She stopped by the avocado tree near the house, picked up Che and placed him on her shoulders. From that vantage point, the boy could reach up and pluck a ripe avocado for their meal.

The following night the family sat on the veranda to watch the night sky. In the distance, they could hear their neighbors talking on their own porches. High-pitched laughter sounded like seagulls fighting over fish. Little children played hopscotch in the moonlight, and older ones told stories about creatures of the night. Adults spoke in dulcet tones of things that had occurred in their lives that day. Two teenagers stole away to the beach to do adult things. Someone down the road was singing "Abide With Me" and bits of it could be heard riding on a lazy wind. A few stray dogs just barked at the night. Abi thought she saw what looked like a part animal part human thing dart behind a tree. Sometimes moonlight can play tricks.

"Breed," Abi broke the silence that lay between them.

"What, my dear?"

"What's with all the demonstrations and the rumors about more conflict in the government?"

"Nothing to squint your green eyes about," said Breed looking protectively at his wife.

"Yes, there is confusion," he continued. "Some of the people who support the deputy saying dat the leader is too soft. School children across the island beginning to demonstrate, and I hear dat some classes have to be cancelled because of the tension."

"Just like Bim Bim say, trouble coming," Abi replied as her shoulders tensed.

"Woi," Che suddenly screamed, pointing at the night sky. "Shooting star. I wish for bicycle, bicycle, bicycle," he said in his childish chirp.

"Don't buy dis boy no bicycle," Popo perked up. "He will break his two foot going down that hill one time."

"Ma," said Breed patiently. "A boy have to be a boy. How many times have I busted open my head, break my hand and what else, eh? Besides, I already promise the boy a bicycle. We going to town to buy a bicycle tomorrow. Abi coming. You are welcome to join us."

"OK," Popo said in a huff. "If I don't come, unu will buy some chupid bike dat the boy can't ride and will end up breaking his neck."

"Enough, Ma," interjected Breed. "You will frighten him."

But Che was absorbed with the thought that a bike was coming his way. He was looking forward to the biggest day in his life.

CHAPTER FORTY-TWO

Baltimore

Hanna Gamble made herself comfortable with her gospel music and a glass of red wine. She picked up Abi's letter with anticipation. The current surge of unrest on Windward, Abi wrote, came about as a result of extensive disagreement and back stabbing by the party's members. The government was actually helping the people move toward a more productive life, so ideally there was nothing to worry about. But the disarray in the capital raised the spectre of an intervention by the United States. The regime's samba with socialism had raised the hackles of Washington, and judging from what Abi had learned from Breed, the islanders were justified in their unease. She wrote that she was impressed at how much the average person knew about what was happening in the world even though they occupied such a tiny corner of it.

Hanna took a sip of wine and wondered where an invasion would leave Abi and her family. Would they be better or worse off? She thought about when might be the safest time to travel to the island again. A suitcase full of gifts was gathering dust in her bedroom.

She had already abandoned her quest to find out more about Madge's death. Abi had discouraged her from becoming the sleuth she thought she was born to be. Even if she managed to uncover the truth, she said to herself, would it be wise to go to the police with the information? No one in her community really trusted them. Could the police be expected to conduct an honest investigation when it involved the wife of a man as powerful as the chief medical examiner? One thing Hanna Gamble knew was that when a person had the clout of Colin Carrington, anyone and anything could be bought, sold or dispensed with.

Feeling discouraged, she reached for the bottle of wine. It was going to be a three-glass night.

Across town, Colin and Deirdra sat in their Charles Village living room having finished their dinner of take-out Chinese food. They were waiting for the proverbial half hour to pass before they got hungry again—often not for food.

"Did you kill Ross Winter?" Deirdra suddenly blurted out. Her words were unrehearsed and her rapidly blinking eyes betrayed her nervousness.

"And how long have you been waiting to ask me that question, Deirdra? Do you think I killed Ross?" Colin asked grimly.

"I think you did. Not that it matters. But he was my friend, so I'd like to know if you killed him and why," Deirdra said, fidgeting in her chair.

"OK," countered Colin, clearing his throat. "Answer this: did you kill my wife? Not that it matters. But she was my wife and I would like to know if you killed her and why."

Without replying, Deirdra got up and left the room. A minute later, she returned with a plastic bag and tossed it at him.

"What is this? A present for me?" he asked cynically as he untied the knot of the bag. His face flushed crimson as he pulled out a cowboy boot.

"Where'd you get this?" he croaked, jerking back his head as if hit with a punch from a heavyweight. "Where is the other one?"

Regaining her composure, Deirdra said as calmly as she could, "We don't need the other boot, Colin."

Turning to face him squarely, she wrinkled her brow thoughtfully. "This is the one that counts. I remember reading how Ross's killer had kicked him in the kidney with a pointed shoe."

"What are you saying?" Colin snarled as he tried to recover from the latest blow. "You really think I did it?"

"Well," Deirdra said, pointing to the purple stain on the tip, "If the boot fits, wear it. This sure looks like dried up old blood to me. What do you think, Mr. Medical Examiner?"

Colin reached into his pocket for a cigarette. He stuck it firmly between his lips and looked at Deirdra out of eyes that had turned to cold slits.

"How long have you had these doubts?" he asked, taking a long drag on his Marlboro. He retrieved the ashtray from on top of the television set and tapped his cigarette angrily against the metal.

"I didn't turn you in for my wife's murder. Are you saying that you will turn me in for this errrr….man? Anybody could have a pointed shoe. In any case, the police thought it was a woman's shoe worn by one of those cross dressers in West Baltimore. Or didn't you read the whole story before you started casting allegations, Madam Prosecutor?"

"Ross told me about you," Deirdra answered, her eyes flashing with anger. "I know all about his paid trip to the Caribbean. He told me he was going to blackmail you for more money. I tried to stop him because I knew it would come to a bad end. But he didn't listen. He told me he was going to meet you that night. And," she stopped for emphasis, "he also told me that if he turned up floating in the Chesapeake, I should go to the cops and tell them it was you that killed him. I didn't go to the police, obviously, but I have his diary. Everything he did with you is written down there. Would you like to read it?"

Colin's face had lost all color. His body turned stiff as the corpses that he came across in a day's work. The two stared at each other intently. Neither spoke. Deirdra put the boot back in the bag, as Colin crushed the end of his cigarette in the ashtray.

"Just so you know, Judge Jackson," he said quietly, "there is no way they can use that blood as evidence. It's too old. Plus you could have planted it there yourself in order to implicate me."

"Why would I want to implicate you?" Deirdra raised her voice, indignant.

"Because we were having an affair, and you wanted me to marry you. I wouldn't, so you hatched up all this. Tread lightly, Dee. You don't know the rules, and I, my dear, am the big bad wolf."

"I know enough of the rules to run with the wolves," Deirdra said defiantly.

Colin twisted his lips in a sneer as he spoke. "If you bring this to the police, you know you are going down for Madge, don't you?"

Deirdra cocked back her head and cried in a choked voice, "If I go down, you going down with me 'cause you covered it up. Either way, I ain't doing time without you."

They sat silently with their thoughts. Hers about Madge and his about Ross.

Colin broke the silence with a short chuckle. "There is no need for us to argue. Let's forget this ever happened. We will destroy all the evidence and just live our lives. People in love don't hurt each other, do they?"

Nuzzling closer to Deirdra, he planted a kiss on her mouth and whispered seductively. "It's very difficult to make love in the pokey. Now that everything is in the open, let's move on. I say we take a nice island cruise. For now, let me take you to do your favourite thing."

Colin had a wicked smirk on his face that Deirdra did not see. She was immediately thinking trinkets. He pulled her to him. They had enough time for a quick roll in the hay before the high-end stores in Baltimore City closed for the day. With his brow still knitted, he unbuckled his belt. Deirdra did not hear him murmur Ross' name as he fell on top of her. She was thinking of that green emerald necklace she had seen the week before at Hecht's.

CHAPTER FORTY-THREE

Windward

The news reached the village before Breed and his family got into their car to head to town to buy Che his bicycle: The leader had been placed under house arrest. Change had again come to the island. Abi was suddenly drawn back to a childhood friend in Baltimore. They had been walking home from school, chattering away about nothing. They did not see the car that had spun out of control down the hill on Union Avenue. Right there, in mid-sentence, her friend was hit by the car. The girl died immediately. A life cut short without rhyme or reason. "Just like a revolution," Abi now thought.

The quiet that fell on the village was frightening. Unusual. People stared blankly at each other uncertain as to what, if anything, they should do.

"What's going to happen to us now?" Abi held on to Che and for his sake, fought off tears.

"Lawd have mercy, chile. Dat is the same ting you asked when this revolution started. We not going to die. We will survive dis, too. For now, we have to go down and see what the people planning to do. We can't leave the leader locked up. Not after all dat man did for dis country."

By now, Che had started to bawl. "No bicycle! No bicycle!" Why couldn't they go to the store and get his bicycle while the others worried about the leader. That seemed simple enough to him. He bawled an octave higher.

"One more sound out of you young man, and …." Breed did not have to finish his sentence because as if by magic, the bawling stopped and quiet prevailed.

"I will dead before I get bike," the boy sniffed, shuffling back into the yard dejected.

Leaving Che with Alister's family, Popo, Abi and Breed caught a bus to town to protest the arrest of the leader. People were demonstrating in parishes around the island. Those who could find transportation took it and flooded the capital. The people wanted vengeance for their leader and for wrongs imagined or remembered.

"Come on," Breed said, grabbing Abi's with one hand and Popo with the other. He propelled them through the dense crowd. They inched their way closer and closer to the top of the hill—towards what was known as "the killing field" in colonial days.

Suddenly there came a rat-a-tat. At first it sounded like somebody's old car trying to start. But then the awful realization hit the crowd as screams pierced through the air. The hail of gunfire persisted as military police poured out of a building, screaming, "Get back, get back."

The heat and smoke was unbearable and forced the stampeding crowd back down the hill. At the bottom, a few cars pulled up and people climbed on top of each other to get into the vehicles before they sped away. The gunfire stopped just as suddenly as it had started, but no one seemed to notice. Some were too busy dying, while others were praying out loud for forgiveness before it was too late.

"Abi," Breed cried out from where they were huddled behind a fence. "Go home and take my grandmother with you. I have to see what's going on."

Abi grabbed Popo's arm and together they negotiated the steep descent with the panicked crowd. But with all the jostling and trampling, she and Popo soon got separated.

"Run, lady, run," an older man yelled, rushing past her. "Dey killing people." Abi saw the fear gripping his face. A pregnant woman stumbled to the ground in front of her. She was holding her stomach and moaning as she fell. Abi's eyes met the woman's briefly before the crowd heaved her forward. All she could think about was a motherless Che.

"Over here, Miss," came a gentle voice that sounded alien under the crazy circumstances. He was standing in an alleyway. The man pointed to a flatbed truck already crowded with people. Abi shoved her way towards the truck and was pulled into the vehicle by two women from the clinic who recognized her. She soon found herself settled on top of them. Her knees were badly bruised and her shirt was partly torn off, but she held herself together.

The truck was old and in ill-repair. It was used to carrying odds and ends and now was tasked to carry terrified humans out of the capital. It putted obstinately out of the alley and began the long climb away from Seaview. The wailing and whimpering in the truck did not cease even when the town became a distant speck against the blue ocean. At intervals, the melancholy blowing of lambi shells could be heard in the distance, fanned by the Atlantic breeze. Everyone half expected that armed soldiers would spring out from the bushes and attack them at any time.

Abi wondered where Popo was. Why was this happening? she asked herself. She closed her eyes and whispered a short prayer asking for the safety of her husband and his grand-mother. But who was she? Would God say to himself, "Oh, wait a minute, I have to save these two people because they are being prayed for. Oh, well, I'll take a different two for whom no one has prayed." Is that how it worked?

At last, they rattled into Marabel. Abi thanked the women for picking her up and headed towards Alister's house to collect Che. Exhausted, she walked up the hill with her son to nurse her wounds and wait for her husband and Popo to come home.

Hours later, one did. A bewildered Popo stumbled into the yard.

"Don't ask me if we going to die because we look like we already dead." Popo said. Abi grasped Popo in her arms and held her for a long time. Popo finally sat down in silence and shock. The day's events had rendered her speechless. Not so with Che.

"I get bike before everybiddy dead?" he demanded of his mother. "Please," he added apologetically, remembering his manners.

"Boy," said Abi, her voice fading as she dropped into a rocking chair next to Popo who was lying face down on the couch.

Sleep came quick and unannounced. It was the next morning before Abi realized that Breed had not come home.

"Don't worry, Abi. He come home soon enough," mumbled Popo, aroused from her slumber. "Is not like it's the first time. Remember when the revolution started, he got caught up and came home late?"

The hours plodded on drearily. Abi and Popo sat close to the radio, but only heard static. After much shaking and banging, they heard a voice say, *"The revolution is over, people of Windward. A provisional government has been formed. The Americans have agreed to assist the new government in any way it can."*

The women stared at each other. Neither spoke. Abi finally broke the silence. "Breed will find his way home to me. To us."

"He always does," Popo replied dubiously.

Before either could say another word, Marshall burst through the front door without knocking. "The leader dead," he announced breathlessly. Tears were running down his cheeks.

"A lot of people dead," he moaned, his arms flopping in the air. "The young and the old. Tell me dis not really happening. Tell me dat I dead and gone to hell."

"I can't tell you dat, Marshall," Popo sighed in a low voice. "No one is ready to die. Everybody frighten."

"Where Breed?" Marshall asked, looking around the room anxiously. His eyes fell on Abi. "He not home yet, but he coming," he added apologetically.

Abi was lost in her thoughts about what all this meant to her. She was an American, after all. Will they find her and take her off the island? She looked around stupidly for somewhere to hide.

Pushing open the door, Abi walked rigidly out to the mango tree and looked up at the sky. "God," she whispered hoarsely, her face tired and flushed. "I beg of You, please keep my Breed safe.

CHAPTER FORTY-FOUR

Windward

C he raced into the house screaming, "Ma, it raining up in the sky and umbrellas coming down."

"What nonsense are you talking about now?" asked his mother. Abi let the boy pull her out on the verandah while he excitedly jumped up and down, pointing to the village green below them.

"Well, I've seen everything now," Abi responded. "It has come to this. Those are not umbrellas, Che. Those are paratroopers."

The villagers clapped and cheered as the soldiers landed. For people used to sunlight, clouds and squawking parrots filling the sky, the audacity of men jumping out of whirring helicopters, was a phenomenal sight.

"The Americans have come to save us," Fish Mouth shouted out as other villagers gathered around him and hooted for joy.

"If Satan himself come, all you would be just as happy," said Malik warily, as he watched the armed troops assemble in the village green.

"Come on, Ma," said Che, trying to pull his mother off the porch and down the stairs. "Let we go and see too."

"You run along with Alister, dear," Abi tapped him on his shoulder. "Mom will stay here in case Daddy comes home." She whispered a prayer to herself, but also crossed her fingers. "Please God, don't let them take me away from this place."

"Where all you staying?" Marshall asked the soldier who seemed to be the leader of the pack.

"We have established a base set up nearer to the capital," the man answered in a pleasant voice. "We won't be long here. Just long enough to make sure that everything is secure and everyone is safe."

The young boys in the village followed the Americans around as they knocked on doors searching for weapons. They shot at each other with guns made out of sticks. Marshall looked at his wife and shook his head. "Do you find it funny dat even if we don't buy toy guns for the children and dem, they still find something and make a gun out of it?"

"Must be the nature of the beast," she replied, looking at Che and Alister. Both boys wanted to be the soldier with the biggest gun. They fell down on the ground, wrestling and screaming each one proclaiming to be the bravest American. Marshall pulled a battered Che out from under Alister before he got another trouncing.

"Mr. Marshall," Che protested. "I the stronger Merican, right?"

"Yes," Marshall answered, without enthusiasm.

The soldiers indulged the children. They showed them some of their gear and handed out little American flags and lots of Wrigley's chewing gum. Many of the children had never chewed gum before, so heaven presented itself to them in little strips of tin foil.

What particularly interested the men in the village was the fact that some of the soldiers were as black as they were. Those that had not travelled out of the Caribbean were impressed by these look-alikes dressed up in camouflage.

"Dis is like a real movie, oui," Boysie exclaimed. The others grinned in agreement. The fact that there were black soldiers in America caused Che to want to become an American soldier all the more with his own umbrella.

"Ma, look," screamed an excited Che, rushing back to the house later. "Choon gum. You want piece?" Che was as happy as Abi had ever seen him. She shook her head to mean "no." The child danced around and chewed his gum vigorously.

After the troops left the village, life returned to a new normal. The meetings in the rum shop became sporadic because of the threat of getting shot for violating the newly establishd curfew.

"I am proud of my people," Old Thief said to the handful of patrons that had gathered in the shop. "Most revolutions in history have the people fighting against de government. Here the people fighting for de government."

"What I want to know is," Malik asked, "what is going to happen after things cool down? What about the children? What kinda adults will they become after all dis fear and violence?"

"We not suffering like in Africa and the Middle East," Marshall said, making his point from his seat in the plum tree.

"So we measuring suffering now?" Debbie interjected. "You want us to raise a generation of people who don't mind killing each other? I asking what going to happen next. My children cry every time they hear a loud noise. What child needs to hear gunfire? And God forbid dey get used to it because then we in big trouble."

"Here's what I think," Abi said with a sigh, addressing the group. "I think that this revolution had to be destroyed by the Americans so that any other nation trying to follow suit would be intimidated. I think they took a gamble coming here, but I believe that it was a gamble that they won."

Abi was solemn while she received a round of applause in agreement. Everyone was worried about Breed and his obvious absence in the room, but no one said anything for fear of distressing her even more. They could see the anguish in her face, and were sorry that she could no longer smile like she used to.

Abi was glad that the soldiers had left without visiting her house. Judging from the reports of the villagers and especially Che's, she felt that they were a friendly lot and were not to be feared. She took comfort in that assumption.

CHAPTER FORTY-FIVE

Baltimore

Colin Carrington glanced at the body on the table in front of him. Another stabbing victim. The body belonged to a white male around the age of forty. Sometimes when he encountered a body of someone his own age, his mind wandered to the circumstances that made the life end like it did. But not today. He was focused on searching the wounds to make sure the kidneys were intact and ready for extraction later that evening when nobody was around. As he looked at the man's face, Kate's face suddenly appeared and replaced it. Her green eyes were holes full of black pus. Colin screamed in terror.

"Dr. Carrington!" Rushing into the morgue's examination room, Suellen observed Colin with his hands deep in the dead man's abdomen and his head turned awkwardly up towards the ceiling. It was not the first time she had found him like this.

"Oh, err," he stuttered. "I must have forgotten where I was."

Suellen faced Colin and for the umpteenth time considered putting in her resignation. If jobs weren't so scarce in Baltimore, she would have left the morgue a long time ago. She did not particularly want to be around when the chief medical examiner fell apart. She noticed that when he pointed out something on the chart at their weekly meeting, his fingernails were like those of a mechanic. Only his were not stained from grease and oil, but from poking around corpses, often without his gloves.

"Damn you, Kate," Colin scowled after Suellen left. "Why do you insist on bothering me? I didn't kill you. Ross did. Go wake him up."

He walked to the men's room across the hall from his office and scrubbed his hands vigorously, dried them on the already dirty towel hanging on a hook and returned to his office. He slumped down in his chair, let his arms droop towards the floor and spun the chair around with a prompt from his foot. Like a child in the playground, he closed his eyes and allowed himself to go around and around until he felt dizzy.

Pulling himself off his merry-go-round, he poured himself a drink from the bottle in the bottom drawer of his file cabinet. He had begun to drink more often to keep his nerves under control. Then he drank to forget that he drank. The more Kate appeared and attached her head to his corpses, the more he and Johnnie Walker conspired. He used the same glass he had been using for two years. The glass had never been washed. What was the point, he had asked himself. Alcohol kills germs. With a glass of Johnnie in one hand and the bottle in the other, he walked over to the only window in his office and peered through the grimy streaks to the street below.

Across town, Mrs. Jackson also looked out of her window. Her thoughts were centered on her daughter and the strange white man to whom she was now married. Deirdra had finally gotten what she wished for. How many times had Mrs. Jackson told her daughter that she should be careful about wishes. In response, Deirdra always made an impatient gesture with her hands and told her mother to please get a life and allow her to live hers. Mrs. Jackson often wondered how life was working out for her only child and, more generally, why people continued to have children.

She did not visit the Carrington home. She spoke with Deirdra once a week on Wednesdays when she was allowed a complimentary hair-do at the Kinky Hair Salon. There she would sit for two hours while Deirdra or one of the other girls worked on her hair. First the dye to camouflage the grey. Then she was put under the dryer to allow the dye to "take." Under the din of the dryer, she could only observe the other women constantly moving their lips and idly mused about their conversations. She was shampooed and conditioned by any available pair of hands, but the final curling of her hair was always done by Deirdra. This was the time that mother and daughter talked about what was hapening in their lives.

During the last appointment, Mrs. Jackson knew that there was something bothering Deirdra. After a fair bit of prodding, Deirdra started whispering so that the other patrons could not hear.

"It's Madge, Ma," she breathed with her lips brushing her mother's ear. The touch made Mrs. Jackson jump and caused her hand to fly up involuntarily and slap Deirdra on the cheek.

"Why you hitting me?" Deirdra raised her voice indignantly, then smiled at the other girls as all the dryers got immediately quiet and the television muted. If a pin dropped it would make a clatter.

"Come to my house later, baby girl," Mrs. Jacksoin said softly. "You sho' is losing yo' cotton-picking mind.

When mother and daughter sat down later in Mrs. Jackson's cramped living room, Dierdra spilled her guts.

"Madge won't stay dead," she shuddered, swallowing hard. "She keeps coming in the house and trying to squeeze in the bed with me and Colin."

"Well, she would still be his wife if you din't go and kill her." Mrs. Jackson sat stiffly on the sofa with her arms folded in her lap, highly satisfied with her theory.

"Not because somebody dead mean they dead, baby," she went on. "Maybe her soul not at rest and she don't want yours to be at rest neither. How your husband sleeping? If only one dead person keeping you wake, I can only imagine he not getting no sleep at all."

Deirdra rose to her feet angrily. "What nonsense you talking, old lady?" she blurted out. "We not murderers."

"If the noose fit, you know what to do. You cain't go round killing off God's chillen and 'spect to sleep."

"You want me to turn myself in? Is that what you want? I know you never loved me. You never did." Deirdra complained, her hands dramatically clutching her breast.

Mrs. Jackson was unmoved. She stood up, straightened her back and exhaled loudly. "I will pray for you. God is merciful. But you still have to pay for what you done did. I know this lady on Aisquith Street."

"Is you crazy?" Deirdra blurted out in frustration. "I am not going to see any of your demon friends."

"This lady know things 'bout dead people." Mrs. Jackson smiled, fascinated by that concept. "She from someplace in the Caribbean. Haiti, maybe. I hear those people very superstitious. Come to think of it, I bet that's what Stevie Wonder was singing about."

Mrs. Jackson paused to consider the brilliance of her connection to Mr. Wonder before continuing with her thought.

"Anyway, Mrs. Clemente, that's her name, have a sister who still living down in the islands."

"I don't have time for what your'e telling me," was Deirdra's peevish answer.

"Whatever, you say, Miss Knoweverything," said Mrs. Jackson, ignoring her daughter's outburst. "Ms. Clemente can give you a potion that you can sprinkle on Madge next time she show up in yo' bed. You want her address?"

Mrs. Jackson looked at her daughter without sympathy. Deirdra reached down to the coffee table to get a pen and paper, which she placed in her mother's outstretched hand.

Neatly printing the address on the piece of paper, Mrs. Jackson kissed her then pointed to the front door.

Deirdra walked out without turning around.

CHAPTER FORTY-SIX

Windward

The thing that Abi feared most would happen, happened one Saturday afternoon. She and Popo were hanging out clothes to dry on the clothes line with their backs turned to the road, when two American soldiers strode into the yard. The women turned around startled, when they heard them approach.

"Good day, ma'am, ma'am," the taller one addressed the women as the shorter soldier looked on sullenly. The man touched the tip of his cap when he spoke. Judging from the stripes on his jacket, he looked like he had outperformed the other soldier. He was strongly built, his hair was blond and dead straight like the hair on the corn in the fields in John John. His eyes were icy blue.

"Which one of you is Mrs. LeGrande?"

271

The women glanced at each other. "I am Mrs. LeGrande," Popo said, taking a step forward and looking him in the eye. He moved back intimidated by her voice and demeanor.

"Uuuh," he cleared his throat. "Well, we seem to have made a mistake here, ma'am. We were told that Mrs. LeGrande was a white woman. Which one of you is married to Breed LeGrande?"

"If you know she white, why you asking?" Popo snapped back.

At the sound of her husband's name, Abi jumped.

"I am Mrs. Le Grande," she said anxiously. "Do you know where he is?"

"Ma'am, who are you?" demanded the second officer of Popo. He was an ugly man with blotchy skin, beady eyes and a shock of red hair that reminded Popo of a bush fire. His super-rigid posture was an advertisement for self-importance.

Not many things in life made Popo LeGrande uneasy. But unsure of what was happening on the island, she was uncomfortable with these two white men standing in front of her.

"Ma'am," the shorter one sneered, inching closer to Popo. His right hand rested on his holster. "We need you to beat it. We need to speak to Mrs. LeGrande alone."

Popo did not budge. Her nature would not allow her to. "I am her mother-in-law and if this concerns my grandson, I not going anywhere."

"Ma'am," the officer repeated himself in a more menacing tone. "You need to leave now. I will not be asking you again."

For the first time since her husband was murdered, Popo felt helpless. Her expression was the same as someone who just realized that the thing he just swallowed was a grenade.

She hadn't obeyed an order since she was a child, and then only from her father.

She looked at Abi, who was just as scared as she was. "I'll be right inside the house. If you need me, I come right back." She directed the last part of her remark to the officer.

Popo walked slowly to the verandah and labored up the front steps. She lingered at the door, turned around to look at Abi, placed her forefinger against her lips to suggest that Abi keep quiet, then went indoors.

When the men were satisfied that they were alone, they sat Abi down on a bench by the clothes line. The ugly one looked her over intently, taking in her tanned skin, auburn dreadlocks and colorful clothing. The blue-eyed one was the first to speak.

"Ma'am," he began, trying hard to sound friendly, "are you here against your will?"

"Against my will? No. What on earth gave you that idea?" Abi protested, trying to remain calm.

"We are here to rescue Americans from the island, ma'am. We understand you're the common-law wife of Breed LeGrande. Mr. LeGrande is wanted by the American government. We consider him a revolutionary and threat to America's interests."

Abi stopped breathing for a second. She felt like she had been flung into space and suspended somewhere between the planets. "Wwwwhat?' she managed. "What are you talking about?" She glanced over her shoulder to see Popo in the window, frantically making a sign that looked like she should keep her chin up. She tilted her chin upward.

"Where are you from ma'am?" the ugly officer asked sharply.

"My name is Abigail Fisherman LeGrande."

"OK, Mrs. LeGrande. Could you please tell us where in the United States you are from? We need your social security number and date of birth, so that we can check your records. We understand you have a boy. Where is he?"

Abi nervously got up from the bench. Her past came flooding into her head. "My son is at a friend's house," she offered reluctantly. "I don't see how this concerns him."

"Mrs. LeGrande, we will take you and your son back to safety in the United States."

"But we are safe here," Abi replied. "I don't want to go anywhere. I just want my husband back."

"Be assured that we will find him. And be just as assured that when we do, we will bring him to justice."

After reciting those words with imperious disdain, the ugly officer grabbed Abi and pulled her roughly towards him so that their thighs touched. He did not budge when she shot him a disapproving look and tried to move her body away. His eyes scoured her face. Abi tried to see if his name was printed on his uniform. It was not.

"What did you say your names were, gentlemen?" She did not address either of them in particular. "When my husband returns, I will be sure to tell him to get in touch with you, if that is what you wish. May I please have your contact information?"

"We did not say and it does not matter," said the taller soldier. "What matters is that we take you with us. And your son." He looked at his companion and nodded.

"Be assured, ma'am," he continued, "we will see Mr. LeGrande long before you do. If you want to have a chance of ever laying eyes on him again, get in the house and get rid of the old lady."

Abi was rooted to the ground.

"Move," the ugly officer demanded as he shoved her towards the house.

"Leave her alone, Jimmy," said his companion. "We can get some native ass in the capital later."

"I don't want native," his friend said belligerently. "I like my meat white. Besides, she ain't bad on the eye."

Jimmy addressed Abi close enough so that she could smell his foul breath. "If you want to stay on this crazy island, bitch, we can make that happen. If you want your African back, we can make that happen. If he is still alive, of course. Do you feel lucky today?"

His mouth twitched and sneered. He grunted like one of Debbie's pigs, grabbed his crotch with one hand and with the other, pushed Abi up the front steps of the house.

"Get in there and get rid of the old lady," he growled. He had shoved Abi so hard that she fell against the steps. He pulled her back up to her feet by her hair and flung her forward. These weren't the nice soldiers that Che and the villagers had told her about, she thought to herself as she scrambled onto the porch and stumbled towards the front door of the house.

"Let's get this show on the road, man," grinned his companion. "We ain't got all day."

Abi burst into the front door and bumped directly into Popo.

"They can take me and Che back to where Colin can find me. They can put Breed away for life or kill him if they haven't done so already. They want you to leave, Ma Po."

"Now," Abi screamed at the startled woman. "Now," she said in a softer tone.

Abi watched helplessly as Popo walked past the men. One of them spat on the ground as she passed by them. She walked slowly down the hill towards the main road. The chimes were silent. There was not a hint of breeze. Abi walked back down the stairs and out into the yard towards the soldiers.

"You want to do this on the ground like the damn natives?" shouted the ugly officer, "or do you want to take us inside on a bed like civilized people?"

Abi gritted her teeth, summoned all the courage she could muster, and walked back into the house, hatred swelling up in her chest. She was strong and she could fight, but she was not strong enough for two men who had her fate in their hands and were bent on rape. The men followed her inside, laughing and leering.

Later that night Popo placed Abi's head in her lap and twisted the water out of her dripping wet locks.

"Shhh, my love," she whispered over and over, in Abi's ear.

"What's done is done. Is not like you had a choice. If you didn't do what they made you do, all now you on a plane to America with my grand baby. Thank you for staying. Shhh. Let's just pray that it not too late, and that Breed come back to us. Dis must be what doing your bit for the war means. I always wondered about dat."

Abi laughed despite herself. She smelled strongly of carbolic soap because she had scrubbed herself hard to get rid of any scent the men might have left on her body or hair.

"It feels like I have experienced more on this island than I have experienced all of my years in Baltimore," she told Popo softly. "What else will life throw my way?"

"I don't know, chile," Popo murmured back. "I am so sorry that you had to endure what you did. Sometimes I feel human beings aren't all human. There should be a different word put aside for some of us. Maybe inhuman beings would be better."

The women hummed and hugged each other as they watched the night sky show off. Darkness wrapped itself around them and in the distance came the mournful hoot of a tired old owl.

"Tomorrow I will write a letter to Hanna and let her know how things stand," Abi told herself.

CHAPTER FORTY-SEVEN

Baltimore

Hanna Gamble opened Abi's letter eagerly. She had read in the newspapers about the coup on Windward followed by the American intervention. Nowhere in the news was anything about the after-effects of this upheaval on the people on the island. She was more than ready for another trip to see Abi and those taut, strong men, but realized that she would need to give the island time to dust itself off and settle again in the sun.

While she had not laid eyes on Deirdra Jackson Carrington since her marriage, she had encountered her husband, Colin Carrington. Taking a shortcut back to the children's nursery after a hearty lunch at Mama Mia's, Hanna walked past the Emergency Room entrance.

"It's the chief medical examiner," she heard someone whisper. With ears and eyes suddenly on red alert, she followed a stretcher that was being pushed down to the swinging doors and asked an orderly about the latest casuality.

"Some guy named Carrington," the orderly told her with studied disinterest. "He ran his car into a fire hydrant on St. Paul Street. Nothing serious. He was blabbering to the medics about some corpse dressed in drag chasing his car. Can you imagine that?"

"Wow," Hanna blurted out. After a long moment of standing motionless, her facial muscles relaxed and her thoughts came into focus. "His deeds," she sighed, stepping away from the orderly, "are catching up with him."

Back in Charles Village, Deirdra was happy to see her husband come home banged up but alive after the accident.

"We need to take that trip," he announced, settling down on the couch with his whiskey. "I need to clear my mind. Why don't I book us a cruise to the Caribbean?"

"Why there?" asked Deirdra, looking at him quizzically. "Isn't that the place where…" Deirdra couldn't finish the question because Colin's hand was firmly plastered against her open mouth.

"Shhh," he breathed against her ear. "I have to find Kate. I need to find her and bury her."

Deirdra's eyes dilated. Slumping against Colin's chest, she managed a wheezing whimper. "Nooo," she hissed.

Colin slowly released his wife from the chokehold, so that he could look her in the face.

"I'll wait here for you," Deirdra managed through chattering teeth. "No point both of us going."

He frowned and shook his head. His voice was high and shrill. "You must come with me. What if she puts up a struggle?"

"She's dead, Colin. D-E-A-D," Deirdra sputtered.

She was no longer afraid of either a dead Madge or an alive Kate because she had taken her mother's advice and had high tailed it to Aisquith Street the moment Mrs. Jackson was out of sight.

She found Ms. Clemente's house to be dark and rather spooky. It made her think of the Halloween Haunted House she had visited as a child. The front parlor was illuminated by flickering candles housed in tall glasses with pictures of the Virgin Mary pasted on the outside. Two brooms turned upside down leaned against a glass menagerie filled with identical statues of an unrecognizable saint. Mismatched chairs covered in various designs of plaids and flowers waited in anticipation of curious occupants. On the mantelpiece next to a ceramic frog that was home to a single plastic flower, was a picture of a younger Ms. Clemente and a young woman that looked exactly like her. They were hugging each other and wearing identical outfits.

"Dats me and my twin sister, Bim Bim," she said proudly, as Deirdra stared at the photograph. "We twins. She living in the West Indies, in Windward." she added proudly.

"I can certainly see the resemblance," Deirdra said softly. She had no clue where the West Indies were, much less a place called Windward.

"You will visit there one day soon," said Ms. Clemente, looking steadily into Deirdre's eyes.

"Me? I don't think so. Why would I?"

Clasping a deck of well-worn playing cards, Ms. Clemente hummed and hissed, her eyebrows bunched together and her eyes squeezed into tiny slits. After much chanting and nodding and the periodical raising of her right eyebrow accompanied by an occasional caustic chuckle, she finally slammed the cards on the table like she just won a domino championship and exclaimed, "Don't fear dead lady now. Dat done."

Opening a bottle of the foulest smelling something Deirdra's nostrils had ever encountered, Mrs. Clemente said, "Sprinkle dis under your bed. It make dead lady spirit disappear. She leaned forward, waving away the smell in the air and speaking earnestly. "Remember your husband still alive but I don't know what to do with that one. He too bad."

Now that Colin had his hand around her throat, Deirdra vividly recalled those last words.

"Maybe Kate's body was washed up on the beach, and we'll find something of hers to bury," she could hear Colin gasp. Deirdra released herself from his grip and dropped into a chair, petrified.

"That was years ago, Colin. There's nothing left of her," she told him quietly.

But Colin could not be appeased. Deirdra was afraid to be in his presence and she was afraid to not be in his presence.

Two months later, they boarded the SS *Tropical Sea* in Miami and headed towards the West Indies, unaware of what was happening back in Baltimore.

Marc Douglas, the robber who had witnessed the murder of Madge Carrington, had earned the moniker, "The Tactful Thief." He was always careful to leave a note after he burgled a house. His mother had taken great pains to raise him "right." His notes were very concise and neatly written in his Catholic School script. "Thanks for sharing," "Sharing is caring" or his favorite one, "You had very nice stuff."

Marcus was finally apprehended by Baltimore's finest. Had he not bothered to leave a note on the day he robbed the house in Guilford, he might have had enough time to escape. His mother's prophesy had finally come true. She had told him on several occasions, "Marc, baby, if your'e not careful, one of these days, you will rob the wrong house." And he did.

When he walked into the Central Police Station handcuffed, he was not especially concerned. He was ready to talk in exchange for a lighter sentence. He would tell them everything he saw on the day that Madge Carrington was killed by the hands of a young black woman. There were still no leads in that case. He was the only eyewitness. He would also be happy to disclose the fact that he had seen that same woman in the company of the city's chief medical examiner on more occasions than he could count. And hadn't he read that they had gotten married in the *Baltimore Times?*

CHAPTER FORTY-EIGHT

Windward

Abi sat silently on the front porch with her thoughts. It was a beautiful morning in the middle of rainy season, so everything was painted in a hundred different shades of green. She could smell the bunch of Julie mangoes that the yard boy had placed on the kitchen table for her. She still loved them best, even if they did not taste quite as sweet as when she had to wrestle them from Breed.

After seven years she had grown accustomed to the sights and sounds of Marabel, but they never ceased to lift her spirits. The view of the ocean peeping out between the hills, dotted with tiny specks of fishing boats made her smile—as did the early morning ruckus of the caribs, the doves and the yellow bananaquit (aka sugar bird). They made so much racket for little creatures, she thought, especially the dove with its mournful cry.

When she prayed, her prayer was always the same—that Breed would return to her unharmed. She became physically sick when Che would insist they go out and find his father. But where would they look? It was like he had disappeared from the face of the earth. She dared not go down to the American Embassy. That would be the same as booking a flight back to Baltimore, never to see him again. She could not imagine her future without him in it. So she prayed and waited and kept a watchful eye on the door in case he just walked in with that sexy gait of his. That thought always sent an electric spark through her body.

She had come to believe that the soldiers would not be back. Her painful experience had receded, but could never be forgotten. If only Breed could comfort her, she told herself, she could erase the memory altogether.

She watched abstractedly as a stray black cat sprang onto the porch, cross in front of her and then jump on the ground from the other side. She had grown as superstitious as the villagers, so when the cat crossed her path, she stood up, turned around three times, made the sign of the cross and sat down again.

If only for old time's sake, Boysie and the men had scheduled a meeting on the verandah that evening. The curfew was no longer in effect, and things superficially seemed to be back to normal. Yet Abi could see from her nursing rounds that the people were growing more and more suspicious of each other and were wary about congregating in broad daylight or even in the dark of night.

"Can you see the invisible line?" Popo asked Abi when they were last at Boysie's rum shop. "It seems like it have two sides now. The side that call dis American ting an intervention, and the side that call it an invasion. Look de line there."

"I can see it," Abi answered. "And I can sense it everywhere."

"Hear ye," Malik announced when the men had arrived and gathered around the porch.

"Shut up," everyone chorused in unison.

"I see all you still chupid," Popo said good naturedly. "Like all dat gunfire ain't do nothing to help unu."

"Hear ye," everyone chorused.

"First tings first," Marshall said solemnly. "A moment of silence for Comrade Breed. May God send him back soon and in one piece." He turned to Abi and added reassuringly, "Hold on Abi. Your man soon come home."

"Thanks everyone," Abi said, touched by the love in the air. "I know you love him, too."

"OK," Popo piped up, "nobody start crying here today. Dats not what Breed would want when so much change happening and so fast to boot."

There remained an obvious American presence in Windward. This presence was not always a physical one. It took on the persona of the proverbial elephant in the room. People were afraid to talk openly about the current political situation for fear of reprimand or worse. On Popo LeGrande's verandah they felt a little ease from prying ears. They trusted each other.

"What all you thinking about this new interim government, eh?" Boysie asked no one in particular.

"I don't tink anyting much," Fish Mouth offered cautiously. Growing bolder, he added, "But one ting I know for sure is dat at least dey bring back some order in de place. I guess we have de Americans to thank for dat."

"So America get rid of the boogyman is what you saying?" Ing laughed derisively.

"Yes, they did," answered Fish Mouth. "I feel so."

"I agree with you, Fish," said Popo. "But dat is not the only ting they help us get rid of. Dey help us get rid of the revolution too. But thank God dey can't help us get rid of the revolutionary spirit. Dat, my comrades, cannot die."

A round of cheers erupted in the night.

"Since the intervention, uhhh… I mean invasion," Debbie stammered, "I feel I can breathe again. Like I was holding my breath de whole time wondering what will become of all of we. Now, I can release my shoulders from up under my ears."

"I know dat feeling. We happy dat dey come and help put tings in order. Now we happy to see dem go back where dey come from," said Peter. "What happening now, is new to us. Neighbours watching each other like they are enemies and people not trusting each other like dey used to. I don't like dat."

"Sometimes," Abi spoke up after a spell of daydreaming. "we need oxygen to survive. We might not like where the oxygen is coming from. We might not even like what we have to pay after the oxygen is given. But we need the oxygen to live, so we take it because we have no choice. And we are grateful for it even though we don't like the donor."

"Hear, hear," said Marshall. "You beginning to sound just like your husband. Comrades, we can't leave everyting to the new government. We have to help pick up the pieces and rebuild our country any way we can. We also can't leave all the education to the schools. We have to teach our children what is what, for ourselves."

Popo pushed back her chair and stood up.

"Dats all well and good, Marshall, but you see all the programs dat the revolution started that stop already? The adult education, the program for women doing non-traditional jobs, the 'plant and eat,' programs, all stop.

Everybody want to buy Chicken of the Sea tuna fish from America because fresh fish not interesting anymore to dem. The fishing expedition program stop. Che only asking me for dis peetza ting it have now. It have cheese and red sauce and can't be good for him. But I have to confess it taste foreign to my tongue but it taste nice." Popo grinned apologetically.

"What happening with your clinic, Abi?" asked Boysie, looking quickly away from Popo, since he had quite enjoyed a slice of that same thing the night before.

"Unfortunately," Abi began, "the young people have abandoned the initiative I started. It was set up to teach them about good health care for themselves and their children. There are not enough funds available anymore, and my own pockets have all but dried up."

"We spinning top in mud. That is what we doing," Debbie said angrily. Her hands were clenched tightly in front of her body. "The literacy program was going so good. Local people were even writing books about the history and geography of the island that the children were reading in the schools. Dats all done, too. We can commence reading about the geography of the so-called civilized Europeans instead. And before we forget, all dat canning local fruits and produce stopping too. But not to worry, we have supermarkets springing up wid package goods for us to eat. Won't be long before we get all kinda medical problems dat comes with dat food."

"All you tink dis stuff happening to kill the memory of the revolution?" asked Ing with a dismissive scoff. "Don't answer dat, because I really don't want to know what anybody tink."

"What you asking questions for if you don't want answers, Big Head?" grumbled Popo.

"Alright now!" Abi tried to sound upbeat to ward off the bickering that was tearing apart Breed's old comrades. "At least plans are on the way to erect a statue of the leader, I heard. That is a positive."

"Ha," Boysie grunted cynically. "Lets wait and see if dat will ever happen."

"Whether it happens or not," Abi said, standing her ground, "it really does not matter much because I am sure his memory will live on for many years to come. So whether there is a stone statue or not, he will remain where he belongs. In our hearts."

The crowd on the verandah hooted in agreement.

Popo and Abi bade their friends good night but not before asking them to pray for all of the men missing after the American occupation, and not just Breed.

CHAPTER FORTY-NINE

Windward

The next morning the sun was a radiant reddish pink. It reflected on the galvanized roof of the pigpen that Popo had constructed to house Che's piglet. The roof looked like it was on fire but the colors did not last long. They disappeared almost as soon as Abi acknowledged them. Like sunsets, they slipped away quickly.

"Can I please go to town with you today, Ma?" Che begged between mouthfuls of salt fish cakes, bakes and dollops of cornmeal porridge.

"You can come with me to help me carry my supplies. And I hope a bicycle can fit on top of the bus."

"Woi," said Che. "I well wait long for dis bike, oui. Thanks, Ma."

The ride to the capital took a little less time this morning. The bus ran faster because it was a school holiday and did not have to make as many stops for people's children. It was a longstanding custom that if a child was not at the bus stop at the appointed time, the driver would stop and the conductor would go looking for the child. Everyone in the bus waited patiently until the child was fetched and placed in the bus. Abi was always tickled that no one complained. In fact, most of the riders waited expectantly for the child to arrive.

Today's bus sped around the narrow corners and behaved like any self-respecting racing car in the Indianapolis 500. The conductor hung himself out of the side and made elaborate signs with his fingers and wrists to walkers who might be wiling to take their lives in their hands that day and climb aboard. The bus was named "One Love."

When Abi and Che hopped off the bus in the market square, the conductor leaned forward and jabbed Che in the ribs.

"Whaggo, Cheboy?" he asked with a playful hoot.

"I cool, man," answered Che. "I cool."

It was the day that the *SS Tropical Sea* was due on the island, so there was hustle and bustle along the seawall. Vendors appeared from everywhere, prepared to sell the tourists anything. Abi and Che joined the throng. First they would go to the main post office to pick up supplies for the Visiting Station, then stop at Mr. Ogilvie's, "Odds and Ends, Bar and Grocery and Bicycle Shop."

Abi waited so that Che could buy a snow cone from the ice lady. One covered in extra red syrup just the way he liked it. When they turned the corner near the old fish house, they could see that the *Tropical Sea* was docked at the new pier that was built with American dollars.

"Lemme take you on a toe aroun de town." The musical voice sounded familiar. Its source turned around after addressing a group of impatient tourists.

"Morning, Roy," Abi smiled at her old acquaintance.

"Morning, Miss," he replied, grinning through fewer teeth than when they first encountered each other. He now wore a weather-beaten black felt sombrero on his head, having long ago retired the multicolored woolen cap that once housed his dreadlocks. Abi suddenly thought about Breed and how he had lost his locks. She hoped Roy did not suffer the same fate.

"What happened to all that hair, Roy? I almost did not recognize you," Abi shook his hand as she spoke.

"Dem fall out. One by one. Too much stress if you ask me," Roy returned her smile. "Is not easy work chasing tourist."

Walking along the harborside, Abi and Che made a curious sight. She with her Caucasian features under a deep tan. Long auburnish hair bleached in the sun, bent on becoming dreadlocks but fighting with indecision. Even wrapped in bright yellow and black African cloth, her emerald eyes stood out. And equally standing out was a cinnamon-colored little boy with red ringlets around his head and a mouth that never stopped moving.

Some tourists stared as they passed. Others made furtive gestures to each other as the statuesque white woman and the curly-haired little black boy went by. A couple of tourists walked towards them. He was a middle-aged portly man. His hair was peppered with white and he sported a short beard to match. At his side was an attractive woman, half his age and as black as he was white. He had an odd smirk on his face and a familiar stiff cadence in his gait.

No. It couldn't be, Abi thought. It was impossible. Then their eyes met, just for an instant, and she knew. Her breakfast immediately tried to push itself back up to her mouth. She pursed her lips tightly and held her breath to prevent it gaining entrance and spilling out.

She heard the woman politely say, "hello," but Abi could not answer. Her tongue had glued itself to the roof of her mouth and her feet had turned to lead.

A few steps after he passed, the man turned back to look at Abi. She felt his eyes pierce the back of her head, but she did not turn around.

"Someone you know?" Deirdra asked casually.

Beads of sweat cascaded down Colin's forehead. He looked down at his feet and leaned helplessly against his wife.

"Someone you know?" Deirdra repeated, this time with some alarm.

"No," he snapped, thrusting his head up abruptly. "How could I possibly know someone on this God-forsaken island?"

Abi stood rooted to the pavement. The voice she had come to loathe many years ago had not changed. It was just the same as she remembered. Sardonic and spiritless, cold and clinical. Like a knife slicing through a cadaver.

Shivering in the morning sun, she grasped Che's hand tightly and willed her feet forward. She did not look back, and walked with an unsteady gait towards her destination.

Colin and Deirdra strolled along the harbor silently. He was not at all interested in the local jewelry and colorful scarves that the natives were selling along the seawall. He looked at Deirdra, her face glistening in the sunlight, and thought of the first Caribbean cruise to the island that had altered his life so dramatically. He bent down and gave his wife a furtive kiss.

"Oh," Deirdra said, startled. "What's that for?"

"I think I have buried a ghost," he grinned.

CHAPTER FIFTY

Windward

Abi sat under the mango tree and tried to regain her composure after her shocking encounter in town. She had felt that something was afoot when she opened her eyes that morning. Even while she boarded the bus with her son, there was a feeling of uneasiness. There was a sense of anticipation or maybe it was apprehension. She did not know which. She was reminded of her experience years ago on the deck of the *Tropical Sea*. But she had so much to live for now. Popo agreed to take Che to the north of the island to visit relatives and to show off his new bicycle. This gave Abi some time to unravel her thoughts and make sense of her experience.

Weary from anxiety and fear, her imagination took flight. What was Colin doing on the island? Did he recognize her? Was he thinking of ways to kill her now that he realized she wasn't already dead?

She anchored her head against the tree and listened to the chimes lament. She was weighted down without Breed. She spoke to him like she usually did when she was uneasy. *Where are you, my love? What's to become of me without you?* Exhausted, her eyes closed and she fell asleep fitfully, the large dent in the tree trunk cradling her head.

She felt herself being transported to a place overrun with an interminable tangle of wild, grotesque plants and where a blood-colored sunset dominated the sky. A sharp contrast to the beautiful sunsets that the people of Windward stood and admired. It was not the place to make a wish or send a dream on a journey.

She was knee-deep in mud and sinking fast. She bent down and squeezed the red earth, to let the warm clumps of soil escape through her fingers, only to find that the earth turned dry and hard in her hands, making them bleed. As dreamers do in nightmares, she struggled to escape from this humid, stifling place where the birds were skeletons of themselves and let out mournful squawks. Long vine-like arms reached out for her. The arms belonged to her mother. Mrs. O'Neill's face was grey and ghoulish. Her body was twisted around itself and her eyes were vacant holes. She was not willing to meet her drunken father so she willed herself forward through the sludge, lest he present himself as something odious. Sharp ammoniacal scents filled the air and an icy dew embraced her.

Instead of her father, she encountered Colin in a bloodied surgeon's coat with large gardening shears in the place of hands. He reached out to her with a howl. He was being chased by a swarm of corpses all with large holes in their bellies. Then Abi saw that the corpses were holding their kidneys in their hands as they chased Colin upstream.

She was floating in black water. Filthy, but familiar. It was the river she remembered in her youth, flowing through The Valley transporting the waste of countless factories to the bay. Who knew the birthplace of the river, she wondered. Was all the muck it held acquired on its arduous journey or was it inherited from the start. She would have to go through it to get through it. She forced herself forward with her face partially held up to the surface.

Turning over on her stomach, she stretched out her arms and began to swim effortlessly towards a light that beamed ahead. On and on she swam until she reached a magnificient sheet of silver glass that covered the surface like a layer of ice. The second her fingertips made contact, the glass broke into a trillion pieces of glimmering sparkles. Diamonds that God had flung down from Heaven. It was the same shimmering water that had shattered her thoughts of suicide aboard the *SS Tropical Sea.*

"Breed." She cried out his name as she heard the familiar strains of *Satisfy My Soul* playing in the water all around her. Now she could feel the friendly, dependable slapping of the water caressing her body and washing her clean. The waves with its rhythmic rock, made her feel like she was dancing the Samba with him in the bedroom with the missing drawer.

"*Oh darling,*" she sang out like Marley, "*I'm calling, calling.*"

Someone was shaking her. Gently at first, then forcibly. Abi opened her eyes and gasped.

"Wake up, Green Eyes," said a deep melodic voice. "I'm home."

Abi realized she had been smothered with kisses. Her face was wet and radiant.

"Wanna wrestle me for dis?" he laughed. In his hand was a plump, crimson colored Julie mango.

Filled with newborn life, she jumped up screaming with joy and chased him into the house, scattering the chickens in her path.

From his throne in the plum tree, Chanticleer crowed.

EPILOGUE

In the wake of his most recent shenanigans, Colin Carrington stepped confidently off the ramp of the *SS Tropical Sea* in Miami. To his surprise, two plainclothes Baltimore detectives approached him.

"Good afternoon, Dr. Carrington," said one of the detectives. "We've been waiting for you."

"A good afternoon to you too," Colin replied cautiously, trying to keep his composure. "How decent of you to welcome me back to civilization," he added with a wink of the eye.

"Dr. Carrington," said the detective, unamused. "We need to talk with your wife. Is she still on board?" The officers scanned the passengers as they continued to come down the ramp of the ship.

"My wife?" Colin asked with feigned alarm. "What on earth could you possibly want with her?"

"We need to question her regarding the death of the late Madge Carrington, sir. We believe that she can shed some light on the case."

Shielding his eyes from the sun, Colin looked at the passengers approaching them. He even stood on his toes so he could have a better vantage point.

"Actually," he addressed both men, "I was wondering where she was myself."

When the last passenger had finally stepped off the ramp and the crew was preparing to lock the gate, Colin wiped the smirk off his face and turned to the detectives.

"Where could she possibly be?" he asked, thinking to himself, well, I didn't bring my gun and I couldn't find a potion...

ABOUT THE AUTHOR

Dawne Allette was born in Grenada, West Indies. She has traveled internationally and has lived in the United States, Europe and the Middle East. She is an author, artist, comedienne and motivational speaker. Ms. Allette has authored seven children's books that are known for their inspiration, lyricism and humor. Her two biographies of Barack and Michelle Obama, are used in schools in Europe and the USA. A number of her poems relating to life in the Caribbean are published in an Anthology of Caribbean Poetry. She has written a textbook for Middle/High School on the life of Henrietta Lacks, which is currently under contract. This is her first novel. Ms. Allette currently resides in Baltimore, Maryland.

CPSIA information can be obtained
at www.ICGtesting.com
Printed in the USA
LVHW101935100622
720908LV00003B/25